W9-BNV-498

The Story of General Dann and Mara's Daughter, Griot and the Snow Dog

By the same author

NOVELS
The Grass is Singing
The Golden Notebook
Briefing for a Descent into Hell
The Summer Before the Dark
Memoirs of a Survivor
Diary of a Good Neighbour
If the Old Could . . .
The Good Terrorist
Playing the Game: a Graphic Novel (illustrated by Charlie Adlard)
Love, Again
Mara and Dann
The Fifth Child
Ben, in the World
The Sweetest Dream

'Canopus in Argos: Archives' series
Re: Colonised Planet 5, Shikasta
The Marriages Between Zones Three, Four and Five
The Sirian Experiments
The Making of the Representative for Planet 8
Documents Relating to the Sentimental Agents in the Volyen Empire

'Children of Violence' novel-sequence
Martha Quest
A Proper Marriage
A Ripple from the Storm
Landlocked
The Four-Gated City

OPERAS
The Marriages Between Zones Three, Four and Five (Music by Philip Glass)
The Making of the Representative for Planet 8 (Music by Philip Glass)

SHORT STORIES
Five
The Habit of Loving
A Man and Two Women
The Story of a Non-Marrying Man and Other Stories
Winter in July
The Black Madonna
This was the Old Chief's Country (Collected African Stories, Vol. 1)
The Sun Between Their Feet (Collected African Stories, Vol. 2)
To Room Nineteen (Collected Stories, Vol. 1)
The Temptation of Jack Orkney (Collected Stories, Vol. 2)
London Observed
The Old Age of El Magnifico
Particularly Cats
Rufus the Survivor
On Cats
The Grandmothers

POETRY
Fourteen Poems

DRAMA
Each His Own Wilderness
Play with a Tiger
The Singing Door

NON-FICTION
In Pursuit of the English
Going Home
A Small Personal Voice
Prisons We Choose to Live Inside
The Wind Blows Away Our Words
African Laughter
Time Bites

AUTOBIOGRAPHY
Under My Skin: Volume 1
Walking in the Shade: Volume 2

DORIS LESSING

The Story of General Dann and Mara's Daughter, Griot and the Snow Dog

FOURTH ESTATE • *London* and *New York*

First published in Great Britain in 2005 by
Fourth Estate
An imprint of HarperCollins*Publishers*
77–85 Fulham Palace Road
London W6 8JB
www.4thestate.co.uk

1

A catalogue record for this book is available from the British Library

ISBN 0-00-715280-9

Typeset in Sabon by
Rowland Phototypesetting Ltd,
Bury St Edmunds, Suffolk

Printed in Great Britain by
Clays Ltd, St Ives plc

A slight move to one side or the other – a mere hand's breadth – and Dann must fall.

He lay stretched, like a diver, and his fingers curled over an extremity of crumbling black rock, the tip of a shelf whose underside had been blasted away by wind and water, and which from a distance looked like a dark finger pointing at the cataract pouring over an edge of black rocks to become, at once, mists and spray that whirled and shifted, hypnotising him with movement: a cliff of thundering white. He was deaf with the noise, and fancied he heard voices calling to him from the thunder, though he knew they were the cries of seabirds. Lengths of white falling water filled all that side of his vision, and then if he shifted his gaze to look ahead, lifting his head from his arm, far away across the gulf he was poised above, those low clouds were snow and ice. White, white on white, and he was breathing a fresh sea air that cleared his lungs of the dull damp smell of the Centre. It was only when he left the Centre and its marshy edges he realised how he hated the smell of the place, and the look of the marshy land, all greys and drab greens and the flat gleam of water. He came here as much for the fresh lively smell as for the swirling movement that filled him with energy. White, and black, and above him the blue of a cold sky. But if he shifted to the very tip of the spit of rock, letting his arms dangle on either side of it, and looked down, far below there was the glint and glide of water, made blue by the sky.

This tip of rock could crumble and fall and he with it: the thought exhilarated him.

That water pouring over the rocks, he knew it; he had been swimming in the sea only a day ago. Salt and cold and strong it was, and the sea far below there was salty and cold but not so strong because of the water that was gushing everywhere from the snow and ice that began where the fall of sea water ended. The water down there was sea water diluted. Yet he saw the seabirds come from the waves to the rocky barrier and let themselves float down to the other sea, the low sea down there, so it was sea enough for them. And how did fish get down from the dangerous salty ocean to that other low sea? he had wondered, thinking that surely fish brought by the waves to the edge of the ocean and the rocks, and dashed over to fall in the white cascades, could not survive such a long gasping whirling descent. But whether they did or not, there was another way fish arrived in the lower sea. The falling masses of water span off foam, masses of it, in clumps many times the size of Dann. And in those clumps travelled fish.

Now the booming of the water was augmented by a loud crashing: he knew what that was. A boulder was being dislodged from the rocky crest and was bounding down, invisible to him behind the white mists, bouncing off hidden projections, and would land out of sight down there, in the water of this end of the Middle Sea. He knew that this chasm, this cleft, so enormous he could easily think it endless, had been a sea. He had known it on the old maps and globes in Chelops. At the Farm he had even tried to copy what was in his mind, on a globe that had drawn on it the Middle Sea, with below, Ifrik, and above it the ice masses of Yerrup, white all the way up to an edge of blue. He had stretched white leather from a goat over a frame of twigs. It was rough, but on it he and Mara had recreated that old Mahondi globe. Ahead, where he stared, more imagined than seen, because he knew it was there, were the regions of the Ice. And it was melting. It was melting into the ocean, and falling down the sides of the Middle Sea to where the sea was, at its bottom. All along a cliffy edge too vast for him to take in, ice water was pouring down into the sea there. So how long would it take to fill? He knew that once it had been full, and the surface of Middle Sea was not far below where he was now. Dann tried to imagine this great hole full of water, a sea almost at the level of the Western Sea – tried, but it was no good. So insistent and present was what he saw – the steep dark sides of the chasm going down to the present Middle Sea, streaked with grass and vegetation.

For weeks he had come to lie here, drawn by the fascination of the place, watching the thundering fall of water, listening, letting his lungs fill with clean salty air. He had looked around and across and down, and wondered about the lower sea. But now he didn't wonder, he knew: he had been down there himself.

During those weeks somebody watching the young man, who was more of a youth, slight, light and from a distance easily mistaken for a bird, must have wondered at his carelessness in that dangerous place. Gusts and swirls of wind came with the mists, and the spray and clumps of foam, but he did not attempt caution – he might sit up, or even dangle his legs over the edge, and stretch out his arms. Was he welcoming the blast that could take him over? And then that was what happened: he was lifted and flung down, landing on a long slippery slope of rock and sliding down it to stop in a grassy cleft. Below him was another descent of wet rock, and again the wind flung him down. These rocks were like glass, and were the work of water: the rub of water over stretches of time he could not begin to imagine had made them. He had slid, his boniness and the thin skin over his bones protected by his thick garments. As he slid, or even rolled, he looked for evidences of a path or at least a way of easier descent, and believed he was catching glimpses of some kind of a path. He knew – he had been told – that people did make this long dangerous descent, because of the good-tasting fish in the clean lower sea. As he clung to a bush, a sizeable clump of foam came to rest beside him, caught on the bush. Inside it he saw little fish wriggling. If they didn't reach water they wouldn't be wriggling for long. Dann stuck his arm right into the foam so that it clung to him, and he went on sliding and falling, down, down, aided by the slippery rocks, and then he was there, by the surface of the lower sea, which like its progenitor, the Western Sea – or part progenitor, the water from the icy cliffs supplied part – was lively, with little waves, but not like the great rollers of the Western Sea.

He flung the mass of foam off him and it lay rocking on the water and he saw little coloured fish swim off into the waves. From down here, the great fall of white water away up on his left hand was half the sky. He found an amenable rock, and crouched there, peering down into the sea, this Middle Sea, which had once filled all this vast space – he knew he was seeing only a tiny portion of its western end – and so he was crouching here on what had been once near the bottom. And would be again. When? So much water pouring in, salt water and fresh ice, and yet behind him the cliffy sides stretched up – and up.

Dann took off his clothes and slid into the water, ready to fish, but with nothing but his ten fingers. There were a lot of fish of all sizes. He swam among them and they crowded around, jostling and nudging, not afraid at all. He embraced a big scarlet fish, stuck his fingers into its gills and wrestled it up and out of the water on to a flat rock where it panted its way to death. He had his knife in his belt. He cut the fish into strips and stuck them on a bush to be cured by the sun. He had nothing like a bag or a satchel with him, and it was a big fish. He stayed for some time, until the sun had gone down behind the great cliff of falling water, and he was in danger of having to climb up that dangerous rocky edge in the dark. He made his way up in the cracks between the rocks. It took a long time and it was dark when he reached the top. He made his way to the Centre, and to his room, avoiding the old woman and the servitors, accepting the heavy damp of the air into his lungs with difficulty.

And next day early he went down the side of the Middle Sea, but this time with a sack to put the strips of fish in. But the fish had gone. Someone, something, had taken it. Alert, looking around, trying to be small and invisible, Dann squatted behind a rock and waited. He could see nothing, nobody. He decided not to swim and try for another fish in case this invisible thief should stop him getting out. The sun was straight above him, and it was hot. He did try a quick dip close to the shore and from the water he saw on a bush strands of coarse white hair. The hair was high on the bush. A largish animal, then. He climbed back up the sides of the chasm to his spit of rock and thought how different it was, believing yourself alone, and then knowing you are not, perhaps being observed.

When he had arrived at the Centre from the Farm – it seemed to him now a pretty long time ago, at least half a sun's cycle – he had found that the man, who called himself Prince Felix, was dead and the old woman, Felissa, mad enough to believe that he had returned as a conqueror with the intention of setting her on a throne. She had an old piece of metal, a shield, from who knew how long ago, with a picture on it of a woman on a high chair, while people knelt around her. Dann wanted to find out from her what the metal was, what time it had come from, from which room in the museums she had taken it, but she only wailed and complained that he was of the royal blood and must assume his rightful place – at her side. He had left her to it.

Then, from the Farm had come after him a youth who had turned up there, looking for work. His name was Griot and Dann remembered those greenish eyes always following him, from as far back as Agre. He had been a soldier, under Dann, who had been General Dann of Agre. The fact was, he had followed Dann from Agre to the Farm, and from there to the Centre. Griot had said to Dann, 'When you didn't come back to the Farm, I thought you might have something for me here.' *Here* meaning the Centre, but his use of the word suggested larger purposes. The two young men had stood together, observing each other, one with need, and Dann wanting to get away. Not that he disliked Griot: he had never much noticed him. A thickset young man, with a strong face, and greenish eyes that had to be noticed because eyes that colour were not often seen. Dann told him the Centre had plenty of space in it. Already all kinds of people sheltered there. It was much bigger than he and Mara had believed when they were here. That it was very large had to be obvious from a glance, but it was only when you knew it that the extent and the intricacy of the place became evident. Rooms led from rooms, rooms above rooms were reached by tiny wriggling stairs, half-ruinous areas that had been abandoned but now had inhabitants who did not want to be noticed, who kept out of sight. Beyond the encircling great stone wall on the side of the Middle Sea were buildings, made long after the main Centre was established, but they were sinking into the marshes. That was why it was easy to see the Centre as smaller than it was. It had been built on the highest place for a long way around, but as the tundra melted, the marshes encroached and the waters crept up. In some places the edges of the Centre were half under water. How long had they been like this? What use asking, when the locals might say of a city whose roofs you could see shining as the boats passed over it, 'My grandfather said that his grandfather remembered this city when the roofs were above water.'

Only such a short time ago he and Mara had been here together, and he could swear that he remembered dry where now there was wet. Perhaps things were speeding up? Once it had taken generations for a city to sink down into the mud, but now, much less?

He had said to Griot that he, Dann, was not looking for company. It was hard to say this into that face full of expectation. Griot had said that he knew a lot of crafts, had many skills; Dann would not find him a liability. Dann asked Griot where he had learned so much, and heard a history not unlike his own: Griot had spent his life on the run, from wars and invasions, as much as from the drought. Dann said there was something valuable Griot could do. Every day more refugees came to the Centre from the wars that were going on in the east, in countries Dann had scarcely heard of. He had had to acknowledge that there was more to the world than Ifrik. On the goatskin where he had sketched his map of the world was Ifrik, in the centre place, and above it the Middle Sea and above that Yerrup, with its ice masses. And, to the west, the Western Sea. That was about it. In his mind now were shadowy eastward extensions of this central Ifrik, filled with images of war. Griot could teach these people his skills, keep them out of mischief and stop them pilfering from the museums. Griot was pleased. He smiled: Dann had not seen this serious youth smile.

Then he watched Griot on a level, comparatively dry area with about a hundred people, not all youths, or men, for there were women among the refugees. He was teaching them to drill, march, run. They were using weapons. From the museums?

Dann said to Griot, 'People trained to be soldiers will want to fight, have you thought of that?'

And there on that stubborn face was an acknowledgement that Dann had said more than he thought he had. Griot nodded, and stared straight into Dann's eyes. What a look that was, asking for so much.

'You were a general in Agre,' said Griot softly.

'Yes, I was, and I remember you, but I am not looking for more fighting.'

And now Dann found himself being examined, most thoroughly, by those unsettling eyes. Griot did not have to say *I don't believe you.*

'It's true, Griot.'

It certainly was odd, the way people again and again expected him to step into some space in their imaginations, fit into their dreams.

He said, 'Griot, when Mara and I came here we found two lunatic old people who wanted us to start a new dynasty of Mahondis. They called us prince and princess.

They saw us as a breeding pair. They saw me as someone who would create an army.'

Griot's eyes did not leave Dann's face: he was searching for what Dann was not saying.

'I mean it,' said Dann. 'Yes, I was a general, and yes, I was, I believe, good at it. But I've seen too much of killing and people being made captives.'

'Why did the old people want you to have an army? What for?'

'Oh, they were batty. To conquer everything. To subdue all of Tundra – I don't know.'

Griot said, 'There is always killing, and people running from wars. And new wars.'

Dann said nothing and Griot asked – and clearly this was the moment of definition for him, 'And so what do you want to do – sir?'

'I don't know,' said Dann. 'No, I really don't.'

Griot said nothing. He had taken in all that Dann had said, but his conclusions were not what Dann would have approved of.

At last Griot said, 'Very well. I'll do what I can with the refugees. Some of them are not bad. They can teach me a thing or two sometimes. And I'm arranging the food supplies. There is plenty of good fish down in the Bottom Sea – not the muddy marsh rubbish around here. And I shall get some seed grain that I saw growing in water. And there's a marsh pig we can breed.'

Dann saw that Griot was taking on the tasks that he had expected Dann to do.

'Thank you, Griot,' he then said.

Griot saluted, and left.

That salute – Dann certainly did not like it. It was establishing some kind of contract between them that Griot needed.

The encounter between the two young men had been some weeks ago.

Dann tried not to run into Griot or even to notice much what he was doing.

On this day after he had noticed the hair of the animal stuck on the bush, he was lying stretched on his rocky spit, and thinking of the Farm and of Kira, who was pregnant with his child. It would be born soon. And Mara's child too. Interesting that Griot had not expected him to return to the Farm, yet Griot had stayed there long enough to learn what was going on, and who belonged to whom. That was a joke; Mara belonged to Shabis. And so Dann wouldn't go back. He thought of Kira and it was painful. How he did love her – and how he did hate her. Love? Well, he loved Mara, so he should not use that same word for Kira. He was fascinated by Kira. Her voice, her way of moving, that slow, lazy, seductive walk . . . but to be with her was to be humiliated. He thought of how, on the night before he left, she had stretched out her naked foot – and she was as good as naked – and said in that sweet singing voice of hers, 'Come here, Dann.' They had been quarrelling. They always quarrelled. He had stood there, a few paces away, and looked at her, and wanted to do what she wanted, which was to get on his hands and knees and crawl to her. She half lay, holding out her naked foot. She was pregnant, but it was too early to show. She needed him to lick her foot. And he desired to, he craved to, he longed to give himself up to her and stop fighting. But he could not do it. She smiled at him, her malicious smile that always made him feel she had cut him with a whip, she had wiggled her toes, and said, 'Come, Dann' – and he had turned and run out. He picked up some clothes, some essentials – and left the Farm. He did not say goodbye to Mara because he could not bear to.

Dann lay on his shelf of unsafe rock and knew it was time he left. He was so restless. Well, hadn't he spent nearly all his life on his feet, walking, walking, one foot after another? He had to be in motion again. But to leave here, leave the Centre, meant going even further away from Mara. She was a few days from here, on the shores of the Western Sea which he was observing for hours of every day from this perch of his, seeing it crash over the rocks down in sheets of foam to the Bottom Sea. The waves he saw break into spray were the same as licked the coast below the Farm. But he had to leave. He told himself it was because of Griot, always spying on him, and now there was this new animal down there, watching him too. He stretched and craned over the edge of his rock finger to see if somewhere was an animal, perhaps expecting more fish from him. For a few minutes he fancied he saw something big and white, but it was too far away. If it was watching Dann, it would be hiding itself. The thought made him feel prickly and caged. No, he must leave, he must go, he would leave Mara.

'Oh, Mara,' he whispered, and then shouted her name into the noisy water. It seemed to him her face was in the patterns the water made. A rainbow spanned the Rocky Gates and little rainbows were spinning off and away with the clumps of foam. The air seemed full of light, and noisy movements – and Mara.

He was heavy with sorrow, felt he could easily roll off that rocky protuberance and let himself fall.

He was leaving Kira too – wasn't he? But he scarcely ever thought of her and the child she was having. His. She had not even bothered to tell him she was pregnant. 'I don't think I'd get much of a look in with that child, even if I were a good father, hanging about, waiting for the birth – which must be soon.' So he excused himself. 'And besides, I know Mara will see that my child will be looked after, and there is Shabis, and Leta and Donna and probably other people by now.' It made him uncomfortable, saying *my child*, though it was. The thought of Kira was like a barrier between him and this soon to be born infant.

He stood up at the very end of the rocky finger and dared the wind to swirl him off. His tunic filled with air, his trousers slapped against his legs: his clothes were willing him to fall, to fly, and he felt the tug and lift of the wind over his whole body. He stood there, upright, not falling, so he left the rock and went to the Centre. There he visited the old woman who screeched at him, and so did the servant: two demented old women, in a bad-smelling room, berating him.

He chose a few things, put them in his old sack, found Griot and told him he would be away for a while.

How those sharp green eyes did peer into his face – his thoughts.

And how much he, Dann, was relying on Griot, and that made him feel even more caged and confined.

'Would you ever return to the Farm, Griot?'

'No.'

Dann waited.

'It's Kira. She wanted me to be her servant.'

'Yes,' said Dann.

'I've had enough of that.'

'Yes,' said Dann, who had been a slave – and worse.

'She is a cruel woman,' said Griot, lowering his voice, as if she might overhear.

'Yes,' said Dann.

'So, you'll be off, then?'

Dann had gone a few paces when he felt the need to turn, and he did, and saw Griot's betrayed face. But had he made Griot any promises? He had not.

'Griot, I'll be back.'

'When?'

'I don't know.'

Dann made himself march away from Griot's need.

Dann set off around the edge of the Middle Sea, going east. He had meant to walk right round the edges of the Bottom Sea, but that was before he had seen it, so rough, often piled with detritus from rockfalls. Up here on the top edge there was a road, more of a track, running between the precipitate fall to the water and the marshes. He had left the stale mouldy smell of the Centre, but the smell of the marshes was as bad: rotting vegetation and stagnant water. He walked, thinking of Mara and the past. His mind was full of Mara, and of sorrow, though he had missed the news of her death. She had died giving birth. The messenger from the Farm had come running to the Centre, but Dann had left. Griot had thought of sending the messenger after Dann, but said that Dann was away. Griot was glad he did not have to tell Dann. During his time at the Farm he had observed, had taken everything in. He knew how close Mara and Dann were: one had only to see them together. He knew the two had walked all the way up Ifrik through many dangers; his own experience had told him what a bond shared danger was. He had seen that Dann suffered, because Mara belonged not to him but to her husband Shabis. To tell Dann his sister was dead: he was in no hurry to do it.

Dann had wanted to leave the Centre – leave the past – because of the weight of sorrow on him, which he believed he understood. It was natural. Of course he was bereft, but he would get over it. He had no intention of subsiding into unhappiness. No, when he got walking, really moving, he would be better. But he had not got into his stride, his rhythm: it was what he needed, the effortlessness of it, when legs and body were in the swing of the moment, a time different from what ruled ordinary sitting, lying, moving about – never tiring. A drug it was, he supposed, to walk like that, walking at its best, as he had done sometimes with Mara, when they were into their stride.

But Mara was not here with him.

He kept at it, thinking of Mara; well, when did he not? She was always there with him, the thought of her, like the reminder of a beating heart: I am here, here,

here. But she wasn't here. He let his feet stumble him to the very edge of the declivity that ended in the Bottom Sea, and imagined her voice saying, *Dann, Dann, what did you see?* – the old childhood game that had served them so well. What was he seeing? He was staring into streaming clouds. Water – again water. His early life had been dust and drought, and now it was water. The abrupt descent before him ended in water and a blue gleam of distant waves, and behind him the reedy swampy ground with its crying marsh birds went on for ever . . . but no, it did not. It ended. And on the other side of the northern cloud mass, he knew, were shores loaded with ice masses. Much more to the point surely was, *Dann, Dann, what do you know?* He knew that the vast emptiness of the gulf before him had been sea that came up almost to where he stood now, with boats on it, and there had been cities all around its edge. He knew that cities had been built all over the bottom of the sea, when it was dry, which were now under water, and on islands, still inhabited, but many of those had emptied, were emptying because everyone knew how fast the waters were rising, and could engulf them. Everyone knew? No, he had met people coming to the Centre who knew nothing of all this. *He* knew, though. He knew because of what the Mahondis knew, fragments of knowledge from distant pasts. 'It is known,' one would say, giving the information to another, who did not have it, because they came from a different part of Ifrik. 'It is known that . . .'

It was known that long ago when the Ice first came creeping and then piling into mountains all over Yerrup, the mass and pack of ice had pushed all those wonderful cities along the edge of that shore that stood opposite to him now, though he could not see it, over the sides and into the great gulf which was already half full of detritus and debris, before the people of that time – and who were they? – had taken up the stones and blocks of cement that had built the old cities and used them for the cities on the land which was now behind him, but then things changed, the Ice began to melt and the cities sank down. That was when the tundra turned into water. Cold, cold, a terrible cold that destroyed all Yerrup but how was it this sea, the Middle Sea, had been a sea but then was empty? 'It was known' that at some time a dryness, just as frightful as the all-destroying Ice, had sucked all the water out of the Middle Sea and left it a dry chasm where cities were built. But it did not fit – these bits of fact did not fit. His mind was a map of bits of knowledge that did not connect. But that was what he did know, as he looked into the moving dark clouds, and heard the seabirds calling as they dropped their way down to the lower sea. And, at his back, the marshes, and beyond them, for they had an end, scrub and sand and dust, Ifrik drying into dust. He and Mara had walked through all that, walked from deserts into marshland, and both were on their way to their opposites, through slow changes you could hardly *see*, you had to *know*.

What do you know, Dann? – I know that what I see is not all there is to know. Isn't that of more use than the childish *What did you see?*

He returned to the track and saw stumbling towards

him a man ill with exhaustion. His eyes stared, his lips cracked with his panting breath, but although he was at his limits he still moved a hand to the hilt of a knife in his belt, so that Dann could see he had a knife. Just as Dann's instinct was; his hand was actually moving towards his knife when he let it fall. Why should he attack this man, who had nothing he needed? But the man might attack him: he was well-fed.

'Food?' grunted the stranger. 'Food?' He spoke in Tundra.

'Walk on,' said Dann. 'You'll find a place where they'll feed you.'

The man went on, not in the easy stride Dann was wanting to find, but on the strength of his will. If he didn't fall into a marsh pool, he would reach the Centre and Griot would feed him.

What with? That was Griot's problem.

Dann went on, slowly, thinking that it was easier to walk fast on dust and sand than on this greasy mud that had already been trodden and squashed by a thousand feet. Plenty of people had been this way. More were coming. Dann stood at the side of this track and watched them. They had walked a long distance. Men, then some women, even a child, who had dull eyes and bad breathing. He would die, this child, before he got to the Centre. In Dann's sack was food, which would save the child, but Dann stood there and watched. How would he ever get into his stride, his own beautiful rhythm, when these refugees came past, came past . . .

He had not made much progress that day, and he was already tired. The sun was sinking over there in the west, behind him. Where was he going to sleep? There wasn't a dry bit of earth anywhere, all was wet and mud. He peered over the edge of the chasm to see if he could find a good rock to stretch out on but they all sloped: he would roll off. Well, why not? He didn't care if he did. He went on, looking down at steep and slippery rocks that had been smoothed by thousands of years of the rub of water – but his mind gave up: it was hurting, to think like this. At last he saw a tree growing aslant, a few paces down. He slid to it on glassy rocks and landed with his legs on either side of the trunk. This was an old tree. And it was not the first that had grown on this site. Remnants and fragments of older trees lay about. Dann pulled out some bread from his sack, hung the sack on a low branch and lay back. It was already dark. The night sounds were beginning, birds and beasts he did not know. Overhead was the moon, for the clouds had gone, and he stared at it, thinking how often its brightness had been a threat to him and Mara when they had been trying to escape notice . . . but he didn't have to hide now. Dann slept and woke to see a large animal, covered with heavy shags of white hair, standing near him on its hind legs, trying to pull down his bag with the food in it. He sat up, found a stone and flung it, hitting the side of the animal who snarled and escaped, sliding and slipping on scree, before reaching some rocks.

It was halfway through the night, and chilly, but worse than that, damp, always so damp. Dann wrapped himself well and thought that if he put the bag with the food under him, the hungry animal might attack him to get it. So he left the bag where it was on the branch and dozed and woke through the rest of the night, waiting for the animal to return. But nothing happened. The sun rose away to the east where – he *knew* – the shores of the Middle Sea ended, and beyond them unknown lands and peoples. For the first time a doubt appeared in his mind. He had been thinking – for such a long time now – that he would walk to the end of this sea and then . . . but how far was it? He had no idea. He did not know. He ate some bread, drank water from a little stream running down from the marshes and climbed back to the path. He was stiff. He must find his pace again, which could carry him all day and – if necessary – all night.

On his right the marshes were opening into larger pools, and places where you could stand and look down through water on to the roofs of towns. And what roofs – what towns. He remembered the boatman who had brought him and Mara north: he had said he didn't enjoy looking down to see buildings so much better than anything anyone knew how to build now. It made him miserable, he said. Yes, thought Dann, exactly, it did make one miserable. Perhaps this weight of sorrow on him was simply that: he was ashamed, surrounded always by a past so much more clever and wonderful and rich than anything they had now. Always now you came up against *long ago . . . long, long ago . . . once there was . . . once there were*, people, cities and, above all, knowledge that had gone.

So, what did he know? When you came down to it? Over there the ice mountains were melting over Yerrup and their water poured all along those coasts he could not see, down into the Middle Sea. Water poured from the Western Sea down over the Rocky Gates into the Middle Sea. The marshes had been frozen solid as rock where cities had been built to last for ever but now they stood down there deep under water. And southwards, beyond the marshes, Ifrik and its rivers were drying into dust. Why? He did not know. He knew nothing.

Dann's thoughts were stumbling as wearily as his feet, he was burdened with the weight of his ignorance. And of his shame. Once, *long ago*, people knew, they knew it all, but now . . .

A man came towards him, tired out, like them all, and Dann called out in Tundra – but saw from the face it was not understood. He tried Mahondi, he tried Agre, and then the odd phrases of the half-dozen languages he knew enough of to say, 'Where are you from?' At last one man did stop. The two were alone on the track. Dann pulled out some bread and watched the starving man eat. Then he said, 'Where are you from?'

Dann heard syllables he recognised.

'Is that far?'

'I have been walking forty days.'

'Is your country near the end of the Middle Sea?'

And now a blank face.

'This is the Middle Sea. We are standing on the edge of it.'

'I don't know anything about that.'

'What do you call this, then?' – Dann indicating the great emptiness just by them.

'We call it the Divide.'

'Dividing what from what?'

'The Lands of the Ice from the dry.'

'Is your land dry?'

'Not like this' – and the man looked with repulsion at the dull low gleam of the marsh near them.

'How far then to the end of the Divide?'

'The end?'

'It must have an end.'

The man shrugged. He wanted to be on his way. His eyes strayed to Dann's sack. Dann pulled out the food bag and gave him another bit of bread. The man hid it in his clothes.

'When I was a child I was told my grandfather had walked to see what lands there were beyond ours and found none. He walked many days.'

And he set off towards the Centre.

Dann stood there, full of dismay and cursing himself for arrogant stupidity. He had taken it for granted that of course he could walk to the end of this shore; why not? Had he not walked all the way up Ifrik? But how long that had taken . . . and between him and the end of this shore were wars; these people walking and running, some of them wounded, with bandaged arms and dried blood on them, had run from wars. Did he really want to walk into a war? Into fighting?

What was he going to do, then? Dann went on, and on, slowly, not finding his pace, as he was continually having to stop because of the parties of refugees coming towards him, and so it was all that day and at evening it was like the last, wet everywhere, the reedy marshes and – this evening – pale mists moving over the water, and the smell even worse, because of the mists. It was getting dark. Dann looked east into the dusk and thought he would never see the end of this coast. What did he think he was doing, why was he here?

On a patch of smooth hard mud at the edge of the road he squatted to draw with his knife's tip a circle, then an oval, then a long thin shape, a circle stretched out – the Middle Sea. Every puddle, every pond, every lake had a shore that went round, enclosing water. Why had he wanted to walk to where the shore of the Middle Sea ended, to turn around on itself? Because he wanted to see the Ice Cliffs of Yerrup for himself, that was the reason. Well, there might be easier ways of doing that than walking for another long part of his life, and marching straight into wars and fighting.

He slid from the edge, as he had done the night before, and landed in a patch of grass where bushes stood about, bent all in one direction, because of the wind from the Ice. He put his sack under his head, his knife ready on his chest, and was pleased with the occasionally appearing moon, which let him keep watch.

He woke in darkness. A large vague white mass was close to him and the moon appeared, letting him see it was another of the great beasts lying there, its eyes open, looking quietly at him. Dann's hand, on his knife's hilt, retreated. This was no enemy. The moon went in. There was a smell of wet fur. The moon came out. What was this beast? Dann had never seen anything like it. Impossible to tell under all that fur what its body was like, but the face was fine, eyes well spaced, a small face surrounded by bursts of white hair. This was a beast for cold; one did not need to be told that; it would not do well on desert sand or anywhere the sun struck down hot. Where did it come from? What was it doing, lying so close? Why was it? Down Dann's face wet was trickling. There was no mist tonight. Tears. Dann did not cry, but he was crying now, and from loneliness, his terrible loneliness defined because of this companionable beast so close there, a friend. Dann dropped off but woke, slept and roused himself so as not to miss the sweetness of this shared trustful sleep. In the early dawn light he woke and the animal was there, its head on its vast shaggy paws, looking at him with green eyes. Like Griot's. This was not a wild animal: it was accustomed to people. And it wasn't hungry; showed no interest in Dann's provisions.

Dann slowly stretched his hand towards the animal's paws, where its head lay. It closed its eyes, in acknowledgement of him, and then again. Dann was crying like a child, and thought, *It's all right, there's no one to see.* The two lay there as the light strengthened, and then the beast's pointed ears stood back and it listened. There were voices up on the road. At once it got up, and slunk down the slope of scree to where a white skeleton bush stood shaking in the wind. There it hid.

Dann watched it go, watched his friend go. Then up he leaped, to face the people up there, face what he had to – though he was not sure now what that was.

With his head just above the edge he watched a group stumbling past, too exhausted to look up and see him. He waited. No one else seemed to be coming. He got back on the track and saw that soon the ground rose dry towards a low hill, with trees. He had to fill his water bottle, if the marshes were ending. He stepped off the track on a dryish edge between pools, and stood, his face to the sun, letting it warm him. He had been dreaming, as he lay with the beast so near, and it had been a bright dream. Mara, yes, he had been dreaming of her because of the sweetness of the beast's companionship. How strange it was, the visit of that animal, in the night.

Dann was looking into a clear pool, with some weed drifting in it. There were three masses of – well, what? Three masses of whitish substance, just below the water. Two large masses and a smaller one . . . bubbles were coming from it, a muzzle, pointing up . . . they were animals, like his night's companion, they were drowned, but wait – bubbles meant life; that smaller thing there, it was alive. He knelt on the very edge of the marshy pool, risking the edge giving way under him, and pulled at the beast, brought it close to his feet, and lifted up the weight of it with a jerk beside him, nearly falling in himself. Dann raised up the sodden mass by the hind legs and watched water stream from the pointed nose. Water was streaming from everywhere. Surely it must be dead? There was not a flicker of the resistance of life, of animation. And still water was pouring from the mouth, from between new little white teeth. The eyes were half open under mats of wet fur. This was a young animal, the cub of those two cloudy masses of white lying so close. Perhaps they weren't dead either? But Dann had his hands too full, literally, with this young beast. Which suddenly sneezed, a choking spluttering sneeze. Dann put his arm round the heavy dense wetness and held it so the head was down, to let the water out. It was so cold, the air, a heavy deadly cold and the animal was a cold weight. Dann did not feel cold because he was used to exposure, but he knew this animal would die if he couldn't warm it. He laid it on some grass tussocks, between the pools, and in his sack found the bundle of clothes he always carried. He used one to wipe the beast's wet skin, where lumps of wet hair lay matted, and then wrapped it in layers of cloth. What was needed here was blankets, thick layers of warmth, and he had nothing. Surely it should be shivering? He could not feel breath. He opened his jacket, of layered cotton, that was warm enough for him, and buttoned the beast against him, head on his shoulder, feet nearly at his knees. The weight of sodden cold made him shudder. What was he going to do? This was a young thing, it needed milk. Dann stood, holding the beast to stop it sliding down, and looked at the two foamy submerged masses which would lie there for days in this cold water before going putrid. Unless something came to eat them?

Marsh birds? There were plenty of small marsh animals. He couldn't concern himself with them; he doubted if he could have saved the great beasts, even if they did have life in them. He doubted whether he could help this one. He stepped carefully between the marsh tussocks to the path, afraid of overbalancing with this dead weight, and wondered if he should return to the Centre? But that was a good two days' fast walking to the west. What if he ran? He could not run, with that weight on him. Ahead was the track, winding along the edge of the cliff, but wait – the ground did rise there ahead and where there were trees must, surely, be people. Despite the weight Dann tried to run, but staggered to a stop, and felt against his chest a small but steady beat. At the same time it began sucking at his shoulder. It wanted to live and Dann had nothing, but nothing, to give it. He was crying again. What was wrong with him? He did not cry. This was an animal, out of luck, and he had watched so many die, with dry eyes. But he could not bear it, this young thing that wanted to live and was so helpless. Although the weight was giving him cramps in his legs, he resumed his stumbling run and then, ahead, the dark edge of the wood showed a path going up and, as he thought, *people* – the beast stopped sucking and whimpered. Dann ran up the path, running for a life, and when ahead he saw a house, more of a shack, with reeds for a roof and reeds for walls, he clutched the animal, because his now fast bounds and leaps were shaking it too much.

At the doorway of the shack stood a woman, and she had a knife in her hand. 'No, no,' shouted Dann. 'Help, we need help.' He was using Mahondi, but what need to say anything? She stood her ground, as Dann arrived beside her, panting, weeping, and opened his jacket and showed her the soaking bundle. She stood aside, put the knife down on an earth ledge on an inside wall, and took the beast from him. It was heavy and she staggered to a bed or couch, covered with blankets and hides. He saw how nimbly she stripped off the soaking clothes, which she let fall to the earth floor. She wrapped the beast in dry blankets.

Dann watched. She was frantic, like him, knowing

how close the animal was to death. He was looking around the interior of the shack, a rough enough place, though Dann's experienced eye saw it had all the basics, a jug of water, bread, a great reed candle, a reed table, reed chairs.

Then she spoke, in Thores, 'Stay with it. I'll get some milk.' She was a Thores: a short, stocky, vigorous woman, with rough black hair.

He said in Thores, 'It's all right.' Apparently not noticing he spoke her language, she went out. Dann felt the animal's heart. It did beat, just, a faint, I want to live, I want to live. It was not so cold now.

The woman returned with some milk in a cup and a spoon, and said, 'Hold its head up.' Dann did as he was told. The woman poured a few drops into the mouth between those sharp little teeth, and waited. There was no swallow. She poured a little more. It choked. But it began a desperate sucking with its wet muddy mouth. And so the two sat there, on either side of the animal, which might or might not be dying, and for a long time dripped milk into its mouth and hoped that would be enough to give it life. Surely it should shiver soon? The woman took off the blanket, now soaked, and replaced it with another. The animal was coughing and sneezing.

As Dann had done, she lifted it by its back legs, still wrapped in the blanket, and held it to see if water would run out. A mix of water and milk came out. Quite a lot of liquid. 'It must be full of water,' she whispered. They were speaking in low voices, yet they were alone and there were no other huts or shacks nearby.

Both thought the animal would die, it was so limp, so

chilly, despite the blanket. Each knew the other was giving up hope, but they kept at it. And both were crying as they laboured.

'Have you lost a child?' he asked.

'Yes, yes, that's it. I lost my child, he died of the marsh sickness.'

He understood she had been going out of the room to express her milk to feed the beast. He wondered why she did not put the animal to her breast now, but saw the sharp teeth, and remembered how they had hurt him when the animal sucked at his shoulder.

Such was their closeness by now that he put his hand on her strong full breast, and thought that if Mara had had her child, she too would have breasts like this. It was hard to imagine.

He said, 'It must hurt, having that milk.'

'Yes,' and she began to cry harder, because of his understanding.

And so they laboured on through the day and then it was evening. During that time they saw only the beast and its struggle for life, yet they did manage to exchange information.

Her name was Kass and she had a husband who had gone off into the towns of Tundra to look for work. He was a Tundra citizen but had made trouble for himself in a knife fight and had to look out for the police. They had been living from hand to mouth on fish from the marsh and sometimes traders came past with grains and vegetables. Dann heard from Kass a tale of the kind he knew so well. She had been in the army, a soldier, with the Thores troops, and had run away, just like him and

Mara, when the Agre Southern Army had invaded Shari. The chaos was such that she imagined she had got away with it, but now the Hennes Army was short of personnel and was searching for its runaway soldiers. 'That war,' she said, 'it was so dreadful.'

'I know,' said Dann, 'I was there.'

'You can't imagine how bad it was, how bad.'

'Yes, I can. I was there.' And so he told his tale, but censored because he wasn't going to tell her he had been General Dann, Tisitch Dann, of the Agre Army, who had invaded Shari and from whom she had run.

'It was horrible. My mother was killed and my brothers. And it was all for nothing.'

'Yes, I know.'

'And now Hennes recruiting officers are out everywhere, to enlist anyone they can talk into going back with them. And they are looking for people like me. But the marshes are a protection. Everyone is afraid of the marshes.'

And all that time of their talk the animal breathed in shallow gasps and did not open its eyes.

The shack filled with dark. She lit the great reed floor candle. The light wavered over the reed ceiling, the reed walls. The chilly damp of the marshes crept into the room. She shut the door and bolted it.

'Some of those poor wretches running from the wars try and break in here but I give as good as I get.'

He could believe it: she was a strong muscled woman – and she had been a soldier.

She lit a small fire of wood. There was nothing generous about that fire, and Dann could see why: probably this rise with its little wood was the only source of fuel for a long way walking in every direction around. She gave Dann some soup made of marsh fish. The animal was lying very still, while its sides went up and down.

And now it began to cry. It whimpered and cried, while its muzzle searched for the absent teats of its mother, drowned in the marsh.

'It wants its mother,' said Kass, and lifted it and cradled it, though it was too big to be a baby for her. Dann watched and wondered why he could not stop crying. Kass actually handed him a cloth for his eyes and remarked, 'And so who have you lost?'

'My sister,' he said, 'my sister,' but did not say she had married and that was why he had lost her: it sounded babyish and he knew it.

He finished his soup and said, 'Perhaps it would like some soup?'

'I'll give him some soup tomorrow.' That meant Kass believed the creature would live.

The cub kept dropping off to sleep, and then waking and crying.

Kass lay on the bed holding the beast, and Dann lay down too, the animal between them. He slept and woke to see it sucking her fingers. She was dipping them in her milk. Dann shut his eyes, so as not to embarrass her. When he woke next, both woman and animal were asleep.

In the morning she gave it more milk and it seemed better, though it was very weak and ill.

The day was like yesterday, they were on the bed with the beast, feeding it mouthfuls of milk, then of soup.

By now she had told him that because of the ice mountains melting over Yerrup, there was a southwards migration of all kinds of animals and that these animals, called snow dogs, were the most often seen.

How was it possible that animals were living among all that ice?

No one knew. 'Some say the animals come from a long way east and they use a route through Yerrup, to avoid the wars that are always going on along this coast, east of here.'

'Some say, some say,' said Dann. 'Why can't we *know*?'

'We know they are here, don't we?' The animals Dann had seen when sleeping out on the side of the cliff were snow dogs. This was a young snow dog, a pup. Hard to match this dirty little beast with the great beasts he had seen, and their fleecy white shags of hair. He was far from white. His hair was now a dirty mat, with bits of marsh weed and mud in it.

Kass wrung out a cloth in warm water and tried to clean the pup, but he hated it and cried.

The helpless crying was driving Dann wild with . . . well, what? Pain of some kind. He could not bear it, and sat with his head in his hands. Kass tried to shush the animal when it started off again.

And so another day passed, and another night and at last the snow pup seemed really to open its eyes and look about. He wasn't far off a baby, but must have been walking with his parents when they fell into the marshes.

'They must have been chased into the marsh,' said

Kass. People were afraid of them. But they did not attack people, they seemed to want to be friendly. People were saying, suppose the snow dogs become a pack, instead of just ones and twos? They would be dangerous then. Yet there were people who used them as guards. They were intelligent. It was easy to tame them.

Kass warmed water, put the pup into it and quickly swirled off the dirt. It seemed to like the warmth. After his bath he was white and fleecy, with large furry paws and a thick ruff round his neck: his intelligent little face looked out from a frame of white ruff.

Then, one day, he actually barked, as if trying out his voice.

'It sounds like Ruff, Ruff, Ruff,' said Kass. 'We'll call him Ruff.'

And now, at night, they set the pup on one side, wrapped in a blanket, instead of lying between them, and they held each other and made love. Both knew they were substitutes for absent loves – her husband, for Kass. For him, that was not easy. Kira was, had been, his lover, but it was Mara he thought of.

Suppose Kass's husband came back suddenly?

She said, yes, she was thinking of that. And what did Dann propose to do next?

Dann said he was going to walk, walk right to the end of this side of the Middle Sea.

He was trying her out and she at once said that he was crazy, he didn't know what he was talking about. And there were at least two wars going on not far along the track. When people came through from there, they brought news, and war was the news they brought.

And Kass knew much more about the Bottom Sea than he did. The opposite north shore did not run in a straight line from the Rocky Gates to – whatever was the end, where it turned to become the southern shore. It was much broken with fingers and fringes of land, and down in the Bottom Sea were a lot of islands, large and small. And that was how the snow dogs came across from the north shore. They swam from island to island.

So what did Dann want to do?

He wanted to walk. He needed to walk. That meant leaving here.

With every day the snow pup was stronger. He sneezed a lot: there was still water in his lungs, they thought. He was a pretty, fluffy young snow dog, who never took his green eyes off them. He loved to lie beside Kass on the bed, but liked better to be with Dann. He snuggled up to Dann and put his head on Dann's shoulder, as he had been on that walk, or rather run, to get here.

'He loves you,' said Kass. 'He knows you rescued him.'

Dann did not want to leave the snow pup. He did not want to leave Kass but what was the use of that? She had a husband. He loved that animal. That angry fighting heart of Dann melted into peace and love when the snow dog lay by him and licked his face or sucked his fingers. But Dann had to move on. At first he had thought the snow pup would go with him, but that was impossible. Ruff was being fed, carefully, on thin soup and bits of fish and milk, not Kass's now, but a goat's, who lived in its pen and bleated because it wanted company.

Ruff could not travel with Dann, and Dann had to move on.

When Dann set forth, the pup wailed and toddled after him along the path. Kass had to run and try to lift him to carry him back. Kass was crying. The snow pup was crying. And Dann cried too.

He told himself that when he was with Kass and the snow pup he had cried most of the time. But he was *not* someone who cried, he repeated. 'I don't cry,' he said aloud, running faster to get away from the snow pup's wailing. 'I never have, so now I must stop.' Then he realised he had found his pace, he was going at a good loping run along the track, and slowed to a fast walk which would sustain him without tiring. It was a wonderful release for him, and he stopped crying and went on, marshes on one side and cliffs on the other, without stopping or changing pace. No refugees came towards him now. That meant the wars had ended, did it? The fighting was over?

Dark came and he slid over the edge to find a bush he could hide in, or a cleft in the rocks. He dreamed of Kass's kindly bed, and of her, and of the snow pup, but woke dry-eyed, and had a mouthful or two of her provisions, and returned to the path, the sun full in his face. He saw the marshes were less. By that night on his right hand were moors, and he slept not on a sloping cliff face but on a dry rock under sweet-smelling bushes. To be rid of the dank reek of the marshes . . . he took in great breaths of clean healthy air and so it was all that day and the next, and he thought he must be careful, or he'd run straight into the fighting, if it still went on.

And all that time no people had come towards him along the track. Then he saw them, two – well, what were they? Children? When they came close, stumbling, their knees bending under them, he saw they were youngsters, all bone, with the hollow staring eyes of extreme hunger. Their skins . . . now, what colour was that? Grey? Were there grey people? No, their skins had gone ashy, and their lips were whitish and cracked. They did not seem to see him; they were going past.

These two were like him and Mara, long ago, ghost-like with deprivation, but still upright. As they came level the girl – it was a girl? – yes, he thought so – nearly fell and the boy put out his hand to catch her, but in a mechanical, useless way. She fell. Dann picked her up and it was like lifting a bundle of thin sticks. He set her by the road on the side where the moors began. The boy stood vaguely, not understanding. Dann put his arm round him, led him to the grass verge, put him near the girl, who sat staring, breathing harshly. He knelt by them, opened his sack, took out some bread, poured water on it to make it easier to eat. He put a morsel in the girl's mouth. She did not eat it: had reached that stage of starvation where the stomach no longer recognises its function. He tried with the boy – the same. They smelled horrible. Their breath was nasty. Then he tried out his languages, first the ones he knew well, then the odd phrases, and they did not respond at all, either not knowing any of them, or too ill to hear him.

They sat exactly where he had set them, and stared, that was all. Dann thought that he and Mara had never been so far gone they could not respond to danger, had lost the will to survive. He believed these two were dying. To reach the Centre would take many days of walking. They could reach Kass, after a few days, but would be met by her broad sharp knife. Beyond them the moors stretched towards Tundra's main towns, a long way off. And if they did manage to get themselves up and walk, and reached the marshes, they would probably fall in and drown, or tumble over the edge of the cliffs.

And then, as he sat there, seeing how the morsels of food he had placed in their mouths were falling out again, they crumpled up and lay, hardly breathing. They would die there. Dann sat with them, a little, then went on, but not in his pace, his rhythm: he was thinking of how Mara and he had been so often in danger, but had always come through, had slid through situations because of their wariness and quickness, were saved by their own efforts or because of the kindness of others. And by luck . . . those two back there had not had luck.

He saw coming towards him a slight figure, walking in a slow obstinate way that Dann knew: this person, a man, was walking on his will, which was far from the ease of how one moved on that rhythm that seemed to come from somewhere else. He was thin, bony, but was in nothing like the bad state of the two youngsters. Dann called out in Mahondi and was at once answered. He could see the man didn't want to stop, but Dann held out some bread, a dry piece, and walked forward with it, and the man stopped. He was a small wiry fellow, yellowish in colour – which was his own real colour and not because of starvation – with dark serious eyes and black locks of fine hair. He had a sparse beard. This was no thug or rough.

Dann started his interrogation, while the man ate, not in a frantic grasping way, but carefully.

Where had he come from?

From a very long way east.

But surely there is a war?

Yes, two, bad ones. The one nearest here had fought itself to a standstill, there was no one left but real soldiers, preparing to make a stand. The one further along was raging. His own country had been invaded; there was civil war. He had left, made a circuit around the further war, knowing it was there, had worked for a farmer for shelter, and some food. And now, what would he find if he went on?

Dann told him, carefully, watching him nod, as he took in the important points. He must not let himself fall into the marshes or over the cliffs. If he went on long enough he would come to a vast complex of buildings, called the Centre, and there he could find a man called Griot, who would help him.

And why did Dann do all this for this stranger? He liked him. He was reminding him of someone, a friend who had helped him, Dann thought, and there was something about that intelligent face . . .

'What is your name?'

'They call me Ali.' He added, trusting Dann as Dann trusted him, 'I was the king's scribe. I had to run away – I was too well known.'

'And your country's name?'

Dann had never heard it. It was beyond Kharab – and Dann scarcely knew where that was.

He gave this Ali a hunk of Kass's bread, and watched him hide it in his clothes, before he went on, hesitant at first, because he was tired, but then stronger, and steadily. Then he turned and looked back at Dann and gave a little bow, hand on his heart.

And as Dann watched him, thinking of him as a friend – why did he feel he knew this Ali? – he heard shouts and the sounds of running feet. What he saw then made him drop over the edge of the cliff, though it was steep there, because he knew these people meant danger. A large noisy crowd and they were hungry, and some wounded, with old dried blood on them, and half-healed cuts. If they knew he had food they would kill him. He could see all this from that one glance.

He did not put his head up over the edge until they had gone on.

He knew Ali was quick and clever enough to hide from them.

And what was Griot going to do with this crowd of bandits when they turned up?

He saw near him a quite large path. Down he went between slabs of dark rock that had been smoothed by water, thinking that previous descents to the Bottom Sea had taken him half a day, but the Middle Sea was deeper here, for darkness fell when there was a long way to go. He ensconced himself for the night in a shelter for travellers, hoping he would not have company, but though he slept with his knife ready there was no knock, or intruding feet, or the strong smell of an animal. He stood outside the hut door as the sun rose, seeing that this part of the Middle Sea was full of islands, some whose tops were level with and even higher than the edges of the sea. And the islands were wooded, he could see that, easily now, and there were lights on them that went out as the sunlight grew strong.

He was thinking of those two who probably still lay by the side of the track, whom he had seen wavering towards him, as if blown by the wind, hatchlings in a storm – and why should he care more about them than so many others? But he did think of them. The crows or other raptors of the wild moor would have found them by now.

He let the sun flush his stiff limbs with warmth and took the path again. Many used it. Before he reached the edge of the Bottom Sea he saw another travellers' hut. Wood. He had become so used to reed roofs, walls, reed everything that it was pleasant to see well-honed planks and solidly encompassing roofs of wooden tiles.

It was well past midday now. The sky blazed and the sea was very blue and full of sharp little waves. Very cold water – his fingers went numb at once. On the shore was a flat place where a post stood on the water's edge. He saw two things; that it was submerged a third of the way up, and that fish traps were tied to it. The post was to hold a boat and so he had only to wait and there would be a boat. There was a bench. He sat and looked across at the nearest island from where he could expect the boat. He could be seen from there. Probably the boatmen kept a lookout and came over when they saw someone waiting. He drowsed – down here he did not feel fearful, or the anxiety of watchfulness. He was woken by a boat scraping at the landing place. In the boat was a youth and a snow dog, which leaped out and ran up the cliff. The youth said, smiling, 'I give them a lift, to save them a swim.'

Dann asked in Mahondi, 'How much to take me over?' but the youth shook his head, and Dann tried Charad and then Tundra and heard, 'What's your money?'

Dann had handfuls of different coinages, and the youth nodded at the Tundra coins.

He was not asking much; Dann got into the boat and they set off.

What was the name of the island? Dann asked all the necessary questions until, when he said, 'Are you part of Tundra?' he encountered a hostile response: Dann saw that he was up against strong local pride.

The islands saw themselves as a unit and they had fought off any attempts to possess them, though Tundra had tried.

'They've given up now. Tundra's lost its teeth,' he said, repeating what Dann had heard from Kass. 'They are not what they were. We hear everyone's had enough of Tundra government.' They were in the middle of the crossing, the sunlight burning up off the water. It was hotter down here than it ever was up on the cliffs.

'So I believe,' said Dann, wanting to hear more, but not what he heard then.

'They say that the old Centre's got a new lease on life. There's a new master now, one of the old line. General, they call him, but he's Prince as far as I am concerned.

We like the old ways, here. If there was a bit of law and order up there again things would be easier for us.'

Dann thought of saying, 'I was recently in the Centre and that's just gossip,' but did not want to define himself too early – if at all. He liked not being known, being free, himself.

They reached the shore and saw a couple of snow dogs half concealed in some trees.

'They wait and hope that one of us'll give them a lift. They can swim, but it's a good bit of a swim for them, with all that hair getting wet. Some of the boatmen give them a hand. I do, but others don't. They're harmless. I think that they never saw humans before coming here. They're curious about us.' And so he chattered, while they balanced on the waves and until they landed at a little town, already lit for the night. It was a cheerful scene, and under Dann's feet was hard dry ground and there was a smell of woodsmoke. The boatman, Durk, said that that inn over there, the Seabird, was a good one, run by his parents.

Dann knew this was advice better ignored, in a town where everyone to do with travelling was in the pay of the police, but he thought he had nothing to fear now, particularly if Tundra's agents were not welcome. He wandered for a while about the streets, enjoying the fresh sea air, and admiring the solid comfortable buildings of wood and stone. Plenty of stone for building here: there was solid rock just below the earth surface. No houses here were going to sink into marsh.

He found himself expected at the inn and spent the evening in the common-room, listening to the talk. A pleasant crowd, of people who all knew each other. They were interested in Dann, but too polite to ask questions. They watched him, though, as he ate his supper of fish, and a kind of porridge made of a grain he did not know.

How unlike they were to the Thores, though they too were a short people, a good head shorter than Dann. The Thores were stubby, with light bones and black short straight hair. Their skin colour – could one say of skin that it was greenish? Compared with the light warm brown of these people, yes. Dann had seen on Kass's cheekbones a sheen of green, and blueish shadows in her neck. Now he saw this, in retrospect, looking at these faces where the brown had reddish tints. And their hair – black – was all waves and curls. What a cheerful crowd they were, and living without fear. Not a weapon in the room – except for Dann's hidden knife.

They were pleased when he asked questions, which were answered from all over the room.

There were a thousand people on this island. All the islands lived by trading fish from this well-stocked sea. They dried it, cured it in many different ways and carried it up the cliffs to sell in the towns along the shore to the east. But the wars had ended all that and fish was piling up at their warehouses. They planned to try an expedition across the moors into Tundra's big towns, though they must expect to be careful: there was disorder now the government was weak.

They also sold fishing nets made from marsh reed, fetched down from what they called, simply, 'up there'.

They made cloth from a variety of the reed, and every

kind of basket and container, some that could hold water. One of the islands was not hilly, was flat enough for fields, and grain was grown. All had goats, which gave milk and meat and hides. They lived well, they told Dann; and feared nobody.

Dann asked if it would be easy to make a journey from island to island until he could stand under the ice cliffs of Yerrup, for he longed to see them for himself.

It was possible, was the answer, but not advisable. The ice masses were so unstable these days you never knew when they were going to crack and fall. Sometimes you could hear the ice cracking even here, so far away.

Dann saw they had no conception that their way of life would soon change, and on some islands, the lower ones, end. Yet 'up there' everyone knew it. The inhabitants of the lower islands would move to the higher ones, and then to the higher ones still – did they know that under the waves that surrounded them were the ruins of great cities? No, they laughed when he mentioned this and said there were all kinds of old stories about that time.

These people did not want to know. And it was not the first time, after all, that he observed this phenomenon: people whose existence was threatened and did not know it. Would not. They could not bear it.

How long before the water rose and covered this pleasantly wooded prosperous island? In the morning he walked to the shore and went a good way along it. The water was rising fast. Not far along the coast houses stood in water, some submerged.

When he mentioned them at the inn there were jests

and laughter, and he heard, 'Oh, yes, we know, but it'll last us our time, and our children's.'

At the inn he shared a large room that had several beds. One of them was the boatman's, Durk, who was a son of the house. Only couples had their own bedrooms. The corresponding room, for women, had a snow dog as guardian, sleeping across the threshold.

This was so comfortable, this inn, these people, but Dann was restless and told Durk he wanted to go to the end of this long island. Durk said there was no inn there, Dann that he was used to sleeping out. Durk was uneasy, and intrigued. 'But it will be cold,' he said.

Dann told him he would take with him goatskin rugs, and added, 'I'll look after you.'

He was seeing this young man as a youth, a boy, even, but they were the same age. Dann lay in the dark, seeing stars bright through the square of the window, thought of Kass and of his snow pup, and then of the hard dangerous histories of everyone he had ever known. Down here it was – but really, another world, safe. They were safe, at least for a time. They were comfortable and safe, well fed and safe, and Dann was seeing them as children, as a childlike people. He lay awake and watched the stars move. Durk was across the room, and a couple of other local youths. Most of the beds were empty: the wars 'up there' were disrupting movement. Sometimes people had come to trade who had walked a whole cycle of the sun to get there. Sometimes they stayed, enticed by the island's way of life, and the safety.

Dann lay with his hand on his knife's hilt, and thought for the first time in his life that perhaps he was mistaken to see people who were fed and unthreatened as inferior. What was wrong with living in what he thought of as a sort of easy dream? They were happy. It was a word Dann did not have much acquaintance with. Content. They did not lock their doors. No one kept watch on any of the islands.

Dann made himself lie quietly, loosened and at ease, not clenched and wary, and thought he might as well stay down here – why not? For one thing, he had promised Griot he would return. He had promised, so he must – soon, not yet. And there was the Farm, where Mara would have her child by now, and Kira, with hers – his. It was not Kira's child he thought of as his, though, but Mara's. Kira might be kin, but she was certainly not his kind.

In the morning at the communal table was a woman who said she was a refugee from the war nearest to here. She had arrived down at the shore last night, waited for someone to come, and had swum over. She was in a poor way, from lack of food, but her eyes burned with the intention to survive. She was claiming asylum. But if she fed herself up a bit she would easily get a husband, he was sure.

Dann set off, with Durk, his sack full of provisions, to see the island. He could not at first understand what it was he was experiencing, a refreshment of his whole self, a provisioning, like a fine and heady food. Then he did. He had not seen ever in his life whole forests of healthy trees, but only trees standing in dust, trees dying of dryness, trees that seemed whole and well until you saw a limpness in their leaves and knew that drought was attacking their roots. And here were trees of a kind he had never seen, dark trees that spired up, their boughs made of masses of thin sharp needles, sending out a brisk aromatic scent; and light graceful trees with white trunks that shivered and shimmered in the smallest breeze. There were bushes that crept about over the rocky earth, laden with berries. Dann told Durk of what he had experienced in the drought-struck lands of southern Ifrik, and saw that he was not being believed. Durk listened to him talk, with an appreciative grin, as if he were a storyteller who had embarked on a tall tale.

When they reached the end shore, with a further island in sight, Dann lay down to sleep on a mat of the springy low bushes, and Durk said he would too, as if this were a great adventure for him. Lying side by side, Dann in his cotton jacket, Durk covered by the goatskin rug, stars closer and brighter than they ever were 'up there', Dann was ready to fall asleep but Durk asked him to go on talking about his adventures. And that is how Dann found how he could keep himself on this trip, when he had so little money, and no means of getting any. There was no shortage of labour here, and it was skilled labour. Fishermen whose fathers and grandfathers had voyaged for fish, travelled in their little boats everywhere in the islands. There were specialists who dried and cured the fish. Others traded it, climbing to 'up there'. Youngsters looked after goats, and women farmed grain. Dann's skills were not needed.

When they returned to the inn, Dann said he would tell tales of his early adventurous life, in return for his food and his bed. That evening the common-room was full. Durk had gone around spreading the news that this visitor of theirs was a storyteller.

The big room, well lit with its fish-oil lamps, was crowded, and Dann stood by the bar counter and looked around, trying to judge how they would take his tales, and wondered which they would like best. He stood frowning, the long fingers of his left hand across his mouth, as if they were censoring memories. He was not like professional storytellers, who are affable and know how to hold people's eyes, how to pause, make a suspense, come in with surprises, spring a joke at tense moments. They saw a tall, too thin young man, his long black hair held by a leather band, standing hesitating there, and that face of his, so unlike theirs, was full of doubt. But it seemed like pain to them.

Where should he begin? If Mara had been here, she would start a long way before he could, because his memories began when he ran away from the Rock Village with the two men who treated him so badly. There were children in the room, who had been promised stories. He could not tell about some of the ways he had been mistreated to children. He began his tale with the dust drifts and dried rivers, with the bones of dead animals lying in heaps where floods had carried them earlier. He saw the children's faces grow dubious, and then a child began crying, hushed by its mother. Dann told of how he had hidden behind a broken wall and saw carried past on the shoulders of porters wooden cages that had in them captives from a war who would be sold in the slave markets. And a child cried out and its mother took him out.

'I see', said Dann, smiling in a shamefaced, desperate way, 'that my memories are not for children.'

'Yes, I think so too,' said another mother.

And so Dann's memories emerged softened and some became comic. When he heard his audience laughing for the first time he felt he could laugh himself, with relief.

Then things became serious again when he said he had met travellers who said that his sister was alive in the Rock Village, and he made his way south, when everyone was running north. He evaded the places where it seemed everything was burning, even the soil, saw the gold and red of the fires flickering through the hills, and found Mara, so near death she was like an old monkey, with filthy matted lumps of hair he had to scrape off with his knife, and skin stretched tight over her bones.

And now, as he told of their journey northwards through all those dangers, they all forgot he had none of the storytellers' skill: he was speaking slowly, as he remembered, so deep in his past that they leaned forward to catch every word.

He reached to where he pushed the sky-skimmers up and down the ridges, and had to stop, to explain sky-skimmers.

'They came originally from the museums of the Centre,' he said, and described them. Machines that had been able to fly once, but, grounded from lack of knowledge and the fuel they needed, became conveyances for travellers able to pay.

They saw he seemed to crouch there before them, imagining how he had pushed the machines up and down the ridges – imagining Mara there, with him.

He stopped, seeing it was late and some children were asleep.

He lay in his bed. Durk, who was across the room, said, 'Did all that really happen to you?'

'Yes, and much more, much worse.'

But he had realised he could not tell them some of his experiences. They would be shocked and hurt by them.

In the day he roamed around, and saw off the western shore the white skeletons of trees sticking up from the sea and around each trunk the fish nosing. They liked these dead trees. Some still green trees were half submerged, the salt water whitening their branches.

He and Durk stood there together, and Dann said, 'The water is rising fast.'

And Durk said, 'Oh, no, you are exaggerating.'

At night Dann told of the water dragons and the land dragons, and heard his audience laugh, and had to say, 'But you have lizards here, don't you? – all kinds of lizard. So why not really big ones?'

But there was always a point in his recitals when his audience was not with him. They did not believe him. Their imaginations had gone fat and soft with the comfort of their lives.

What they liked best were tales of the Mahondi house in Chelops, and the girls in their pretty coloured dresses, preparing herbs in the courtyard, and how they tended the milk beasts.

He said nothing about the horrors of the Towers of Chelops. What he remembered hurt him to think of, and yet he knew he had forgotten the really bad parts.

He said how Mara had come into the Towers to rescue

him, and how he had been nursed back to health by a woman who knew about herbs and healing. They could not get enough of all that, and he never told them that this idyll of lovely living had ended in civil war and exile.

Soon he was off again, with Durk, to another island, which was like the first, with small quiet towns, and inns that were full of people in the evenings. Durk said this ought to be a short visit, because he wanted to get married. He and his girl had been promised their room. The custom was that the new couple was accompanied after a celebration to their room, which was kept decorated with boughs and flowers for a full month. Then, if either wished to end it, there was no criticism or opprobrium, but if they stayed together they were considered bound and there were penalties for frivolous or lightly considered severance. But really Durk seemed content enough to linger on this island, where he had not been before. It was large, with a stream that provided sport and fishing: otherwise there were no novelties. All the islands were the same, Durk said, as far as he knew. Why should they be any different? He had not remarked, it seemed, that the islands being all the same suggested a long, stable history. When Dann pointed this out he was struck by it and said, yes, he supposed this must be so. He was so incurious, Dann was often impatient. Nothing in these beautiful islands was ever questioned. When he asked about an island's history, the reply was vague: 'We have always been here.' What does that mean, *always*, Dann asked, at first, but then did not bother.

He, too, liked this island and then Durk pointed out that they had been here so long people were asking if they intended to make their home there. And Dann's tales in the evenings at the inns were becoming repetitious. They moved on, and then again, from island to island, always moving nearer to the north shore's ice cliffs. Durk did make rueful jokes about his girl – that she would have found another man by now. He stayed with Dann because, as he said, 'You make me think, Dann.' And on the last island there was plenty to make Dann think too.

In the inn there on the walls of the common-room were two maps, just as there had been in Chelops. But these two were of when the Middle Sea had been full of water, and of how it was now. Goatskins had been stitched together and stretched. On the first were islands, big ones, which were the tops of those that could be seen now, mountains reaching high up, to the level of the cliffs. Sticking out into the sea from the north shore were promontories and fringes of land. One was long and thin, like a leg. The person who had made this map 'long, long ago' had drawn little boats balancing on steep waves. At one end to the west were the Rocky Gates, but they stood apart, with sea between. On the other end, to the east, was the word 'Unknown'. There were towns indicated all around this sea.

The other map was of the Middle Sea, as it had been before the Ice began to melt. Cities crowded all over the bottom – and they were here now, far down under these new waves. So these people did know that there had been cities – but when asked, some said that the artist must have had a fine imagination. Who was he, she – who were they? The maps were skilful, much finer than those back in Chelops, which had been crude. (And where were those maps now, after fire and fighting? Did they still survive, and did the new people see them and understand what they said?)

You had to have an eye to read a map – as Dann discovered when he found that Durk could not make sense of them. Dann stood there, with Durk, using a clean stick to show how this ragged shape was that island – 'Over there – do you see?' – this black charcoal line the shore. Durk was reduced to sighing wondering incoherence, standing there, watching Dann's patient indicator. And he was not the only one. Others in the common-room, seeing them there, came to stand and marvel at the maps they had known all their lives but never understood, maps that had not been used to teach children. Those that could read them had not instructed those who could not. Here was this incuriosity again, that made Dann uneasy.

'See here' – and his stick pointed at where they were now, the group of islands scattered across the sea, from the southern shore to near the northern shore. 'This is where we are now. Once these were just little bumps at the bottom of the dry Middle Sea.' And will be again, he stopped himself saying, for this kind of thing was making people fear him.

Already his reputation as a know-all and a show-off was growing. His tales about his life – not everyone believed them, though they laughed and applauded.

As for Dann, his mind was hurt by the enormity of it

all. Yes, he knew the Middle Sea had been full and fresh, and ships went everywhere over it, and now it was nearly empty; yes, he had joked with Mara about the 'thousands' and the 'millions' that it was not really possible for their minds to grasp, let alone hold. But now, standing on land protruding from the Bottom Sea that had once been deep under it, when the seabirds cried over the waves, and disappeared, that was how he felt: who was Dann? – standing here where . . .

Once this enormous gash in the earth's surface had been filled with water. So, it had boiled away in some frenzy of heat, or it had frozen into a great pit of snow and then some unimaginable wind storm had carried the snow away? All at once? Surely, over – here he went again – thousands of years.

A sea, sparkling and lively, like the one he looked at now through the windows of the inn, but high above his head, at the level of the top of the cliffs where he had walked and would walk again and then – gone, gone, and his mind felt hurt, or something was hurting, and – he saw Durk, frowning up at the maps and turning a doubtful face to him. 'Tell me again, Dann, it's so hard to take in, isn't it?'

Then, seeing his interest in the maps, the inn's proprietress, the young woman, Marianthe, showed Dann something he did not understand, at first. Standing against a wall in the common-room was a large slab of white rock, about the thickness of half his hand, very heavy, covered on one side in a story. There were men, of a kind Dann had never seen, smiling faces with pointed curling beards, and expressions of crafty cleverness.

They wore garments held with metal clasps, much worked. The women had elaborate black curls framing the same crafty smiling faces, and their garments were twisted and folded, and one breast was bare. They wore necklaces and bracelets, and ornaments in their hair. To look at them was to know how very far these people were above anybody that lived now – as far as he knew – and he had after all seen many different people. Perhaps it was these people who had made all the things in the Centre no one knew now how to use? Who were they? – he asked Marianthe, who said, 'It was a long time ago.' Neither did anyone know where the white slab had come from. That it had been a long time in the water could be seen; the sharp edges of the carved figures had been dulled. So it had been pulled up out of the water, at some time, somewhere, or fallen over the cliff with the melting ice.

Marianthe was as intrigued by the people on the slab as Dann was. And looking at her, it was at once evident how fascinated she was. She was tall, she was slim, she had black hair in curls around her face, for she modelled herself on the women carved on the slab. She was paler than anybody Dann had seen, who was not an Alb. And her face, though not fine and subtle like the smiling slab women, did have a look of them. She had a long, thin, always smiling mouth and long, narrow, observing eyes. She was the widow of a seaman drowned not long ago in a storm. She did not seem oppressed by this fatality, but laughed and made fun with her customers, who were mostly seamen, for this island was the base of the main fishing fleet. And she liked Dann, giving him not only his food and shelter but herself, when she had heard his tales of 'up there'. She laughed at him, knew that he was making it all up, but said her husband had liked a good tale and told them well. Dann was telling them well by now, with so much practice.

Durk meanwhile went out with the fishing fleet. He was not jealous, but said that now Dann had found this easy berth, he should stay in it.

Dann was tempted to do just that. This woman was quick and clever, like Kira, but not unkind; seductive, like Kira, but did not use her power. How could he do better than stay with this prize of a woman, down here on the islands of the Bottom Sea, with the aromatic forests, and where it was hard rock underfoot, never marshy and sodden. But he had promised Griot – hadn't he? Well, who was Griot that Dann had to honour a promise he felt had been pressured out of him? But Griot *was* waiting for him. And at the Farm Mara did too – although she did slide into another man's arms every night to sleep.

'Stay with me, Dann,' coaxed Marianthe, winding her long limbs around him.

'I can't,' he conscientiously replied. 'There are people waiting for me to come back.'

'Who, who, Dann? Are you married? Who is she?'

'No, I am not married,' said Dann – but could not bring himself to say, 'I have a child – you see, there's a child,' which would have settled it.

To say that would have acknowledged Kira who, with every day, seemed to Dann more of a lump of showy charms displayed like a visual equivalent of 'Look at me!

Look at me!'. Well, he was very young when he first fell for Kira, he tried to excuse himself and knew he could not then have imagined a woman as delightful, as candid, as subtly clever as Marianthe. Whom he would have to leave . . . yes, he must . . . yes, soon . . . but not yet.

First, he wanted to see the ice cliffs that so haunted his mind and called to him. This island was the last inhabited one. Within sight, on the horizon, was another, a half-day's rowing away, uninhabited, though it had been once, and abandoned because of the cracking and roaring of the falling ice. From there, he was sure, he could get close enough to see what he so acutely imagined. No one wanted to accompany him: they thought he was mad. Durk, though reluctantly, said he would go too. Young men taunted them for being foolhardy, a little envious perhaps, since none of them had thought of going. Dann and Durk went quietly about preparations, and then four others said they would go. Durk, who had actually been planning to use his little boat, was now glad to leave it in favour of a bigger one that needed several rowers. 'But we need six oarsmen,' protested the four brave ones and Dann said that he had earned his living once as a boatman.

Marianthe's eyes never left Dann that last evening, and in bed she held him and said, loudly, to reach the ears of some god of the islands, that she was being expected to sacrifice another man to the sea. And she wept and kissed the scars on Dann's body.

It was a clear morning when they left, six strong young men in the fishing boat, that had its nets and pots removed. Instead there was food and piles of goat rugs.

They rowed all morning, to the north, to the island which as it neared showed itself standing clear of the waves, well-wooded and, in the sunlight, inviting. They pulled the boat up on a beach and went into the interior where at once they found an abandoned town that was already falling down. They put their gear into a house that had shutters that could be fixed across the windows, and a door that could be barred. They had glimpsed on the edge of the wood a snow dog, standing watching them – and then another. It was a pack, which had decided to stay here on this island and not make the effort to cross. And indeed, it was hard to see how the others had made the trip; it would be a dangerous swim for any snow dog, no matter how strong.

Then the six walked carefully to the northern end of the island, not speaking, because the sound of crashing ice, cracking ice, groaning ice, was so loud. No wonder the people had left here.

There was a beach there, and bollards that had once held boats safe. They were staring across a white sea at what looked like icy clouds, shining white, higher than any had imagined the Ice could be, and behind them were taller reaches of white. They were staring at the ice cliffs of Yerrup, that seemed undiminished, in spite of how they cracked and fell. As they gazed, a portion of the lower shining mass groaned and fell, and slid into the waves, leaving a dark scarred cliff which from here looked like a black gap on the white. Although they were far away, the noise was unpleasant and any remark anyone made was silenced by a fresh roar of complaint from the packed and ancient snows.

'There,' said Durk, 'now you have seen it.'

'I want to go closer,' said Dann in an interval in the noise. At once the others, all five at once, expostulated. And as he persisted, went on protesting.

'Then I shall go by myself,' said Dann. 'I can manage the boat.'

This put them on the spot. He could not be allowed to go alone, and yet they were afraid and their faces showed it. And it was frightening, standing there, the sea chopping about so close, disturbed by the blocks of falling ice and behind them the dark woods, where they knew a pack of snow dogs was bound to be watching them, and probably wondering if it were safe to attack. There couldn't be so much food here, not enough to keep a pack of large animals well fed.

Clouds slid across the sky and without sunlight it was a dismal scene.

'Why don't we spend the night here?' said Dann. 'We've got plenty of food. And then you decide if you'll come with me.'

This was taunting them; he had a small, not very pleasant grin on his face. They would have to come with him. Otherwise back on their island it would be said they had left Dann to challenge danger alone.

Durk said, 'Yes, why don't we sleep on it? And if the sea is bad tomorrow morning, then we'll forget it – eh, Dann?'

Dann shrugged.

They walked back on an overgrown path and caught sight of the big white animals keeping level with them. They were pleased to get inside the house, start a fire with the driftwood that still was stacked in a corner, light the rush lights they had brought, and eat.

Durk asked Dann where he had been a boatman. He told them of the boat on the River Cong, the river dragons and the old woman Han, and the sun trap. They listened, sometimes exchanging glances, so that they could not be thought gullible, believing these tall tales. When Dann got to the place where the war had filled the water with corpses, he left all that out; exactly as, talking to children, he softened and made pleasant, so now he felt that this innocence should be spared. These were good, peaceful people who had never known war.

They slept, without a guard, knowing the shutters and the door were solid, though they could hear the animals roaming about and testing the entrances.

In the morning the sky was clear and Dann said, 'If the sea is all right, I'm going.'

They walked to the landing place and this time the animals openly accompanied them.

'They want us to help them across the sea,' said Dann.

'Let them want,' said one of the lads, and the others agreed. Dann said nothing.

At the sea's edge the waves were no worse than yesterday, choppy and brisk, but Dann went to the boat without looking to see if the others came too and pushed it out; then they did join him. They were sulky, resistant, and Dann knew they hated him.

Dann was soon rowing fast, straight towards the nearest cliffs. The sun was burning their faces and shoulders, and now they could see slabs of ice lying along the bottom of the cliffs, and they were rowing between blocks of ice like houses.

Still Dann went on. The noise was frightful today, a cacophony of ice complaints, and Dann shouted, 'Stop!' as they saw the cliff nearest to them shed its ice load in a long single movement like a shrug to remove a weight. Now they were close, too close, to a tall shining cliff face, bare of ice, though water was bounding down, off rocks, in freshets and rivers, and the sea was rocking and rearing so badly that the boat was in danger of overturning. They were clutching the sides and calling out, while Dann was yelling with exultation, for this was what he had dreamed of, and it was what he was seeing – there were the ice cliffs of Yerrup and the sounds they made as they fell was like many voices, all at once, shouting, groaning, screaming – and then, crack, another ice face was peeling off, and Dann found that the others had turned the boat and it was rocking its way back to the shore, a long, dangerous way off. 'No,' cried Dann. 'No, I want to stay,' but Durk said, across the noise, 'We are leaving, Dann.'

And so Dann, in the back of the boat, sat staring at the retreating ice cliffs. And before they reached shore and safety, a large block of ice that shone blue and green and dusky pink was coming straight for them. To get out of its way they all had to row, Dann too, and then sat resting on their oars to watch it rock past.

They reached the shore and the waiting snow dogs.

Dann was white-faced and miserable. He wanted more, more, and closer, and he knew these men would not give him what he wanted.

He was thinking they were cowards. These were soft people, on these islands. Tender living had made them so. Well, he would talk in the inn of the wonders of the creaking and sliding cliffs, and use what was left of his money to pay others to go with him.

Dann stood on the shore, gazing at the cliffs, at the black places on the white cliffs, and wondered how long the ice had clung to those frozen sides, how long had it taken to form. He did not know, could not know; he was back in the realm of 'long, long ago' and the bitterness of it. He wanted so badly to know . . . surely answers could be found if only he could go further into the cliffs and then along them, and perhaps even climb up on to the ice and see – what would he see? For one thing, how did the snow dogs survive in all that wilderness of ice? How did they come down the cliffs? He stood and stared and the others, pulling up the boat and making it safe, sent wondering looks at him. There were tears on his face. This was a strange one, this Dann, they might have been saying aloud.

It was latish in the day, the sun would soon be gone behind the cliffs. It would be better to spend the night and go early tomorrow.

And so they did. They did not ask Dann for more of his tales, but first Durk, then the others, treated him gently, because of the unhappiness in his face.

'Dann,' said Durk, in consolation, as they lay down on their goatskins to sleep. 'You did it, didn't you? You saw what you wanted?'

And Dann said, as if to a child, 'Yes, I did, you're right, I did see them.'

Next morning, when they had eaten and left the house clean and tidy, they went out and a pack of snow dogs was sitting about, looking at them.

'Are we going to give some of them a lift over?' said Dann, and at once the others said, 'No, we aren't.' And 'Let them swim' and 'There's no room in the boat'.

As they walked to the boat, Dann saw an old abandoned craft, large, that did not seem to be holed, or useless. Without asking the others, he put rope that he always carried with him into its prow and pulled, and then Durk helped. Dann and Durk pushed the boat on to the waves and Dann tied it to their boat.

The dogs crowded closer, seeming to know what was being done.

The young men got on to their boat and were ready to row, their faces, all but Durk's, critical and sullen.

'The dogs won't stay on this island,' said Dann. 'They always want to go on.'

'They'll drown, if that boat sinks,' said one.

A bold snow dog jumped into the boat, then another, and then there were five in the boat. Others hung back, afraid.

'You'll have to wait a long time,' said Durk to them, laughing. 'No one's going to come back here if they can help it.'

But the big animals whined and moved about on the sand, and could not make themselves get on to the boat.

The first boat set off, all of them rowing, and the boat with the dogs followed on the rope.

The water was very cold. Surely any dog attempting that swim must drown?

The waves were tall and sharp, and seemed to be attacking the boat. The winds were belligerent. They had not gone more than a short way when one dog jumped into the sea to swim back. They watched it, but the waves were too high and soon they could not see it.

'Drowned,' said one youth and did not need to add, 'I hope.'

Dann thought of his snow pup and remembered the little beast's nuzzling at his shoulder.

Back at their landing stage they watched the animals leap off the old boat, swim to the shore and disappear into a wood.

Dann descended with Marianthe from their bedroom to the inn's common-room, expecting hostility, but saw the young men who had gone with him being bought drinks and questioned about the trip. They were enjoying their fame, and when Dann appeared mugs were lifted towards him from all the room.

Dann did not join the five, but let them keep their moment. He sat with Marianthe, and when people came to lay their hands on his shoulders and congratulate him, he said that without the others, nothing could have been achieved.

But no one had ever gone so near the ice cliffs, until he came to this island.

And now Marianthe was saying that it was time for their room to be decorated with the wedding branches and flowers; it was time to celebrate their union.

Dann held her close and said that she must not stop him leaving – when he did leave.

In the common-room people were joking about him

and Marianthe, and not always pleasantly. Some of the young men had hoped to take the place of her husband and resented Dann. He never replied to the jokes. Now he began to press them for another excursion. Had they ever seen the great fall of water from the Western Sea into this one? Marianthe said her husband wanted to make the attempt, but had been talked out of it. The feeling was that it would take days in even the largest fishing boat and it was not known if there were islands near the Falls where they could restock. But the real reason for the reluctance was the same: what for? was the feeling. Weren't things all right as they were?

They were talking of a wildly dangerous event, which they knew must appeal to Dann's reckless nature, and were satisfied with the trip to the ice cliffs: Dann and the fishermen and Durk were great heroes, and Dann did not say that compared with some of the dangers in his life it was not much of a thing to boast about.

He began going out with the fishermen; they seemed to think he had earned the right, because of his daring adventure to the ice cliffs. He learned the art of catching many different kinds of fish, and became friends with the men. All the time he was thinking of the northern icy shores and their secrets, hoping to persuade them to take him close again. He asked many questions, and learned very little. He was up against their lack of curiosity. He often could not believe it when he asked something and heard, 'We've never needed to know that,' or some such evasion.

The bitterness of his ignorance grew in him. He could not bear it, the immensity of what he didn't know. The pain was linked deep in him with something hidden from him. He never asked himself why he had to know what other people were content to leave unknown. He was used to Mara, who was like him, and longed to understand. Down here on this lovely island, where he was a stranger only in this one thing – that these people did not even know how ignorant they were – he thought of Mara, missed her and dreamed of her too. Marianthe said to him that he had been calling out for a woman, called Mara. Who was she? 'My sister,' he said and saw her politely sceptical smile.

How it isolated him, that smile, how it estranged her. He thought that back in the Centre Griot would not smile if Dann talked of Mara, for he had lived at the Farm.

The pain Dann felt was homesickness, but he did not suspect that: he had never had a home that he could remember, so how could he be missing one?

He must leave. Soon, he must leave, before Marianthe's disappointment in him turned to worse. But still he lingered.

He liked being with the girls who helped Marianthe with the inn's work. They were merry, teased and caressed him, and made fun. 'Oh, why are you so serious, Dann, always so serious, come on, give me a smile . . .' He thought that Kira could be one of them – but even as he did, knew her presence would end the laughter. Well, then, suppose she had been born here, in this easy pleasant place, rather than as a slave, with the threat of being taken for breeding by the Hadrons, would she then have been kind and loving, instead of always looking for an advantage, always ready to humiliate? Was he asking, then, if these girls, whose nature was to caress and charm, had been born for it? But here Dann was coming up against a question too hard for him: it was a matter of what people were born with. Had Kira been born hard and unkind? If these girls had been born into that city, Chelops (now gone into dust and ashes), would they have been like Kira? But he could not know the answer, and so he let it go and allowed himself to be entertained by them.

Now a thought barged into his mind that he certainly could not welcome. If Mara had been born here, would she, like these girls, have had adroit tender hands and a smile like an embrace? *Was he criticising Mara?* How could he! Brave Mara – but fierce Mara; indomitable and tenacious Mara. But no one could say she was not stubborn and obstinate – she could no more have smiled, and yielded and teased and cajoled than . . . these girls could have gone a mile of that journey she and he had undergone. But, he was thinking, what a hard life she had had, never any ease, or lightness, never any . . . fun. What a word to apply to Mara; he almost felt ashamed – and he watched Marianthe's girls at a kind of ball game they had, laughing and playing the fool. Oh, Mara, and I certainly didn't make things easier for you, did I? But these thoughts were too difficult and painful, so he let them go and allowed himself to be entertained.

He stood with Marianthe at her window, overlooking the northern seas, where sometimes appeared blocks of ice that had fallen from the cliffs – though they always melted fast in the sun. Below them was a blue dance of water that he knew could be so cold, but with the sun on it seemed a playfellow, with the intimacy of an invitation: come on in, join me . . . Dann asked Marianthe, holding her close from behind, his face on her shining black curls, if she would not like to go with him back up the cliffs and walk to the Centre, and from there go with him to see that amazing roar and rush of white water . . . even as he said it, he thought how dismal she would find the marshes and the chilly mists.

'How could I leave my inn?' she said, meaning that she did not want to.

And now he dared to say that one day he believed she would have to. That morning he had made a trip to the town at the sea's edge that had waves washing over its roofs.

'Look over there,' he said, tilting back her head by the chin, so she had to look up, to the distant icy gleams that were the ice mountains. Up there, he said to her, long long ago had been great cities, marvellous cities, finer than anything anywhere now – and he knew she was seeing in her mind's eye the villages of the islands; you could not really call them towns. 'It is hard for us to imagine those cities, and now anything like them is deep in the marshes up there on the southern shore.' Marianthe leaned back against him, and rubbed her head against his cheek – he was tall, but she was almost as tall – and asked coaxingly why she should care about long ago.

'Beautiful cities,' he said, 'with gardens and parks, that the ice covered, but it is going now, it is going so fast.'

But she mocked him and he laughed with her.

'Come to bed, Dann.'

He had not been in her bed for three nights now and it was because, and he told her so, she was in the middle of her cycle, so she could conceive. She always laughed at him and was petulant, when he said this, asking how did he know, and anyway, she wanted a child, please, come on Dann.

And this was now the painful point of division between them. She wanted a child, to keep him with her, and he very much did not.

Marianthe had told her woman friends and the girls working at the inn, and they had told their men, and one evening, in the big main room, one of the fishermen called out that they had heard he knew the secrets of the bed.

'Not of the bed,' he said. 'But of birth, when to conceive, yes.'

The room was full of men and women, and some children. By now he knew them all. Their faces had on them the same expression when they looked at him. Not antagonistic, exactly, but ready to be. He was always testing them, even when he did not mean to.

Now one fisherman called out, 'And where did you get all that clever stuff from, Dann? Perhaps it is too deep for us.'

Here it was again, a moment when something he said brought into question everything he had ever said, all his tales, his exploits.

'Nothing clever about it,' Dann said. 'If you can count the days between one full moon and the next full moon, and you do that all the time, then you can count the intervals between a woman's flows. It is simple. For five days in the middle of a woman's cycle a woman can conceive.'

'You haven't told us who told you. How do you know? How is it you know this and we don't?' A woman said this, and she was unfriendly.

'Yes, you ask me how I know. Well, it is known. But only in some places. And that is the trouble. That is *our* trouble, all of us – do you see? Why is it you can travel to a new place and there is knowledge there that isn't in other places? When my sister Mara arrived at the Agre Army – I told you that story – the general there taught her all kinds of things she didn't know but he didn't know about the means of controlling birth. He had never heard of it.'

Dann was standing by the great counter of the room where the casks of beer were, and the ranks of mugs. He was looking around at them all, from face to face, as if someone there could come out, there and then, with another bit of information that could fit in and make a whole.

'Once,' he said, 'long ago, before the Ice came down up there' – and he pointed in the direction of the ice cliffs – 'all the land up there was covered with great cities and there was a great knowledge, which was lost, under the Ice. But it was found, some of it, and hidden in the sands – when there were sands and not marshes. Then bits and pieces of the old knowledge travelled, and it was known here and there, but never as a whole, except in the old Centre – but now it is in fragments there too.'

'And how do you know what you know?' came a sardonic query, from the eldest of the fishermen. Real hostility was near now; they were all staring at him and their eyes were cold.

Marianthe, behind the counter, began to weep.

'Yes,' said one of the younger fishermen, 'he makes you cry; is that why you like him, Marianthe?'

That scene had been some days ago.

And now, this afternoon, was the moment when Dann knew he had to go . . .

'Marianthe,' he said, 'you know what I'm going to say.'

'Yes,' she said.

'Well, Marianthe, would you really be pleased if I went off leaving you with a baby? Would you?'

She was crying and would not answer.

In the corner of the room was his old sack. And that was all he had, or needed, after such a long time here – how long? Durk had reminded him that it was nearly three years.

He went down to the common-room, holding his old sack.

All the eyes in the room turned to see Marianthe, pale and tragic. People were eating their midday meal after returning from fishing.

One of the girls called out, 'Some men were asking for you.'

'What?' said Dann, and in an instant his security in this place, or anywhere on the islands, disappeared. What a fool he had been, thinking that the descent to the Bottom Sea and a few hops from island to island had been enough to . . . 'Who were they?' he asked.

A fisherman called out, 'They say you have a price on your head. What is your crime?'

Dann had already hitched his sack on to his shoulders and, seeing this, Durk was collecting his things too.

'I told you, I ran away from the army in Shari. I was a general and I deserted.'

A man who didn't like him said, 'General, were you?'

'I told you that.'

'So your tales were true, then?' someone said, half regretful, part sceptical still.

Dann, standing there, a thin and at the moment grief-stricken figure, so young – sometimes he still looked like a boy – did not look like a general, or anything soldierly, for that matter. Not that they had ever seen a soldier.

'Nearly all were true,' said Dann, thinking of how he had softened everything for them. He had never told them that once he had gambled away his sister, nor what had happened to him in the Towers – not even Marianthe, who knew of the scars on his body. 'They were true,' he said again, 'but the very bad things I did not tell you.'

Marianthe was leaning on the bar counter, weeping. One of the girls put her arms round her and said, 'Don't, you'll be ill.'

'You haven't said what they looked like,' said Dann, thinking of his old enemy, Kulik, who might or might not be dead.

At last he got out of them that there were two men, not young, and yes, one had a scar. Well, plenty of people had scars; 'up there' they did, but not down here.

Durk was beside Dann now, with his sack. The girls were bringing food for them to take.

'Well,' called a fisherman, from over his dish of soup and bread, 'I suppose we'll never hear the rest of your tales. Perhaps I'll miss you, at that.'

'We'll miss you,' the girls said, and crowded around to kiss him and pet him. 'Come back, come back,' they mourned.

And Dann embraced Marianthe, but swiftly, because of the watching people. 'Why don't you come up to the Centre?' he whispered, but knew she never would – and she did not answer.

'Goodbye, General,' came from his chief antagonist, sounding quite friendly now. 'And be careful as you go. Those men are nasty-looking types.'

Dann and Durk went to the boat, this time not stopping at every island, and to Durk's, where his parents asked what had kept him so long. The girl Durk had wanted was with someone else and averted her eyes when she saw him.

At the inn Dann heard again about the men who had been asking for him. He thought, *When I get to the Centre I'll be safe.* In the morning, he sat in the boat as he had come, in the bows, like a passenger, Durk rowing from the middle, his back to Dann, like a boatman.

Dann watched the great cliffs of the southern shore loom up, until Durk exclaimed, 'Look!' and rested his oars, and Dann stood to see better.

Down the crevices and cracks and gulleys poured white, a smoking white . . . had 'up there' been flooded, had the marshes overflowed? And then they saw; it was mist that was seeping down the dark faces of the cliff. And Durk said he had never seen anything like that in all his time as a boatman and Dann slumped back on his seat, so relieved he could only say, 'That's all right, then.' He had had such a vision of disaster, as if all the world of 'up there' had gone into water.

Closer they drew, and closer: as the mists neared the Middle Sea they vanished, vanquished by the warmer airs of this happy sea . . . so Dann was seeing it, as the boat crunched on the gritty shore.

That pouring weight of wet air, the mists, was speaking to him of loss, of sorrow, but that was not how he had set out from Durk's inn, light-hearted and looking forward to – well, to what exactly? He did not love the Centre! No, it was Mara, he must see Mara, he would go to the Farm, he must. But he stood on the little beach and stared up, and the falling wet whiteness filled him with woe.

He turned, and saw Durk there, with the boat's rope in his hand, staring at him. That look, what did it mean? Not possible to pretend it away: Durk's honest, and always friendly, face was . . . what? He was looking at Dann as if wanting to see right inside him. Dann was reminded of – yes, it was Griot, whose face was so often a reproach.

'Well,' said Dann, 'and so I'm off.' He turned away from Durk, and the look which was disturbing him, saying, 'Some time, come and see me at the Centre. All you have to do is to walk for some days along the edge.' He thought, *and the dangers, and the ugliness, and the wet slipperiness* . . . He said, his back still turned as he began to walk to the foot of the cliffs, 'It's easy, Durk, you'll see,' and thought that for Durk it would not be easy: he knew about boats and the sea and the safe work of the islands.

He took his first step on the path up, and heard an oar splash.

He felt that all the grey dank airs of the marshes had seeped into him, in a cold weight of . . . he was miserable about something: he had to admit it. He turned. A few paces from the shore Durk stood in his boat, still staring at Dann, who thought, *We have been together all this time, he stayed away from his island and his girl because of me, he is my friend.* These were new thoughts for Dann. He shouted, 'Durk, come to the Centre, do come.'

Durk turned his back on Dann and sat, rowing hard – and out of Dann's life.

Dann watched him, thinking, he must turn round . . . but he didn't.

Dann started up the cliff, into the mists. He was at once soaked. And his face . . . but for lovely and loving Marianthe he did not shed one tear, or if he did, it was not in him to know it.

He thought, struggling up the cliff: *But that's what I've always done. What's the use of looking back and crying? If you have to leave a place . . . leave a person . . . then, that's it, you leave. I've been doing it all my life, haven't I?*

It took all day to reach the top, and then he heard voices, but he did not know the languages. He sheltered, wet and uncomfortable, under a rock. He was thinking,

Am I mad, am I really, really mad to leave 'down there' – with its delightful airs, its balmy winds, its peaceful sunny islands? It is the nicest, friendliest place I have ever been in.

After the soft bed of Marianthe his stony sleep was fitful and he woke early, thinking to get on to the path before the refugees filled it. But there was already a stream of desperate people walking there. Dann slipped into the stream and became one of them, so they did not eye his heavy sack, and the possibility of food. Who were they, these fugitives? They were not the same as those he had seen three years before. Another war? Where? What was this language, or languages?

He walked along, brisk and healthy, and attracted looks because of his difference from these weary, starving people.

Then, by the side of the track, he saw a tumble of white bones, and he stepped out of the crowd and stood by them. The long bones had teeth marks and one had been cracked for the marrow. No heath bird had done that. What animals lived on these moors? Probably some snow dogs did. The two youngsters – these were their bones. Dann had never imagined what he and Mara might have looked like to observers, friendly and unfriendly, on their journey north. Not until he saw the two youngsters, seemingly blown towards him by the marshy winds, until he caught them, had he ever thought how Mara and he had been seen, but now here they were, scattered bones by the roadside. That's Mara and me, thought Dann – if we had been unlucky.

And he stood there, as if on watch, until he bent and

picked little sprigs of heather and put them in the eye sockets of the two clean young skulls.

Soon afterwards he saw a dark crest of woods on the rise ahead and knew it would be crowded with people at last able to sit down on solid ground that was dry. And so it was; a lot of people, very many sitting and lying under the trees. There were children, crying from hunger. Not far was Kass's little house, out of sight of these desperate ones, and Dann went towards it, carefully, not attracting attention. When he reached it he saw the door was open and on the step a large white beast who, seeing him, lifted its head and howled. It came bounding towards him, and lay before him and rolled, and barked, licking his legs. Dann was so busy squatting to greet Ruff that he did not at once notice Kass, but she was not alone. There was a man with her, a Thores, like her, short and strong – and dangerously alert to everything. Kass called out, 'See, he knows you, he's been waiting for you, he's been waiting for days now and the nights too, looking out . . .' And to the man she said, 'This is Dann, I told you.' What she had told her husband Dann could not know; he was being given not hostile, but wary and knowledgeable looks. He was invited in, first by Kass: 'This is Noll,' and then by Noll. He had found them at table and was glad of it: it was a good way to the Centre and his food had to last. The snow dog was told to sit in the open door, to be seen, and to frighten off any refugees sharp enough to find their way there.

Noll had come from the cities of Tundra with enough money to keep them going, but he would have to return.

The food and stores he had brought, and the money, were already depleted. This was an amiable enough man, but on guard, and sharp, and Dann was feeling relief that Noll was the kind of fellow he understood, someone who knew hardship. Already the islands were seeming to him like a kindly story or dream, and Durk's smiling (and reproachful) face – but Dann did not want to recognise that – a part of the past, and an old tale. Yes, the fishermen had to face storms, sometimes, but there was something down there that sapped and enervated.

In spite of the damp, and the cold of the mists that rolled through the trees from the marshes, Dann thought, *This is much more my line*.

Kass did not hide from her husband that she was pleased to see Dann and even took his hand and held it, in front of him. Noll merely smiled, and then said, 'Yes, you're welcome.' The snow dog came from his post at the door to Dann, put his head on his arm and whined.

'This animal has looked after me well,' said Kass. 'I don't know how often I've had desperadoes banging at the door, but Ruff's barking sent them off again.'

And now Dann, his arms round Ruff, who would not leave him, told how he had gone down the cliffs to the Bottom Sea and the islands, but did not mention Marianthe, though Kass's eyes were on his face to see if she could find the shadow of a woman on it.

These two were listening as if to tales from an imagined place, and kept saying that one day they would make the trip to the Bottom Sea and find out for themselves what strange folk lived down there, and discover the forests of trees they had never seen.

When night came Dann lay on a pallet on the floor, and thought of how on that bed up there he had lain with Kass and the snow puppy, now this great shaggy beast who lay by him as close as he could press, whining his happiness that Dann was there.

Dann was thinking that Kass had been good to him, and then – and this was a new thought for him – that he had been good to Kass. He had not stopped to wonder before if he had been good to or for a person. It was not a sentiment one associated with Kira. Surely he had been good to Mara? But the question did not arise. She was Mara and he was Dann, and that was all that had to be said. And Marianthe? No, that was something else. But with Kass he had to think first of kindness, and how she had held him when he wept, and had nourished the pup.

In the morning he shared their meal, and at last said he must go. Down the hill the woods were still full of the fugitives, new ones probably. And now the snow dog was whining in anxiety, and he actually took Dann's sleeve in his teeth and pulled him. 'He knows you are going,' said Kass. 'He doesn't want you to go.' And her eyes told Dann she didn't want him to go either. Her husband, in possession, merely smiled, pleasantly enough, and would not be sorry when Dann left.

Ruff followed Dann to the door.

Noll said, 'He knows you saved his life.'

Dann stroked the snow dog, and then hugged him and said, 'Goodbye, Ruff,' but the animal came with him out of the door and looked back at Kass and Noll and barked, but followed Dann.

'Oh, Ruff,' said Kass, 'you're leaving me.' The dog whined, looking at her, but kept on after Dann who was trying not to look back and tempt the animal away. Now Kass ran after Dann with bread off the table, and rations for the animal, and some fish. She said to Dann, out of earshot of her husband, 'Come back and see me, you and Ruff, come back.' Dann said aloud that if she kept a lookout she would see new snow dogs coming up the cliff and one could take the place of Ruff, for a guard dog. She did not say it would not be the same, but knelt by the great dog and put her arms round him, and Ruff licked her face. Then she got up and, without looking back at Dann and Ruff, went to her husband.

'So, Ruff, you remembered me so well after all this time' and before he reached the stream of refugees, he knelt by Ruff and held him. The dog put his head on Dann's shoulder and Dann was crying again. *He's my friend*, Dann was thinking.

The stream of refugees became agitated when they saw Dann with the snow dog. Heads turned, hands went to knives and sticks were raised. Dann called out, 'It's all right, he's tame,' in one language and then another but no one understood. More effective was how he stepped into the stream, his knife in his hand. People fell back behind him and left a space on either side of him. Dann was afraid of a stone thrown from behind his back, but was reassured by Ruff's thick coat – no stone could make an impression on that – although there was his long tender muzzle, his bright eyes, emerging from the ruff, his small, neat ears. So Dann kept turning to make sure no one was creeping up to attack the beast. No one did. They were too full of frightened thoughts of their hunger, of how to get to safety. And they went along, Dann and his snow dog, who kept looking up at Dann to see if all was well, and so the day went by until he began looking for the place where he had stepped off the path and seen whitish masses floating in a pool.

It was further than he expected. So slowly were they travelling today, because of the wariness over Ruff and having to stop, whereas when he had run to find help for the pup he had been going as fast as he could – faster than he had known. At last he saw a pattern of pools he recognised and stepped from the stream of people on to a soggy path between the pools. And there in the water he saw two foamy white masses. Ruff was by him, looking where he looked. He glanced up to see Dann's face, looked back at the water. Then he began to whine anxiously and it seemed he was going to jump into the water. Dann took a good hold of the snow dog and said, 'No, Ruff, no, Ruff, no.' The water was very cold. Films and crinkles of ice lay here and there on it and enclosed the stems of reeds. All that time had passed, but the bubbling white was still there: not the flesh and the bones, only the mats of hair. Ruff let out a howl, causing the travellers on the path to stop and look. Dann smoothed his head, thinking how he had stood here with the dead weight of the soaked young animal against him. Dann led him to the soggy path and all the way Ruff was looking back, even when the pool became screened with reeds. He remembered, or half remembered, and Dann kept his hand on the animal's head as they rejoined the people and talked to him: 'Ruff, Ruff, you're safe, I'll look after you. I'll always look after you.' The snow dog barked, in answer, and kept looking up at Dann for reassurance.

Now the night was coming and there was a difficulty. On this path there was nowhere to shelter, as he knew from his journey the other way. A place would have to be found down the side of the cliff. There were bushes, but quite a way down and the stronger refugees would try to reach them. He was hungry and so was Ruff, but Dann had seen people eyeing his bulging sack and he knew what they would do if they saw him giving precious food to a hated snow dog. At last he saw a great boulder, resting on another. There was a ledge. It would take ingenuity to climb up there and Dann doubted whether anyone would try it. He slid down over shale to the boulder and found a way up; Ruff followed him and lay down. There below them was the gleam of the Bottom Sea, and to the east dark blobs that were the islands. The evening sky was a pearly lake, flushed pink. The bushes back near the path were crowded with people, already fighting off others who were trying to crowd in. Now Dann could open his sack and give some bread and some fish to Ruff. The animal had been drinking from the marshes as they came. Soon there was a moon and Dann was glad of it: he saw shadows creeping towards the boulder and he shouted and saw scuttling off some lads, who had planned to join them. Ruff was moving about restlessly, and whining, but Dann held his muzzle shut and whispered, 'Don't bark, don't.' And

Ruff lay down, head on his great white paws, and was silent, watching the side of the cliff. So passed the night and the first light saw the refugees crowding back to the path. Some had used their clothes to scoop up marsh fish, and soggy fishbones lay about.

That next night was spent in a hollow between rocks a good way from the travellers. Ruff lay close to Dann, who was glad of the warmth.

More days passed, and then a wide enough track ran off south through marshes that were shallower here, not so dangerous. Part of the refugee stream turned off on the track, which lay on a route through Tundra to its frontier. Well, they wouldn't find much comfort there, and he tried to tell them so, but one after another they turned sullen and uncomprehending eyes on him. Those who still kept to the path on the cliff's edge were, it seemed, because there were fewer of them, relieved of the necessity for keeping the peace. They began quarrelling and fighting, if they suspected one had food hidden. They surrounded Dann and the snow dog, for Dann's sack, which was much depleted now, but still had a promising bulge. Ruff barked and made short rushes at them, and they fell back; Dann led off the track into a path that went south-west, still through bogs and marshes, but they were not so bad. The ground soon became a little higher, there were some bushes and clumps of tall reeds. There came into sight a building, not more than a shed, on the right of the track. On the door of this shed was scrawled 'No Refugees Here. Keep off'. He knocked and shouted, 'I'm not a refugee. I can pay.' No sound or movement from inside. He knocked again, a shutter moved and the face of a scowling old woman appeared.

'What do you want?'

'Let me in. I'll pay for food and shelter.'

'I'm not having a snow dog here.'

'He's tame, he won't hurt you.'

'No, go away.'

'He can keep guard,' shouted Dann.

At last the door, which was made of thick reeds held together by leather thongs, moved open and an old man's voice said, 'Be quick, then.'

Two old people stood facing him, but looking at the great beast, who sat down at once and looked at them.

The room was not large, and it was dark, with a single fish-oil lamp on a rough table. The walls were of turves and the roof of reeds.

Dann said, 'I'll pay you for some food for me and the animal.'

'Then you must leave,' said the old woman, who showed that she was afraid of Ruff.

'I'll pay you for letting us sleep here, on the floor.'

At this moment there were shouts and knocks on the door, which would give way in another instant. The old woman swore and shouted abuse. The old man was peering out through cracks in the shutter.

'Bark, Ruff,' said Dann. Ruff understood and barked loudly. The people outside ran off.

'He's a guard dog,' said Dann.

'Very well,' said the old woman. She said something to the old man, and Dann didn't recognise the language.

'Where are you from?' asked Dann. Their faces, under

the dirt, were pallid, and their hair pale too. 'Are you Albs?'

'What's that to you?' demanded the old man, afraid.

'I have friends who are Albs,' said Dann.

'We are half Albs,' said the old woman. 'And that half is enough to make us enemies, so they think.'

'I know the trouble Albs have,' said Dann.

'Do you? That's nice for you, then.'

'I am from Rustam,' said Dann casually, to see what they would say.

'Rustam, where's that?'

'A long, long way south, beyond Charad, beyond the river towns, beyond Chelops.'

'We hear a lot of travellers' tales – thieves and liars, that's what they are,' said the old woman.

Outside, moonlight showed that some refugees had found this higher drier track and were lying on it, sleeping.

'There are quite a few children out there,' Dann said – to see what they would say.

'Children grow up to be thieves and rascals.'

Dann was given a bowl of marsh fish, muddy and grey, with a porridge of vegetables thickened with meal. Ruff got the same: well, he didn't have much better at Kass's house.

Then the old woman said, 'Now, you and that animal sit near the door and if there's knocking, make him bark.'

Dann settled near the door, the dog beside him. He thought that there would probably not be disturbances now it was late. But once knocks did rouse them all, and the dog barked and the intruder left.

'We don't like snow dogs,' said the old woman, from her ragged bed on the floor. 'We kill them if we can.'

'Why don't you make one into a guard dog?'

But in the corner she muttered and gloomed and the old man, who clearly did what he was told, said that snow dogs were dangerous, everyone knew that.

Dann slept sitting, with the snow dog lying close, both glad of the warmth. They must be very cold out there, those poor people . . . Dann surprised himself with this thought. He did not see the use of sympathising with people in trouble, if he could not make cause with them, in some way. But he was thinking that once he and Mara had been – often enough – two frightened youngsters among refugees and outcasts, just like those out there in the cold moonlight that sifted over them from wet cloud.

In the very early morning, as the light came, he woke and looked at the mud floor, the turf walls, the low reed roof that leaked in places, and thought that this was called a house. It was worse by far than Kass's. Under the marshes were the marvellous great cities that had sunk through the mud. Why was it such cities were not built now? He remembered the towns he and Mara had travelled through, fine towns, but far from the drowned cities around him – and such a longing gripped him for the glories of that lost time that he groaned. Ruff woke and licked his hands. 'Why?' he was muttering. 'Why, Ruff? I don't understand how it could happen. *That* – and then this.'

He coughed, and Ruff barked softly, and the two old ones woke.

'So, you're off, then?' said the old woman.

'Not without our breakfast.'

Again they got a kind of porridge, with vegetables.

'Where are you going?' the woman wanted to know.

'To the Centre.'

'Then what are you doing in a poor place like this?'

Dann said he had come from the east, had been down in the islands, but the old people were uneasy, and did not want to know any more.

'We hear the islands do well enough,' said the old man angrily.

Dann asked, as casually as he could, what was heard about the Centre these days.

'There are ruffians there now, they say. I don't know what the old Mahondis would say.'

'I am a Mahondi,' said Dann, remembering what it had once meant to say that.

'Then you'll know about the young prince. Everyone is waiting for him to put things right.'

Dann was going to say, *Hasn't the time gone past for princes?* – but decided not to. They were so old: in the cold morning light they were like old ghosts.

A banging at the door. Ruff barked; again the sound of running feet.

'It seems to me we've done well enough by you, keeping them all away,' said Dann.

'He's right,' said the old man. 'Let him stay. He and that animal can keep watch and we can get some sleep.'

'Thanks,' said Dann, 'but we'll be off. And thanks for your hospitality.' He had meant this last to be sarcastic, but those two old things were making him feel as if he were hitting babies.

'Perhaps you could ask your Alb friends to visit us?' said the old woman.

'There's an Alb settlement not too far from here,' he said, and she said, 'They don't want to know us, because of the half of us not Alb.'

These two old toddlers could not get much further than the clifftop track, if as far as that.

'It would be nice to see something of our kind' – and even the nets of wrinkles on her face and the old sunk eyes seemed to be pleading.

Dann thought of fastidious Leta in this hut but said nevertheless, 'I'll tell them to visit you.'

The old woman began to cry, and then the old man, in sympathy.

'Don't leave us,' she said, and then he said it too.

'Why don't you invite the next snow dog in?' said Dann. 'They make good companions.'

He and Ruff left, making their way on little-used paths back to the track westwards, and there they went on until one crossroad led to the Centre and the other to the Farm. *Mara, there's Mara*, he was thinking, longing to go to her, but he took a few steps and came back, hesitated. The snow dog went forward and Dann followed, but stopped. The snow dog stopped, his eyes on Dann's face. It was as if the way west were barred with a NO, like a dark cloud. He wanted so much to go to the Farm, but could not. Ruff came and sat by his knees, looking up, then licking his hands, and by this Dann knew the dog was sensing more than his indecision. When Dann was sad, Ruff knew it. 'Why can't I go, Ruff?' he enquired aloud, standing there by the grey watery wastes, the white marsh birds standing in their pools, or calling and looking for fish and frogs as they floated low, the wind in their feathers. 'Why can't I?' And he set himself northwards, to the Centre.

Long before he reached it he saw it rise up there, its top gone into low cloud. How large it was, how imposing – if one didn't know about the ruins and half-ruins, the waters soaking its northern and western edges, the smell of damp and rot. No wonder it had dominated the whole area – no, the whole of Ifrik – for so long. With the sun coming on to it from the western sky it gleamed, it glowed, the golden cloud crowning it, the outer walls shining. Dann went towards it, thinking now of Griot, who had every reason for reproach, noting changes, one of them being the sentry who challenged him at the gate. He wore something like a uniform: brown baggy top, baggy trousers, a red blanket over one shoulder. A surge of rage overwhelmed him; he pushed aside the youth, whose eyes were on the snow dog. Ruff disdained even to growl.

In the great hall, where he and Mara had waited to be recognised, he saw Griot sitting at a table, which had on it the frames with beads used for counting, and piles of reed tablets. Dann approached quietly. Griot raised his head and at once a smile appeared, like an embrace. Griot stood and his arms did rise, but fell again as he put on an expression more suitable for a soldier, though he need not have bothered: he was an embodied cry of joy.

'Dann . . . Sir . . . General . . .'

'Yes, I'm sorry,' said Dann, who was, at that moment.

'You've been such a long time.'

'Yes, I know. I was detained by a witch on an island in the Bottom Sea.' He was trying to jest, but amended, 'No, I was joking, it is pleasant down there.'

Now Dann saw something in Griot's face that made him stand, quietly, on guard, waiting: was Griot going to speak? No. Dann asked, 'Tell me how things are going.'

Griot came out from behind his table and, standing at ease, as he had been taught when a new soldier under Dann's command, 'We have six hundred trained men now, sir.'

'Six hundred.'

'We could have as many as we like, so many come to the Centre from the east.'

Here Ruff went forward to inspect this new friend, his heavy tail wagging.

'We have quite a few of these snow dogs trained as guards,' said Griot, stroking the animal's head.

'People seem to be afraid of them.'

'Enemies have good reason to be afraid of them.'

'So, what are those reed huts I saw coming in – they're new.'

'Barracks. And we must build more.'

'And what are we going to do with this army?'

'Yes, that's it, but you'll have heard about Tundra. It's falling apart. There are two factions. There will be more, we think.'

Dann noted the *we*.

'The administration is hardly working. One faction has sent us messages, to join them. It's the prestige of the Centre, you see, sir.' Griot hesitated, then went bravely on. 'It's your prestige, everyone knows you're here, in command.'

'And the other faction, presumably the weaker?'

'They're just – useless. It will be a walkover.'

'I see. And do you know how many refugees are pouring into Tundra from the east?'

'Yes, we know. Many turn up here. The majority. I have a friend in Tundra, he keeps me informed.'

'So, Griot, you have a spy system?'

'Yes – yes, sir, I do. And it is very efficient.'

'Well done, Griot. I see our army in Agre trained you well.'

'It was Shabis.' And at the mention of Shabis Griot's eyes were full of – what? Dann was on the point of asking, but again evaded with, 'And how are you feeding all these people?'

'We are growing grains and vegetables on the foothills of the mountain, where it's dry. And we have a lot of animals now – there are so many empty buildings on the outskirts.'

'Why did you build the huts, then?'

'First, if people are in the Centre they pilfer, and then, keeping the men in barracks makes for uniformity. The empty buildings come in every size and shape, but the huts take two men each or two women and no one can complain about favouritism.'

There was a pause here. Griot was standing on one side of the table, Dann on the other, the snow dog sitting where he could observe them: his eyes went from face to face and his tail wasn't wagging now.

'Are you hungry?' Griot asked, postponing the moment, whatever it was.

'No, but I am sure Ruff is.'

Griot went to the door and Ruff went with him. Griot shouted orders and returned.

'You're honoured, Griot, he doesn't make friends with everyone.'

'I get along with snow dogs. I train ours.'

'Tell me more abut the provisioning,' said Dann, and Griot did so until a bowl of food arrived and was set down. The soldier who brought it kept his distance from the snow dog. Ruff ate, the two men sat and watched.

'Better than he's had in his life. I don't think much meat has come his way.'

A pause, and now Dann could not help himself. 'Out with it, what is it?'

Griot sat silent, and then said in a low voice, 'Don't blame me for what I have to tell you. Bad enough to have to sit on the news for so long . . .'

'Out with it.'

'Mara's dead. She died when the child was born.' Griot averted his eyes from Dann's face.

Dann said in a matter-of-fact way, 'Of course. I knew it. That makes sense. Yes.'

Griot risked a swift glance.

'I knew it all the time, I must have,' said Dann. 'Otherwise, why . . .' and he fell silent.

'The message came just after you left.'

Dann sat on, not moving. The dog came to him, put his head on his knee and whined.

Dann rose up from his chair mechanically, slowly,

and stood, hands out, palms up. He stared down at them. 'Of course,' he said in the same reasonable voice. 'Yes, that's it.' And then, to Griot, 'You say Mara's dead?'

'Yes, she's dead, but the child is alive. You've been gone a good bit, sir. The child . . .'

'It killed Mara,' said Dann.

He began moving about, not consistently or purposefully, but he took a step, stopped, and again there was that way of staring at his hands; he took another step or two, whirled about as if ready to attack someone, stood glaring.

Ruff was following him, looking up at his face. Griot watched them both. Dann took another jerky step or two, then stopped.

'Mara,' said Dann. 'Mara' in a loud emphatic voice, arguing with someone invisible, so it seemed, and then threatening: 'Mara dead? No, no, no,' and now he shouted, all defiance, and he kicked out wildly, just missing Ruff, who crept under the table.

Then in the same erratic jerky way he sat down at the table and stared at Griot.

'You knew her?' he said.

'Yes, I was at the Farm.'

'I suppose the other one, Kira – Kira had her baby and it's alive?'

'Yes.'

'I suppose we could count on that,' said Dann grimly, and Griot, knowing exactly why he said it and feeling with him, said, 'Yes, I know.'

'What am I going to do?' Dann asked Griot, and

Griot, all pain for Dann, muttered, 'I don't know. I don't know, Dann, sir . . .'

Dann got up again and began on his jerky inconsequential progress.

He was talking nonsense, names of places and people, ejaculations of protest and anger, and Griot was not able to follow it.

At one point he asked about the old woman, and Griot said that she was dead.

'She wanted me as a stud, and Mara as a brood animal.'

'Yes, I know.'

This tale, like the others of Dann's and Mara's adventures, was known generally, but sometimes told fantastically. The custodians of the Centre had waited for the rightful prince and princess to arrive and start a new dynasty of the royal ruling family, but they had refused. So far so good. But then the public imagination had created a battle where the old pair were killed because they would not share the secret knowledge of the Centre, and Dann and Mara escaped to found their own dynasty, and would return to the Centre to take over . . . all of Ifrik, all of Tundra, or however far the geographical knowledge of the teller extended. And in these versions Dann had become a great conquering general who had fought his way here from far down Ifrik.

Dann talked, then muttered, while Griot listened and Ruff watched from under the table. Dann was more than a little mad, and at last Griot got up and said, 'Dann, sir, General, you must go to sleep. You'll be ill. You are ill.'

'What am I going to do, Griot?' And Dann gripped

Griot by the shoulders and stared close into his face. 'I don't know what I'm going to do.'

'Yes, sir. Just come with me. Now come.'

For all the time Dann had been gone, two rooms had waited for his return. One was Dann's and Griot knew this, but the other had been Mara's, and that Griot did not know. When Dann stumbled through this room and looked down at the bed where Mara had been, he began crying.

Griot led him through this room and to the next. It had a door open on to the square where the soldiers drilled, and this Griot shut. He led Dann to the bed and, when he did not do more than stare down at it, Griot helped him lie down. Ruff lay by the bed, keeping his distance.

Griot went off and returned with a sticky black lump which he showed to Dann. 'It's poppy,' he said. 'You'll sleep.'

At this Dann shot up, and grabbed Griot by the shoulders and shook him. With a terrible laugh he shouted, 'So, you want to kill me.'

Griot had seldom smoked the stuff, he did not care for it. He had no idea what Dann meant; Dann saw that anxious puzzled face and let him go.

'It did nearly kill me once,' he said and, of his own accord, lay down again.

'The soldiers use it. They burn it. They like the fumes.'

'Then forbid it.'

'There's not much of it in the camp.'

'I said – forbid it. That's an order, Griot.' He sounded sane enough.

Griot covered Dann's legs with a blanket and said, 'Call me, if you want me,' and went out.

He sat on the bed in the room next door and heard howling. Was that Ruff? No, it was Dann, and Ruff was whining in sympathy. Griot put his head in his hands and listened. At last there was silence. He crept to the door; Dann was asleep, his arms round the snow dog's neck. Ruff was not asleep.

Now Dann was ill, and it went on, and time went on, and Griot looked after Dann, not knowing if what he was doing was right. Yet Dann did take some responsibility for himself. First, he told Griot that if he ever asked for poppy Griot must refuse. 'That's an order, Griot.' He demanded to be kept supplied with jugs of the beer the soldiers made, alcoholic if enough of it was drunk, and he stayed in his room, sometimes walking about, sometimes lying on the bed, and he talked to himself or to Mara, or to the snow dog. He kept himself drunk. When he walked about, Ruff went with him, step for step, and at night Ruff lay close, and licked his hands and face. Dann told Griot he must call Ruff to go out, have his meals and run around a little. Ruff went willingly with Griot and he made the acquaintance of the other snow dogs – a tricky thing this, because Ruff had not been with others of his kind. But they got on well enough, provided Ruff kept his distance. He never became one of their pack. He always wanted to return to Dann. Weeks passed. Griot was thinking that now was the time to invade the Tundra cities; all the news he was getting confirmed this, but he needed Dann because he was General Dann and known through all of Tundra. And, too, Griot needed Dann for his superior military knowledge.

Though Dann was quite crazy at this time, this did not prevent him from emerging on occasion, to sit at the table with Griot, advising on this and that. The advice was sensible and Griot relied on it.

The soldiers talked among themselves, of course, because they were on duty as guards outside Dann's room, and sometimes inside the room, when Dann was worse than usual. Their General was mad, they all knew, but for some reason this did not seem to alarm them. They spoke of him always with respect – more, it was love, Griot thought, and this did not surprise him.

But Dann did not seem to be getting better, so Griot decided to make the trip to the Farm, to talk to Shabis and ask help from Leta, who had so much knowledge of plants and medicines. He told Dann he was going to make a reconnaissance trip to Tundra's cities. Dann said he wanted a soldier in Griot's place, male, not a woman.

Because this man organised Dann's bathing, bringing the big basins and the hot water, and persuading Dann into the water, he saw the scars around Dann's waist, which he could not account for, but which looked as if at some point Dann had worn a slave chain, whose barbs had torn him; and he saw, too, the scars on Dann's buttocks radiating out from his anus. The word got around the camp about these cruel scars, and Dann's reputation was enhanced, in the direction of awesomeness and the unknown. And their General had been a slave – that helped them to understand his present illness. Then the guard soldier let drop that Griot had gone to the Farm and, while Dann understood the deception, it hurt to think of Griot there, at that place which in his mind was like a soothing dream, with its windy Western Sea, its streams of running water and the old house . . . but Kira was there, and he did not want to think of his child, who was now getting on for four. And he certainly didn't want to think of Mara's child.

Griot set off, four soldiers marching behind him. With Tundra collapsing the roads were even more unsafe. He could watch out for attacks from the front. The soldiers were just within hearing distance. He listened to gossip from the camp and on the whole liked what he overheard. The soldiers had all been refugees, and often did not know each other's languages. Griot had instituted compulsory lessons in Tundra, and this is what they were talking, saying they looked forward to when they could spread themselves over the spaces of Tundra: it was so cramped in the camp.

Griot began thinking about his own life, but from that point in it when he could match this Griot here with that Griot, who had arrived as a fugitive boy at the Agre camps in Charad and was at once put into training to become a soldier. Before that – no, he did not much enjoy thinking about it. He would make himself remember it all – later. Agre had made him: now he knew it was Shabis who had made him, who was then the big General so far above him he knew only his name and sometimes saw him: 'There, there he is, that's Shabis.' He was under Dann's immediate command, the handsome, daring young officer, whom he hero-worshipped. Griot marched to Shari behind General Dann, as he had become, and when the Hennes armies invaded Shari and he heard that Dann had run from Shari, Griot did too. He had been in that mass of refugees that flooded Karas, but then he lost Dann's trail and could not get news. He was a runaway soldier and in danger of being recaptured and punished – perhaps executed. He had heard there was a price on Dann's head. About Mara he did not know. He had actually heard her address the soldiers in the public square in Agre, but he had not immediately connected that lanky fishbone of a girl with the beauty he had seen at the Farm. He made his way to Tundra, always in danger, worked when he could and, when he thought of the safety of the Agre Army, wished he had not run away. Then he heard by chance that General Dann, with his sister, was in a farm away to the west, and there he went, arriving just after Dann had left.

Griot recognised Shabis at once, but did not know Mara. He asked for work. He knew about farming, having served with the agricultural detachments in the Agre Army. They gave him a room and their trust but he knew Kira did not like that. For her, he was a menial. But Mara and Shabis, and the others, Daulis and the two Albs, treated him like one of them. He had never known a family, but suspected this must be one. And soon it would be more of one, because both Mara and Kira were pregnant. Kira complained: that was her style. Pettishly or angrily, she complained. Mara soothed her and kept her in order; that was how Griot saw it. The couple, Shabis and Mara, were at the centre of this family, and Kira was like the awkward child.

Griot had spent his life – that is, the one before arriving in Agre – watching, always on guard, seeing everything, faces, gestures, little movements of the eyes, a hardly perceptible grimace, or smirk, or sneer, or smile; that is how he had learned about life, about people. And he knew that not everyone had his perceptiveness: he was often surprised at how little they ordinarily saw. Here, at the Farm, he was returned, as far as dangers and threats went, to his pre-Agre condition. Not because of Shabis, or Mara – it was Kira he had to watch. Now he worked hard, was careful never to presume, kept out of Kira's way and watched them all. He knew Mara missed her brother, not because she complained, but because they talked often of Dann and she sighed, and Shabis would put his hand on hers or draw her to him in an embrace. Kira saw this satirically – unkindly. When she spoke of Dann it was as of a possession she had mislaid. As her pregnancy went on she grew very large and did really suffer. The winds were blowing dry and cold, and then dry and warm, while Kira lay around with her feet up and began ordering Griot about, until he said to her, with the others all present, that he was not her servant.

'You are if I say you are,' she snapped, and at once Mara and Shabis corrected her.

'We are having no servants or slaves here, Kira.'

Then she began prefacing her commands with a sarcastic *please* – fetch her this and get her that. When she got him to wait on her she smiled, and smirked – like a child, Griot thought.

Mara was not well either, and it annoyed Griot – and,

he could see, the others – that she consoled and helped Kira but got no kindness in return.

Then there was a fearful row, not long before the women were due to give birth, with Kira shrieking that if Griot wanted to stay he must do as he was told. Griot knew that his labour was needed at the Farm, and tried to stick it out but then Kira actually tried to hit him and he left, apologising to Shabis and Mara. He went to the Centre, and there was Dann. That Dann did not greet him with the inward upwelling of feeling – you could call it rapture or at least intense happiness – which Griot felt, seemed to Griot only right: he had been one of Dann's soldiers, that was all. But to be with Dann, working for him, serving him, seemed to Griot not only a reward for his long worship of Dann, but it had a special rightness, like a gift from – Fate, or whatever you called it. Griot had not gone in for gods and deities, though he had seen many different kinds in his short life, but now he was wondering if there wasn't one who had a specially kind eye out for him. Otherwise, how to account for his good fortune – landing in Agre, under officer Dann, hearing about Dann at the Farm, then finding him here at the Centre, which was so wonderfully equipped to accommodate Griot's plans.

He could say – he was prepared to – that Dann's going away for so long was hardly a kindness to Griot, but then he had made good use of the time, moulding and making his army, examining the resources of the Centre.

He could have said that Dann being so very ill was hardly a beneficent provision of Fate, or whatever little god it was – Griot was modest, he awarded himself only a minor deity – but having nursed Dann now for weeks he at least knew his hero had faults. However, those he decided to see as signs or guarantees of a future largeness of destiny.

And now he was going back to the Farm, and it was Kira he thought of, but carefully warding off misfortune with the kind of wary respect a spiteful and anarchic person does demand.

He left the soldiers at the inn, not wanting to burden the Farm with their lodging and food, always short, he knew, and said he would be back in a day or so.

As he walked up to the house, the Western Sea noisy on the right hand, two dogs came down to greet him: they knew him. On the veranda Kira stood, fatter than she had been, a large woman in a purple gown, her hair curled and oiled, a flower in it, watching his approach.

'Good greetings to you,' he said, getting in first, to establish the note he intended for his stay.

'Have you come to see me?' she demanded.

Now this was really odd of her, and it set Griot back.

'No, Kira, I've come to see Shabis.'

'Oh, no one comes to visit me,' she complained and he noted that peevishness was still the rule.

Down the side of the house, on a level sandy place, two little girls were playing, and the two Albs were with them.

Daulis was on the veranda, and his greeting smile was genuine. Griot sat, and the two dogs lay down beside him. To see these creatures tamed in the service of people was to know Ruff's wildness, and the large freedoms of the snow dogs, who owed only some of their allegiance to people. Griot thought for the first time how easily those great white beasts could become a pack and turn on their guardians. Could Ruff turn on Dann? Hard to think that.

Kira settled her billows of purple skirt into a chair and enquired, 'And how is my dear Dann?'

Griot was not going to tell Kira how Dann was, knowing she would take advantage of it if she could. Yet, with people coming this way from the Centre on their way down the coast, she must have heard, or would hear.

'Dann has been on a long visit to the Bottom Sea,' he said and, as she pressed for more, he kept fending her off, saying, 'He went fishing with the fishing fleet.' 'He saw the ice mountains from up close,' and then Shabis came and Griot stood, waiting for his greeting, knowing from that kindly face that Shabis was pleased to see him – and that he was muting his greeting because of Kira.

Shabis nodded at Griot to sit, and sat himself. He looked older and his loss of Mara had sapped him of some vital substance, some buoyancy that had infused his whole being when Mara had been with him. He was a tall, too thin man, and greying. It had to be acknowledged that this soldier was very far from what he had been.

Griot wanted to talk to Shabis alone, and now began an unpleasant little game, where Kira prevented Dann and Shabis from going aside to talk. When at last they went into the house to evade her she went with them and all that evening during the meal she kept up a chatter designed to prevent her being forgotten, even for a moment.

And she had changed: Griot's covert glances at that

pretty face, with its many little tricks of lip and eye and look and smile, told him that whatever had been there to like, and admire, had gone: and her voice, too, had changed.

Everything had changed since Griot had left. Mara had been some sort of centre for this family, but it was not one now. She had held it together. And she had kept Kira out of its centre, where she tried to be.

The two little girls, both delightful and – well, like little girls, Griot supposed, who had had no contact with children since he had been one – were well behaved, but Griot noted that Tamar, Mara's child, stayed close to her father, and when she looked at Kira she was apprehensive.

Kira ordered not only her own child, Rhea, to do this and that, sit up, not fidget, not eat so fast and so on, but Tamar too, though the two Albs, Leta and Donna, were in charge of them. At last Shabis said, 'That's enough, Kira,' a rebuke with an authority that went far beyond the present situation. Kira pouted, and sulked.

When the time came for goodnights, Tamar was going past Kira, who said, 'What's this, no kiss for Kira?'

The child blew Kira a kiss, but she was not going to be allowed to get away with that. Griot saw how they all, Shabis, Leta, Daulis and Donna, watched as the child ran up to Kira and lifted her face up for a kiss – Tamar was pretending to laugh but she was frightened. And Kira made a great ugly face – a joke, of course – and when she bent to the kiss, made the face even more threatening, so that the child broke away and ran to Leta.

'What a little cry-baby,' said Kira.

The little girls were taken off by the two Albs – into separate rooms, as Griot saw – and Kira said, 'Another of those long boring evenings. Do tell us something interesting, Griot.'

Griot said, 'I'm sorry, Kira. I have to leave in the morning early and I must talk to Shabis.'

'Then talk away.'

Griot looked for help to Shabis, who rose and said, 'Come, we'll go for a walk. It's quite light still.'

'I want to walk too,' said Kira.

'No,' said Shabis. 'Stay where you are.'

'Oh, Shabis,' cajoled Kira, but Shabis frowned. Griot saw that Kira had wanted to move into Mara's place, still wanted to, but it had not happened, and that was the reason for her petulance and her complaints. The idea of Kira where Mara had been shocked Griot, and he stood looking at Kira with such dislike that she removed her attention from Shabis, gave it to Griot and said, 'So, what's the matter, Griot? You've got your way, haven't you? It's more than I ever do.' And she actually seemed about to cry.

This was such a new thing in Kira, this childishness, that Griot was again set back by it, and Shabis called to him, 'Come on, Griot.'

The two men went out into the dusk, with the dogs.

They stood well away from the house. Kira was in the doorway trying to overhear. Griot told how Dann had been ill since the news of Mara's death; he explained why Dann had heard so late. He told as much as he had gathered of Dann's adventures at the Bottom Sea and at last made himself say that Dann was mad, and he didn't know what to do.

'Let us go further,' said Shabis, with a glance back at the looming purple shape that was Kira. They walked down a stony path while the noise of the Western Sea loudened, and stopped close together where spray came hurtling over a cliff, but the noise was not too bad.

'He was very ill once before,' said Shabis and told Griot of the events in the Towers at Chelops.

'Yes, when he is rambling he talks about it.'

'Usually he never mentions it. Mara said he was afraid of thinking about it.'

'And now he is afraid of poppy.' Griot told Shabis of Dann's orders never to give him poppy.

'Then that's the main thing,' said Shabis. 'And I'll ask Leta, she has medicines for everything. But meanwhile tell me about the Centre. What's all this about a new army?'

Griot told Shabis his story, not boasting, but proud of what he had achieved, and he ended saying that Tundra's cities should be invaded. Now was the right time.

'You talk easily about invasions and killing, Griot.'

'I think Tundra will soon start invading us. The Centre is a rich prize. And the old people are dead. They want Dann, for his reputation.'

'Really, and what reputation is that?' said Shabis, surprising Griot, who then saw the older man's ironical smile. 'But it seems to me there are two. One, General Dann – and he deserved that; when I promoted him so young I think I can say I knew what I was doing. But this other reputation, the wonder worker Prince Dann? That's all just moonshine and talk.'

'It's not Prince Dann, or prince anything, people talk about. But he does seem to have some kind of – authority that it's hard to explain. And my spies tell me that all over Tundra they are waiting for him.'

'I see. I seem to have been here before. I spoke against the invasion of Shari. That is why I became the enemy of the other three generals. And I was right. Nothing was achieved except the usual tale of refugees and deaths. In my experience easy talk about wars and invasions means weakness, not strength.'

'It's a question of need. The refugees keep coming and coming – I am sure you must see them here – and they have to be fed and clothed and looked after. I remember how you used to give us lectures and lessons, and I try to do the same, Shabis. We are all so crowded, there's no room. And Tundra is mostly empty.'

'Everything is so unstable, can't you see that? The wars along the road to the east – they show no signs of ending. On the contrary, new wars flare up . . . The great unknown quantity, Griot – it's the masses of refugees. Are you going to control armies of displaced people with some talk about a wonder worker called General Dann? And down south, there is bad trouble in Charad, in my country. The three generals were killed in a coup and the army is wanting me back.'

Griot could see that Shabis, standing there so close, was talking to himself, though loudly, because of the sea noise; he was rehearsing thoughts that he went over when he was alone.

'And yes, Griot, you are too polite to say it, but you're thinking I am too old for generalling and war. Yes, I am, but I'm not too old to be a figurehead. I am General Shabis, who was against the three bad generals, and they are dead. So I am wanted back to unify Agre and protect them against the Hennes. But how can I leave, Griot? You must see . . .'

Griot saw. Shabis could not take the child with him on a long and dangerous journey south. And she couldn't be left here with Kira, who wished her ill.

'I have a wife in Agre,' said Shabis. 'She's a good woman but she would not welcome Mara's child. Why should she? She longed for her own child but – we weren't lucky. If I arrived there with Mara's – no, I can't even think of it. And so – you do see, Griot?'

'You could come to the Centre, with the child,' said Griot.

'I feel I have responsibilities here, apart from Tamar. Daulis, I know, would go back to Bilma if there weren't Leta to consider. And Leta knows it. If Leta returned to Bilma she would find herself back in the . . . did you know Leta was in the whorehouse there?'

'Yes. When Dann rambles he tells a good deal. But you forget, I was living here before and Leta is not exactly shy about her life as a whore.'

'You don't understand. She's so ashamed of it, and that's why she has to talk.'

'If you came to the Centre, you and Dann together could lead us invading Tundra.' Griot's voice trembled, telling how this seemed to him the apotheosis of the best he could hope for – General Shabis and General Dann . . . 'You and Dann,' he said again.

'Have you thought that Dann might not be so pleased

to see me? He lost his sister to me – that's how he sees it. Rather, how he feels it. He was always generous to me – to us – to me and Mara. But when I think of how he *feels* – well, I try not to, Griot.'

Griot was silent. The sea crashed and washed below them and stung them with spray.

'So, you see, Griot, there's a stop to any path I might want to take.'

Griot, who had been a child left to fend for himself, was thinking that the little girl, Tamar, was surely too small, too unimportant – was that it? – to stand in the way of General Shabis and his duty to heal his country.

'Back to the house, Griot. I'm glad you came. Don't imagine I'm not thinking about all this – it's what I think about all the time.'

Kira met them on the veranda, and she was glittering with anger in the lamplight.

'In a minute, Kira,' said Shabis and the two men went past her. In the main room Leta and Daulis were playing dice. Donna was with the children.

Shabis asked Leta to go with him. They left Kira with Griot.

'So, what's the big secret?' said Kira. 'Has Dann gone completely crazy at last?'

This was most unpleasantly acute.

'I'm sure you would be told if he were,' said Griot.

Leta returned with packets of herbs, which she spread out and began instructing Griot.

'These are all sedative herbs,' said Kira.

'We have people who are ill,' said Griot, refusing to surrender Dann to Kira.

'Well, tell Dann it is time he saw his child,' said Kira. 'Tell him to come and see me.'

'Yes, I will. And he would want to see his sister's child too,' said Griot.

He was using a tone to Kira he never had when he was here before. He stood his ground while she sparked off anger, muttered something, turned and went out.

'Never mind her,' said Leta, her voice full of dislike.

This must be a jolly company of people, Griot thought. He was glad he was not trapped here.

He asked to sleep on the veranda, so he could slip off in the morning. He slept lightly. In the night he watched Kira come out and stand at the top of the steps, looking out. She only glanced at him, and then went out into the dark.

Very early he woke and saw her a little way down a slope to where some sheds stood, talking to some people who he knew were newly arrived refugees. They must have come by the marsh roads, not seeing the Centre. The two dogs were with her; when they saw he was awake, they left her and came to wag their tails and lick his hands, and then went a little way with him.

Before he turned a corner on to the road, he saw Leta on the veranda. Her hair glistened in the early light: it was like sunlight. Her skin was so white: he could never decide what he thought about Albs. They fascinated but they repelled him. That hair – how he wanted to touch it, to let the smooth slippery masses run through his fingers. But her skin . . . he thought it was like the white thick underbelly skin of a fish.

Donna's hair wasn't fair, like Leta's, but dark and

fine, and where it was parted, or when a breeze blew, the skin showed dead white. Once, Griot knew, all of Yerrup had been filled with these Alb people, all with white fish skins. He didn't like thinking about it. A lot of people said Albs were witches, the men too, but Griot did not take this seriously: he knew how easily people said others were witches, or had magical powers. And why should he complain? When his soldiers said Dann had magic in him, Griot merely smiled and let them think it.

Before Griot had even reached the gates of the Centre he heard the commotion in Dann's quarters: shouts, the snow dog's barks, Dann's voice. He ran, and burst into the room where Dann was standing on his bed, arms flailing, eyes and face wild. There was a sickly smell. Dann saw Griot and shouted, 'Liar. You tricked me. You went to intrigue with Shabis against me.' The two soldiers on guard, minding Dann, stood with their backs to a wall: they were exhausted and they were frightened. The snow dog sat near them, as if protecting them, and watched Dann, who jumped off the bed and began whirling around, so that his outflung hands just missed first one soldier's face and then the other's; he whirled so that his fingers flicked Griot's cheek, then a foot went out as if to kick Ruff, but the animal sat there, unflinching. He let out a low growl of warning.

'Sir,' said Griot, 'General . . . no, listen, Dann . . .'

'Dann,' sneered Dann, still flailing about, 'so it's Dann, is it? Inferior ranks address their superiors like that, is that it?'

Now Griot had had time to see that on a low table was a greasy smeared dish and on that a lump of poppy which had been burning and was still smoking.

Dann leaped back on the bed and stood, knees bent, hands on his thighs, glaring around. His dark pupils had white edges. He was shaking.

'And there's another thing,' he shouted at Griot. 'I'm going to burn down your precious Centre, full of rubbish, full of dead old rubbish, I'm going to make a fire big enough to scorch all of Tundra.' He fell back on the bed, obviously to his own surprise, and lay staring up, breathing in fast sharp gasps.

One of the soldiers said, in a low voice, which was dulled by fear, 'Griot, sir, the General set fire to the Centre, but we stopped him.'

'Yes, I did,' came the loud voice from the bed. 'And I will again. What do we want with all this old rubbish? We should burn it and be finished.'

'General, sir,' said Griot, 'may I remind you that you asked me not to let you have poppy. It was an order, sir. And now I'm going to take it away.'

At this up leaped Dann and he jumped off the bed towards the poppy, and then changed his mind, to attack Griot, who stood there as if hypnotised. And he was: he was thinking that in the fearful strength of his seizure Dann could overmaster him easily and in a moment.

The snow dog walked in a calm considered way to where the two men faced each other and took Dann's right arm, lifted to strike, in his big jaws and held it. Dann whirled about. A knife had appeared in his other hand, but it was not clear if Dann meant it for Ruff or for Griot. The snow dog let himself move with Dann's movement but did not let go.

Griot said, 'Sir, you ordered me to keep the poppy from you.'

'Yes, but that wasn't me, it was The Other One.'

And now, hearing what he had said he stood transfixed, staring – listening? He was hearing . . . what?

'The Other One,' muttered Dann. Yes. Mara had said it, *the other one*, she had said it reminding him of what he was capable of, reminding him of how he had gambled her away. The Other One . . . and Dann. Two.

Just where he was standing now, he and Mara had stood and he had heard her tell him, because of some folly he was about to commit, 'You *wouldn't do it but the other one would.*'

The Other One. Which one was he now? The snow dog let Dann's arm fall from those great jaws and returned to where he had stationed himself, near the two bemused soldiers.

'The Other One,' Dann said. He whirled about, so that they all thought he might be beginning again with his flailing and his threatening, but instead he took up the dish with the smoking poppy on it and thrust it at Griot.

'Take it. Don't let me have it.'

Griot beckoned one of the soldiers, handed him the dish and said, 'Get rid of it. Destroy it.' The soldier went out with the dish.

Dann watched this, eyes narrowed, his body quivering; he slackened and let himself fall on the bed.

'Come here, Ruff,' he said.

The snow dog came, jumped up on the bed and Dann put his arms round him. He was sobbing, a dry painful weeping, without tears. 'I am thirsty,' he croaked.

The remaining soldier brought him a mug of water. Dann drank it all, began to say, 'More, I need more . . .' and fell back, and was asleep, the snow dog's head on his chest.

Griot ordered the soldier to go and rest, and see to it that there were replacement guards. He needed to sleep, too.

That scene with Dann – but he had seemed more like a demented impostor – had gone so fast Griot hadn't understood what was happening. He needed to think about it. Afraid to go too far from Dann, he lay on the bed in the adjacent room and left the door open.

The other one, Dann had said.

He, Griot, needed to ask someone – Shabis? It was Mara he needed to talk to. If he could bring her back, even for a few moments, he would know exactly what to ask her.

Through the open door Griot watched the two replacement guards enter from outside and stand by the wall. Ruff growled a soft warning, but let his great tail wag, and fall. He slept. Dann slept. Griot slept.

And woke to silence. In the next room Dann had not moved, neither had the snow dog, and the two soldiers dozed, sitting with their backs to the wall. A peaceful silence.

Griot withdrew, washed, changed, ate, inserting himself again into this life, in the Centre. He then took up his position at the table in the great hall. There he spent the hours after the midday meal, thinking, calculating supplies and seeing any soldier who wanted to see him. Usually he could be sure of a stream of supplicants, with their interpreters, since there might be a dozen languages Griot did not know in the course of an hour or two. Today there were none. The soldiers were confused. Worse, they were afraid. Everyone knew that their General whose absences, whose unpredictability, added to his prestige, had gone very mad and that he had tried to set fire to the Centre. They would not know how or what to ask Griot, if they did come to speak to him, which was every soldier's right. Griot sat on at his table. They were in their huts in the camp, waiting. For Griot, for explanations. For Dann, most of all.

If they didn't know what to think, Griot didn't either. His feeling for Dann had been not far off awe, something much higher than the respect for a superior. For days, before going to the Farm, he had been nursing that scarred body, with its weals around the waist, which could only be from the sharp claws of a slave's punishment chain. Well, Griot had been a slave: they all feared that tight metal chain with its spikes more than any other punishment. He had seen Dann rave, from poppy, and if it hadn't been for the snow dog Dann might easily have killed Griot.

So what did he think now? One thought was the obvious one. He, Griot, had created the army out there, for it was that, if a small one. He, Griot, ran it, maintained it, fed it, planned for it. If Dann died, or finally went mad, or walked away again somewhere, Griot would be its ruler, and what did he think about that?

There was one central thing here, not to be encompassed in an easy fact, or statement: Dann's fame, or whatever the emanation from him could be called, had spread everywhere through the cities of Tundra. Griot had discovered this for himself. He had gone in disguise into Tundra, taking the dangerous way through the marshes, and had sat about in eating houses and bars, drinking for long tedious evenings in inns, gossiping in market places. Everyone knew that the old Mahondis were dead, but there were new young ones, and it wasn't just 'the Mahondis' but one, the young General, Dann. Some said his name was Prince Shahmand, but where had all that come from? Not Griot! It was the old woman, spinning her webs, using her network of spies – which now was Griot's network. But the name was General Dann, and that had not been the old woman's. It was a strange and unsettling thing, listening to that talk. Dann had not been so very long at the Centre before he had gone to the Farm, had not been long there again before going on his adventure to the Bottom Sea. Yet that had been enough to set the talk running, to fire imaginations. He had a life in the thoughts of the peoples of Tundra. They expected that he would fill the Centre with its old power and that once again it would dominate all of Tundra. Tundra power was weakening fast and so they waited for the Good General, for Dann. What name could you put to that fame of his? It was an illusion, as Shabis had said. It was a flicker of nothing, like marsh gas, or the greenish light that runs along the tops of sea waves – Griot had seen that, in his time. It had no existence. Yet it was powerful.

It was nothing. Yet people waited for General Dann.

Griot had created an army, an efficient one, but Griot was nothing at all, compared with Dann, who possessed this – *what*?

Griot sat pondering this, sitting quiet and long in the great hall, a small figure underneath the tall pillars and airy fluted ceilings that still held traces of long-ago colours, clear reds, blues, yellows, green like sea water. He did not much care about all that but supposed that old grandeur did connect somewhere with Dann's glamour. Did it? But why should he care about Dann's qualities, if he did not care now about Dann, who would have killed him? But he did. Griot's not very long life, his hard and dangerous life, had not taught him love or tenderness, except for a sick horse he had tended in one of the places he had stopped – for a while – before having to run away again. He understood Dann's feeling for the snow dog. But now Griot was thinking that if he had loved Dann, there was nothing left of what he had loved him for. But that word, *love*, it made him uncomfortable. Could the passionate admiration of a boy for an officer far above him be called love? He did not think so. Where was that handsome, kindly young officer – captain, then general? There was only the unreal thing, his ability to set fire to the expectations of people who had never even met him.

Griot thought of that terribly scarred body, which he had nursed like – well, like the wounded horse whose life he had saved.

He was really very unhappy. Where there should have been General Dann, a strong healthy man, there was a sick man who was at that moment sleeping off a bout of poppy.

Then he saw coming from Dann's apartment Ruff, the snow dog, and behind him, Dann, white-faced, frail, cautious of movement, but himself.

Himself. Who? Well, he wasn't *the other one* – whoever *he* was.

Why was Griot so sure? He was. He was conscious that to say it was no answer to terrible questions – which he did not feel equipped to deal with. But he *was* equipped to say, 'That's Dann, there he is.'

Dann sat down opposite Griot, yawned and said, 'Don't be afraid. I'm not mad now.' (He could have said, 'I am not *him* now.')

Then Dann said, and it wasn't careless, or casual – no, he had been thinking he must say it, and mean it: 'I am sorry, Griot.' Did he remember he could have killed Griot if Ruff hadn't stopped him?

'First,' he went on, in this considering way he was using, as if checking off things he had planned to say, 'first, Griot, there is the question of your rank. I was stupid – what I said.' (He didn't say, 'what *he* said.') 'You are responsible for everything. You've done it all. And yet the soldiers don't know what to call you.'

Griot sat waiting, suffering because Dann was, looking at Dann who was not looking at him, and that was because his eyes were hurting, Griot could see: light from high up, where the many windows were, fell in bright rays. Dann moved his head back, out of the brilliance, and blinked at Griot.

'If Shabis could make me a learner general – did you

know that, Griot? I and others of Shabis's – pets, we were learner generals. But they called us general.'

'Yes, I know,' said Griot quietly, but hurt: he found it so hard to accept that he had made so small an impression on Dann at a time when Dann had been everything for him.

'So, how about it, Griot? I suppose I am General Dann, if you say I am, but you should be a general too, General Griot.'

'I'd like to be captain,' said Griot, remembering the handsome young captain Dann who was in his memory still as something to aim for.

'Then we'll have to be careful no one gets promoted above captain,' said Dann. 'We are making up this army from scratch, aren't we, Griot? So we can say what goes. General Dann and Captain Griot. Why not?' And he laughed gently, looking through the bright light at Griot with eyes that watered; he wanted Griot to laugh with him. There was something gentle and tentative about all this, and Griot found himself wanting to walk round the table, lift Dann up and carry him back to his bed. Dann was trembling. His hand shook.

'I am going to address the soldiers,' he said, and Griot heard another item on Dann's mental list ticked off.

'Yes, I think you should,' said Griot. 'They are pretty disturbed.'

'Yes. The sooner the better. And at some point we must talk about the Centre . . . it's all right, I'm not going to burn it down. I'm not saying I don't want to.' He lifted his head and sniffed, as Ruff might have done – as Ruff did, too, because Dann did. Griot allowed the smell of the Centre, which he usually shut away from him, in his mind, to enter, and wrinkled up his nose, as Dann was doing. A dank grey smell, and now it had a hint of burning in it, too.

'Dann, there is something I found out about the Centre and you'd be interested . . .'

Dann waved this away. 'Call the soldiers,' he said.

Griot went out, looking back to see Dann sitting blinking there in the light, which was about to slide away and leave him in shadow. The snow dog put his head on Dann's thighs and Dann stroked it. 'Ruff,' he said, and he said it passionately, 'you're my friend, Ruff. Yes, you're my friend.'

And I am not, Griot said to himself. *I am not.*

Soon a thousand soldiers stood at ease on the space called the parade ground, or the square, between the main Centre buildings and the camp of shed and huts. Too small a space, but there was nowhere for it to expand. On one side of the camp were the cliffs of the Middle Sea and on the other the marshes began. The camp could expand only one way, along the edge of the Middle Sea, and it was, and too fast. On the north side of the Centre its walls were sinking into wet. Between them and the cliffs were the roads needed to bring the crops and the animals from their pastures, and the fish catches from the sea.

Dann stood at ease, wearing the old gown he slept in – lived in, these days. Beside him sat Ruff, his head as high as Dann's chest. Opposite Ruff sat the phalanx of snow dogs, with their minders, one to a dog. The animals were very white and they glistened in the gloomy scene. Behind the snow dogs were the soldiers. They were of every kind and colour. The majority were stocky, strong, solid people, probably Thores, or of Thores stock, but there were many Kharabs, tall and thin, and mixes of people from all along the coasts, from the wars; they were still coming in every day. The presence of people from the River Towns, so far south, was evidenced by the ranks of shiny very black faces, and there was even a little platoon of Albs, with skin like Leta's or modified shades of it. The hair was of all kinds. Not one of them had Leta's pale hair, like light. All colours, all sizes, and hair long and black, like Dann's, to the tight close curls of the River Towns, and the many shades of brown from the East. There were all kinds of clothes. Some still wore the rags they had arrived in. Griot simply could not get enough clothes for them, of any sort, let alone standard clothes that would make a uniform. Despairing, Griot had bought fleece cloth from Tundra and dyed it red, and every soldier, no matter what he wore under it, had over his or her shoulder a red woolly blanket, needed on most days of the year, chilly, cold, always damp. Without these red blankets they would have nothing to identify them. Throw them away and they would be a rabble.

Dann stood there, silent, for a while, smiling, letting them have a good look at him. Then he said, 'I am sure you know that I have been ill.' He waited, watching those faces, which would show – what? Derisive smiles? Impatience? No, they all stood and waited, serious, attentive.

'Yes, I have been very ill.' He waited. 'I was ill from

the poppy.' Now a different silence gripped the soldiers. A seabird speeding along the cliff edge cut the silence with its wings. It screamed and another answered from where it floated far out beyond the cliffs.

'When I was young I was captured by a gang of dealers in poppy and ganja – I was forced to take poppy and I was very ill then. I have the scars of the poppy on me – as I think you must know.'

Silence; a deep and powerful attention.

Dann had picked up a red fleece on his way out to the square and had held it in his hand, and now he shifted it into his arms and stood sheltering it, like a child: like something young that needed protecting. There was a breath of sympathy from the soldiers, a sigh.

'So I know very well how poppy gets a grip on you.

'It had a grip on me.

'It still has a grip on me.

'I do not believe that this will be the last time it makes me – ill.'

Between each quiet, and almost casual, statement Dann waited, and took his time looking over the faces. Not a sound.

'Griot – where are you?'

Griot stepped out from the doorway that led to Dann's room and came forward to stand in front of Dann, where he saluted and, at Dann's gesture, stood beside him.

'You all know Griot. This is Captain Griot. That is what you will call him. Now, I am speaking for Captain Griot and for myself, General Dann. If any one of you, any one wearing the red fleece, catches me with poppy, it will be your duty to arrest me and take me at once to Captain Griot – or anyone else who is in command. You will take no notice of anything I say or do when under the influence of poppy. This is my order. You will arrest me.'

He paused a long time here. Ruff, standing between Griot and Dann, looked up at Griot's face and at Dann's, and then barked softly.

A ripple of laughter.

'Yes, and Ruff says so too. And now for you. If any one of you is found with poppy, in the camp, let alone smoking it, you will be arrested and severely punished.'

Here a tension communicated itself from Griot to Dann, who said, 'The degree of punishment has not yet been decided. It will be announced.'

A movement of unease through the soldiers.

'You will remember, I am sure, that you chose to come here, to the Centre. No one forced you. No one stops you from leaving. But while you are here, you will obey orders. And now, look to Captain Griot for orders and for what you need. I am not well yet and I shall rest, though I am sure I will be well soon. Captain, dismiss them.'

Dann retired back to the great hall and Griot's working table, where Griot joined him, with the snow dog.

Dann sat carefully, disposing his so thinly covered bones among the folds of his Sahar robe, which had been Mara's, though Griot did not know this.

Griot waited and, when Dann said nothing, asked, 'And how are you proposing to punish, sir?'

'I thought we could dismiss any soldier caught with poppy.'

'No, that is how I was punishing the looters from the Centre, and all that happens is that they became gangs of outlaws and thieves.'

'So, what else?'

'I have put offenders into a punishment hut on half-rations but, you see, some of these people have starved for weeks, and our half-rations and a warm hut are hardly a punishment.'

'Well, then?'

'When I was in the army in Venn, they branded offenders with marks denoting their offence.'

'No,' said Dann at once, 'no.' His hand went to his waist where the scars were.

'No,' said Griot, 'I agree. When I was in the army in Theope – that's on the coast, and it's a cruel place – they flogged offenders, in front of the whole army.'

'No, no flogging. I've seen it. No.'

'This is an army – General.'

'Yes, it is, and congratulations. And how are you going to enforce discipline?'

'Sir, in my view there is not much we can do. This is an army but it is a voluntary one. What we are depending on is . . .'

'Well, out with it.'

'It's you – sir. No, I know you don't like that, General, but it's true. Everyone is waiting – for you. What we lack is space. You can see that. We are badly overcrowded now. There are parts of the Centre fit for occupation, but if we had the soldiers in it, they would be a rabble in no time.'

'Yes, you are right. And then?'

'And the food. You have no idea what a job it is, feeding everyone.'

'Then tell me.'

'We've got a road zigzagging down to the Bottom Sea and the fish comes up that. We have fishing villages all along the shores of the Bottom Sea now – well, for a good little distance. We have our farms on the slopes of the mountain. The animals are doing well. But there's never enough of anything.'

'So, it's Tundra. I get your message, Griot. So what are your spies saying?'

'There will be civil war. There's already fighting in some places out on the eastern edges of Tundra.' He saw the strain on Dann's face. Dann was trembling. He seemed hardly able to keep his seat.

'They want us to invade and keep order and – they want you, sir.'

'A Mahondi general?'

'I don't think they remember that. To tell the truth it is hard to understand how they see it. You are a bit of a legend, sir.'

'What a prize, Griot. What a general. What a ruler – that's what they want, I suppose.'

Griot's eyes were going to overflow if he wasn't careful. He could hardly bear to see Dann sit shaking there: he was actually putting his weight on the snow dog, for support. Griot could not stop thinking about the handsome young captain in Agre, or, for that matter, the healthy Dann who had returned from his wanderings so recently. And here was this sick unhappy man who looked as if he were seeing ghosts, or hearing them.

'You'll get better, Dann – sir.'

'Will I? I suppose I will. And then . . .' Here there was a good long pause and Griot had no idea what Dann might say next. 'Griot, do you ever think of – of the cities – the cities under the marshes? Did you know they were all copies of the cities that long ago – long, long ago – were all over Yerrup? That was before the Ice. They were built here on permafrost. That is, permanent frost, that would last for ever – that is how we think, you see, Griot, that the things we have will last. But they don't last. The cities sank down into the water. All of us, we live up here and just down there are the old dead cities.' Now he was making himself lean forward to hold Griot's eyes, trying to make what he was saying reach Griot who, he was sure, was not taking it in.

'Dann, sir, you've forgotten, I've had bad times too. And when you're frightened or you're hungry you have all kinds of bad thoughts. But there's no point in that, is there? It doesn't get you anywhere.'

'No point in starting again. Yes, Griot, exactly; no point. Over and over again, all the effort and the fighting and the hoping, but it ends in the Ice, or in the cities sinking down out of sight into the mud.'

Now Griot leaned across the table and took Dann's hand. It was cold and it shook. 'It's the poppy, sir. It's still in you. You should go to bed, have a rest, sleep it off.'

The snow dog did not like Griot touching Dann and he growled. Griot removed his hand.

'We live in these ruins, Griot, these ruins, full of things we don't know how to use.'

'We know how to make some of them. And there is something else I discovered while you were away. I'd like to talk to you about it when you wake up.'

'Rubbish, ancient rubbish, Griot. I had the right idea when I set fire to it. No, I won't do it again, don't worry.'

'There are things here you haven't seen.'

'Mara and I explored the place.'

'There's a hidden place. The old people didn't know about it. They didn't care about all that. All they cared about was you and Mara – well, that's the past.'

'Yes, it is.'

'But the servants – the Centre had hereditary servants.'

'It would.'

'Yes. They knew the Centre and the hidden things. They never told the old people. Only the servants knew. And there are things . . .'

'More old rubbish.'

'No, wonders. You'll see.'

Dann got up unsteadily, his weight on the snow dog who adapted himself to him.

'And you haven't heard what is going on at the Farm.'

'Do I want to hear it? Yes, of course I have to hear it.'

He stood by the table, balancing himself there with one hand, but his weight was on Ruff's back. He listened.

'But my child isn't in danger – Rhea, you say? Because it is Kira's.'

'It is Mara's child who is in danger. But Leta and Donna – they never let Tamar out of their sight.'

'I was going to suggest you ask Leta to come. She has all that knowledge of medicines.'

Griot knew that there were people in the camp with this knowledge, or some, but he did not want to discourage Dann's interest, so he said, 'I'll send for Leta. Donna can keep watch on Mara's child.'

Dann said, 'If Shabis goes back to Agre, the child could go with him.'

Griot repeated what Shabis had said.

'Then . . . that's it,' said Dann, shaking off these problems, because they were too much for him – as Griot could see.

Dann walked to his quarters, with that cautious steadiness people use when they are afraid of falling. The snow dog went with him.

Griot sat on in the empty hall. The airy apertures of its upper parts showed a light snow whirling about the sky.

Snow: and that mass of people out there he was responsible for might never have seen it. Against extreme cold all they had was fleecy red blankets. Soon they would be streaming into the hall to complain: and so it was, in they came. How were they to make fires when there was no firewood, and reeds burned so fast they were ash before they gave out warmth? Well, it made a change from the problem of too many people in too small a space.

He was expecting Dann to rejoin him: it was his need that made him think so. So much weight on him, Griot, so many difficulties. But Dann did not emerge and when Griot went to see, he was lying as still as a stunned fish and seemed hardly to breathe. The guards were dozing, the snow dog lying stretched out asleep beside him.

It occurred to Griot that he must postpone his expectations of Dann. Perhaps next day, or the next . . . Griot had plenty to think about. He was rehearsing how he would report his discoveries.

When Dann had gone on his walk to the east, Griot had decided to explore the Centre's resources. This plan lasted a day or two. Griot had had no idea of the vastness of the place: it would take too long. It was immediately obvious that some parts had been so thoroughly plundered there was nothing to hope for from them. Halls so long and wide you could hardly see their edges, were empty: these had held guns, weapons, of the kind to be seen in armies in every part of Ifrik. What had been left were samples of what had gone. In a space that could have housed an army would be displayed a single sword of workmanship which no one could match now: a musket; a bow made of unknown wood; guns Griot had seen in use, that fired iron balls; but of course many of these had gone too. Empty halls: and the need for space. But these vast spaces had leaking roofs and in some places puddles that were not from the roof: excuse enough not to put them into use. The sheds and huts the soldiers lived in were drier and warmer than these frigid leaking halls. Many of the fugitives and outcasts that had found hiding places in the Centre had sneaked themselves places in the soldiers' camp and Griot pretended ignorance.

Other halls, as vast, were full of artefacts whose use was now known, and stood in a crammed order that had not been touched for – but Griot did not enjoy talk of thousands of years.

The places that interested him had machines that he believed might be copied and used now, for agriculture, or boats of intriguing designs. He put some soldiers on to examine all these, and found – not for the first time – what a treasure of expertise and skills were in that crowd of runaways out there, now his army.

He left them to it, demanding that they should memorise what they had found, well enough to describe it all to Dann.

He had become absorbed in an unexpected direction: the water that was welling up, so it seemed, from deep under the Centre.

He asked for volunteers to dig, who had some knowledge of wells, or shafts, and within a few days they had come to say they had found layers of wood.

They had stood all around a pit and looked down at beams laid in a cross-hatch, on which had been built foundations of stone.

First of all, the wood. There were no big trees for many days' walking in any direction. On the mountain were light trees, useless for building. These beams would have been heavy, even before they were soaked. Wood. Anywhere they dug, and not too deep down, were beams, and no one, none of these people from so many different countries, had seen trees that could have provided this wood. In one spot, the highest place in the Centre, Griot put the soldiers to dig further and they came on layers of wood and then more, deeper still. Once there had been forests here. Probably if you dug deeply enough into the marshes there would be trees lying pickled in that sour water. And then there was the stone. The Centre, or parts of it, was built of stone. Other parts were of bricks made of mud and reeds. Layers of time here: Griot knew that this interested Dann and so he stored up the information that was being brought to him by the soldiers. So much. All were interested, in their various ways, and some knowledgeable. Griot, who had never had a day's schooling until he reached Agre and Shabis's lectures for the troops, listened while his soldiers talked of things far above his head. Griot did not pretend to knowledge he did not have and was eager to listen – for Dann, who would soon return and be ready to hear all this. Griot remembered Mara, and how she talked of the Centre and of its stores of information, its lessons, and that is why he was sure about Dann. But Dann did not return.

All the wells and pits – and this was true anywhere in the Centre – held water. The northern edges of the Centre were sinking into wet. The truth was, and there was no evading it, the whole enormous expanse of the Centre was undermined with water, and it was not far down, either.

And then something else happened, and its importance was brought to Griot by some of his soldiers, who had been scribes and teachers in their native lands.

There were, and there were bound to be, tales of ghosts: so many peoples had lived here, builders in wood from long, long ago, builders in stone, generations upon generations, and of course ghosts walked the Centre, and people inclined that way had seen them. And there were tales, that Griot took as little notice of as he did of the ghosts, of a secret place in the Centre so well hidden no one could find it without a guide. It was people from far away in the east who took this kind of thing seriously: they had heard it all as part of their tales of the Centre, which had been known everywhere, because of its fame and its influence. Griot listened to soldiers whom he had to respect, for their education, talking about sand libraries, and sand records. He had heard Mara use these words, not knowing what they meant. Well, then, so there was this hidden place, but it was hidden, wasn't it? And then, one of the refugees, newly arrived, said that he had been told as part of the stories he was brought up with, that the secrets of the Centre were known by its servants.

The old princess, Felissa, was alive, but demented, and when Griot took a Mahondi speaker to visit her she screeched at both of them, not to tell lies. If there were secrets in the Centre she would have known them.

Two servants had looked after Felissa. One, the old man, had died, but the old woman was sharp and alert and suspicious.

Griot and his Mahondi interpreter said that they knew there was a secret place and that she, as an hereditary servitor of the old couple, must know about it.

She said it was all lies.

Griot cut this by saying that Dann had instructed him to get the secret, and emphasised his command by standing over her with a long deadly knife – he had found it rusting in one of the museums and had had it sharpened.

The old servant might have been as near death as made no difference, but she was afraid for her life, and agreed to show Griot the way. At first she wriggled and evaded and said she had forgotten, and that anyway she believed the place had fallen in, and there was a curse on anyone who told the secret, but at last the fact that she was going to tell the truth showed in her terror: she believed in this curse, and wept and whined as she led the way.

The Centre could be viewed perhaps as a pot being shaped on a wheel, its shape changing, then changing again. Long ago – but the phrase meant a stretch of time shorter than the great age of the Centre – someone – who? – had ordered builders – who? – to make a place hard to find. Walls curved and evaded, disappeared as other walls intervened, and no wall was made of the same substance as its neighbour. Inside formidable weights of stone were long slim bricks made of clay and reed, that became stone again, and a wall had patterns on it you could memorise, but in a moment the patterns had changed, and slid into other messages, and, it seemed, other languages. The walls were like a magician's tricks: designed to hold your attention while they did something else. No matter how carefully the invader approached a place, which he had been inveigled into thinking must be the right one, somehow he was deflected and found himself where he had started.

Griot had taken just one soldier with him, a man from the east, and both followed the weeping and sniffling old woman, never taking their eyes off her, so easy was it to believe she shared the deceiving properties of the walls, that slid, and slipped away, and misled. That clever old builder, or school of builders, knew how to make fools of intruders. Though Griot was holding plans of where he had been in his mind, there was a moment when he knew he and his soldier were lost: if the old woman chose to leave them here, they might not be found again. They were deep under masses of stone. Griot stopped, stopped the old woman, made her retreat with him until he recognised a mark he had made on a stone, then advanced again, with her in front, the interpreter sweating and afraid. And now, this time, there was a place where walls slid past each other so cunningly you could hardly see a gap, because it was concealed by an outjut of old brick, but Griot and his companion did slide in, watching how the old woman had to bend and slide, and then at last he began to see what was hidden. But he did not understand anything.

The old woman stood gibbering with terror. At what? A large room, or small hall, held in its centre a shape in something like glass, but as soon as Griot touched it he knew it was not – he had never before seen this transparent, hard substance. It was difficult to see through the shine of the not-glass, because it was shaped like an inner room, square, and all over the inner side were stuck packs of leaves, stacked together. 'Books,' said his Mahondi interpreter, sounding relieved that the fearsome thing had turned out to be something he knew. But not something Griot knew.

'The sand libraries?' the soldier asked the old woman, but she was clinging to the rock of the wall and blubbering too hard to speak, or, probably, to hear.

Griot saw that this man from the east was interested, was impressed, was now moving around the inner shape, looking at one scribbled page, and then another.

The air was fresh – clean air was coming in from somewhere – but there was a smell of damp too.

In the middle of the squarish transparent room – but it was larger than that, more like a smaller inner hall – were piles of the same packs of leaves of pressed reed that were held on to the walls. What held them? Each was pressed to the surface with a kind of clamp, that adhered to the walls on either side by, presumably, some sort of glue.

The soldier from the east was transfixed with all this. He was moving from one of the exposed leaves, that had writing or pictures on, and saying, 'This is . . .' some language or other. 'This is . . . I don't know this one.'

It was clear that the old servant was ill; she was trembling enough to shake to pieces.

Well, so now two people knew the way, Griot and this eastern man, whose name was Sabir. They and the old woman. They set her face to the narrow slit which was the exit and had to push her through. They were afraid she was in such a state she would not remember the difficult way, but at last they were back outside in the air, and the route had been memorised by both men.

That night the old servant died. So did Felissa; from shock. At once in the camps spread the rumour that the curse had killed them. Would the soldier, Sabir, die? Would Griot? But no, they remained healthy and uncursed. Not a moment too soon had they discovered the Centre's secret, because without the old servant no one could have found that clever, concealed way in.

What Sabir was telling his mates in the camp, Griot did not know: all he cared about was that it was not the route in, but when asked, Sabir said not many people were interested in the old sand libraries. There was one, whom he wanted to recommend to Griot; his name was Ali and he was a very learned man who knew everything about old books and languages.

In the great hall, along from Griot's table, was set another, for Sabir and Ali, not so close that their talk could be an interruption to Griot's work, but within earshot because he hoped to understand something of what they discussed. They had piles of the sheets of pulped and dried reed that were used for writing, and sticks of burned wood that made the marks, and the two went into the secret place every day, bending and slanting and oiling their way in the thin gap, returning, excited, their hands full of their notes. They came to Griot, to say, perhaps, 'Most are languages that were lost a long, long time ago.' Or, 'We think there's someone in the camp who knows . . .' whatever it was. Griot listened, feeling stupid, and told them to save all this up for General Dann, who would be here soon. But where was Dann, where was he?

The spillage from a war does not run smooth, or clear: there are breaks in the flow. More than once Griot thought the wars had stopped and was thankful, for he was so overstretched, but then the refugees came again, all of them hungry, all shocked because this terrible thing had happened to them, all with a history of killings and pillage and fire. There were assemblages of clothes so various that this diversity itself united them; never had there been such a multi-hued and many-shaped mass of people. Some were almost naked, because their clothes had been stolen; some had stolen what they wore and this mass of ragged people, this patchwork, was what Griot was calling an army, and drilling and marching them in platoons and companies and regiments, as he had seen done in the Agre Army.

He walked with some of them to the trading posts on the Tundra border and came back with bales of the red fleeces, and then the camp blossomed into scarlet and on every left shoulder hung the mark of Griot's army, the unifying red blanket. Never had so simple an act created such an immediate result. He was secretly proud of himself and perhaps a little afraid: this one thing he had done, an inspiration, yes – but he could describe it as an impulse of desperation – had created his army for him. What other similarly clever actions was he overlooking?

Griot achieved his army, his Red Blanket army, about halfway through Dann's long absence – while he was expecting Dann to turn up every day.

Now, watching the two men at the companion table, so busy, so absorbed, Griot knew that he was ignorant, and did not even know what he was ignorant of: he was continually being surprised by randomly, accidentally dropped bits of information.

He had understood that in his army – his lovely Red Blanket army – were people who were learned: some had been powerful – like Ali, so Sabir said. Talk of the 'sand libraries' among some of the soldiers was as easy and commonplace as talk of rations or the eternal cold mists. Sabir and Ali were not from the same country, but from adjacent countries, far to the east; 'sand-eaters' was the camp nickname for them, and they told him that the countries of eternal sand were where 'everyone' knew, 'had always known' of the sand libraries of North Ifrik, where there had been no sand for – who knew? Thousands of years would do.

Now, when the new petitioners arrived, begging for admittance to this army, Griot's army, two of the soldiers, Ali and Sabir, told him when they were learned and knew languages. Ali and Sabir sat by them, asking each one what they knew about the sand libraries. But no one knew more than that they existed and deserved to be spoken of with awe.

As for Griot, he wanted to know what could be so precious about these sheets of – well, it looked like old bark or half-digested pulp, dried and pressed – what? He wanted someone to tell him. Ali said, speaking to Griot carefully, choosing words, as if to a child, or as if he were using a spell or a charm whose words had to be perfect to be heard – as if words could be like a key in a lock – that 'the sand libraries had held all the records from the past – secrets, some of them from before the Ice, secrets that in some ages only kings and their queens and their keepers of the libraries knew'.

Griot was wondering – and wondered that he had not thought of it before – what other information was at large in the minds of the soldiers, men and women in the camp. And now there was a new rule, that every new arrival must be asked what was the most important thing he knew – or she knew. What knowledge did he, or she, bring from their country that could be of use here?

The answers to that were like stabs of light in the dark of Griot's mind. He had scribes from the camp, chosen by Sabir and Ali, to write down these answers and pile up the tablets or reed sheets – for when Dann came.

But Dann didn't come.

Griot was feeding more and more, housing them, clothing them, creating the fisheries down at the Bottom Sea, the farms, the looms where fleeces were made into cloth for tunics and trousers. It was only the red blankets that united so many people – hundreds now.

Why did they submit to him, to Griot? he secretly wondered. Why should they? Some were so much cleverer and some really learned, and who was he? Who was Griot, a man without a country, a man who sat at his table in the great hall and called a rabble an army.

Griot made his plans, thought his thoughts, watched the two men from the countries of sand at their nearby table, in the great hall where the high windows or apertures let in patterns of sunlight when there was sun and where sometimes birds flew across high above, and one even made a nest among the coloured tiles. Tiles that no one knew how to make now, and Ali said the art wasn't known in his country either . . . Ali, how often things did come back to Ali . . . the little brown man, who did not smile much. He had lost all his children and, he thought, his wife, too, in the war he had fled from.

Ali, always there to answer the questions that Griot had to ask, because he knew himself to be so ignorant. But it was all right, Dann would come and then . . .

Dann didn't come. And he did not send a message.

When he came, there would be all these new things to hear, about the secret place, about the information in it. There would be this army, General Dann's army, for Griot knew very well that without Dann's reputation, the legend of Dann, he would be nothing. Griot would be nothing, and it was not for him people stayed here, in discomfort, at the camp outside the Centre. People talked about General Dann, who was coming – soon.

All these new things to tell Dann – but wait, there was this business of his sister, of Mara being dead. Mara had died, and Dann didn't know it and he would have to be told. Griot registered this from time to time; he did remember, and think, it will be hard for him, he loved his sister.

Griot had never loved anyone – except, of course, Dann, if that was the word for it.

Griot, waiting, always waiting, thought about himself, and what had made him and why he sat here, waiting for Dann.

He tried to send his thoughts back, and back, but they were always blocked by a barrier of smoke and flame, of shouting soldiers and screaming people among whom were his parents. But that was as far as he could get.

Later he learned that on that night he had been nine years old.

After that he was a boy soldier, in an army on the move, that raided, and stole, and made slaves of people he was taught to think of as enemies. He was one of many child soldiers, without parents. He used a spear and could kill with it, a club and used that, a catapult, his favourite, and killed birds and animals as well as people. He was well fed and slept in a shed with other children. He was stunned, he knew now, did not think, only obeyed orders and slept when he could.

Then one day he stood in front of an officer who was sitting – as Griot was sitting now – in authority, with soldiers being brought before him, one after another, until it was his turn. This man said to him, 'What's your name?'

'It is Griot.'

'Do you have another name?'

The child shifted unhappily as he stood: he knew there had been another name; he knew . . .

'Never mind, Griot will do. What was your father?'

Griot shook his head.

'Did you have brothers and sisters?'

Griot believed he had, yes; but all his thoughts ended in fire and shouting and killing.

This man, the officer, who was in charge of the children, said gently, 'Griot, can you remember anything before – that night?'

Griot shook his head.

'We attacked your village. There was a lot of killing. The village was burned down. But before that – do you remember?'

'No, I remember nothing,' said Griot, and though he knew he was a soldier and soldiers do not cry, tears were trickling.

He saw that this man's eyes were wet too: he was sorry for Griot. It occurred to Griot to ask, 'How long ago was that night – I mean, the night you came to my village?'

'It was nearly a full year ago. It was the rainy season. Do you remember? When we marched away from the fires there was a big storm and lightning.'

And now, all these years later, Griot was thinking of the night the officer told him he was ten years old: he had in his memory on that night only a year of living.

'You're a good boy,' said this officer, whom Griot knew only as 'sir'.

And Griot, hearing the words, began to cry again in gratitude for them, hard and painfully, since soldiers do not cry, and he did not remember how he got back to the shed where his bed was. Next day they were on the move again, and there was an ambush and a big fight. Griot was captured, together with other children – those who had not been killed – and the kind officer who had told him he was ten years old was dead. Then he was a boy soldier in this other army, which he had known as the enemy, and from there he had run away, at night, hungry and sore from beating, and found a refuge in a village, he did not know what village or where. He was a servant to an old woman who beat him and he ran away again, in a flood of refugees escaping from war and wars. During this time, all he knew about himself was his name, Griot. He kept a record of how he grew older, ten, then eleven, then . . .

He knew how to kill. He knew how to make himself be like the people around him, when there were people around him. He knew how to run fast and unseen through the bush, and how to be a servant. He could cook, clean, do a hundred things in the way of mending, patching, making. But in all this time he met no one who taught him anything like writing or reading. As for numbers, he had learned how to calculate on an abacus, or with stones collected in a leather bag and used in counting barter.

Then, after adventures, he was in the Agre Army, and he was not ten now, but fifteen, and behind him his memories were only of running, fighting, keeping out of trouble, killing . . . and he had his name, Griot.

In the Agre Army he was in a platoon with boys who had had the same experience of running away, being a slave (once, in his case), being a soldier, never belonging anywhere. This platoon was part of a regiment under Captain Dann, who several times picked him for special tasks. 'You're a good boy, Griot.'

In the Agre Army there were classes; the soldiers were taught all kinds of things and Griot was going to be in a class that taught how to read and write Agre, and Mahondi and Charad, which was spoken, so he heard, all over north Ifrik. By now he knew phrases in a dozen languages. Then the Agre Army moved to attack the Hennes and Griot was with it. He heard General Dann had run off from the army and Griot ran after him, or rather, after what, at odd times, and by chance, he heard of him. It was like following a ghost on a dark night.

Then he had heard of the Farm, and that Dann was there, with his sister. When he got there, he was asked questions again – and again – but always came up against that night of flame and noise and killing.

In what he remembered the brightest thing was Dann, Captain Dann, for whom he had come here to the Centre.

Griot sat at the table in the great hall, where the light changed as the weather came and went outside, and waited for Dann.

Then Dann did come. He came, and was told about Mara being dead – and now he lay on his bed in his room. When Griot went in to see how he did, Dann said, 'It's all right, Griot. Leave me. Leave me alone, Griot.'

For three years Griot had sat and waited for Dann to come back. Now he sat and waited for him to wake up and become Dann again, become General Dann, take his place in the army, his army, General Dann's army, the Red Blanket army – which was how the soldiers talked of it.

But he didn't get up.

Ali, who had been a doctor in his country, said to Griot that he must be patient. When people have a bad shock, when they lose someone they love, sometimes it can take a long time to be able to live again.

Griot thanked Ali, whom he admired, to whom he was always grateful, but he thought privately that there was no one in that mass of people out there he called an army who hadn't lost someone or several; lost wives, children, parents, lost everything . . . but they weren't lying on their beds sometimes for hours on end, not moving at all. Sometimes it looked as if Dann was not breathing, he was so still.

Often, when Griot saw that Dann had not moved and that the snow dog waited there, patiently, he took Ruff out for a walk, and to be with the other snow dogs. Because Ruff was not always with them, they were cautious with him, and they all stood around for a while with their tails wagging, but Ruff didn't want to leave Dann: when he went out with Griot he always looked back at Dann and barked softly. It was clear he was saying he would be back soon.

Sometimes Griot knelt by Dann, one hand on the snow dog's head to restrain him, and said, 'Dann, sir, Dann, General . . .'

And Dann would at last stir himself and sit up. 'What is it, Griot?'

Dann was so thin, and ill, and it was as if he were being interrupted in some long thought, or dream.

'Sir, I wish you would come out for a bit – a bit of a walk, perhaps? It would do you good. It can't be good for you to be always lying here.'

'Yes, it is good, it's good, Griot,' and Dann would lie back.

Then Ali told Griot to talk to Dann, even though it seemed he was not listening.

So Griot would say, 'Perhaps you would like to hear what's going on, sir?'

And though Dann did not answer, Griot told him what he was doing, how the food was being organised, how they were weaving now and dyeing, and that so many of the refugees had skills which could be learned.

He really wanted to tell Dann about the secret place and the sand libraries conserved there but was waiting for the right time, when Dann could hear, and perhaps sit up and listen.

'Dann, sir, perhaps we could take a little walk along the edge of the cliff?'

'Yes, we'll do that tomorrow. Tomorrow, Griot.'

And after talking sometimes till his breath ran out, Griot left him, lying as flat as a sand fish, and apparently not breathing.

Two soldiers always sat with Dann, watching over him.

A soldier came running to the door after Griot, 'Sir, the General does talk sometimes, he talks to himself and to us too.'

'What does he talk about?'

'He is remembering all kinds of things. Well, I'd not like to have to remember some of them. And he talks about Mara. We hear that was his sister, sir.'

'Yes, she died, and that is the trouble.'

'Yes, sir.'

'But don't worry, he'll get over it.'

And why had he said that? Why should he? Dann didn't seem to want to.

Suppose Dann died? What then? Would Griot lie on his bed, limp as a newly dead thing? But even the thought shocked him into a kind of panic. He could not conceive of life without Dann. Dann was what he lived for – *his* General Dann.

It was no good, he could not come to terms with it. Dann was ill because of his love for his sister. Because of love. Mara, yes, she was a nice enough woman, yes, she was – had been.

Back there in my life, beyond that night of fire and killing and fighting, I had a family. I must have. In that first army where I was a boy soldier they called me an orphan. If they called me an orphan I must have had a father and a mother.

Perhaps I had a sister, too.

There were girls in armies.

There were girls out there in his army. He already had a battalion of boy soldiers, and soon there would be one of girl soldiers. Girls meant babies. If that happened, this army of his would be more like a town than a camp. What was he to do? All these people to feed and clothe, and it was time they went into Tundra – but for that he needed Dann, and Dann lay on his bed and would not get up.

'What am I to do?' he whispered to himself, sitting at his table in the great hall. Ali heard and said to him, 'Patience, sir, be patient. Grief is like a poison; it can poison.'

So were all those people out there, each with a tragedy to tell, poisoned? Was Ali? Griot did not think so.

The soldiers guarding Dann said that the sick man was talking about someone called Leta.

Griot sent a message to Leta by a traveller, saying that it must be delivered only to Leta herself, or to Shabis.

Griot and the snow dog were walking on the road that would lead to the Farm, when around a bend came running a figure Griot at once recognised because behind her streamed a flood of pale hair. She was shouting, 'Help, help,' and behind her ran and yelled 'Albie, Albie' two louts with sticks. She saw the snow dog and stopped. The two persecutors stopped. The white-skinned woman and the great white animal shone out against the dull mud of the road, the greasy-green of the marshes, the low grey sky. A struggling ray of sun found that hair, and it gleamed and glimmered. Ruff had not been taught attack and pursuit, and he had never seen

Leta, but he knew what to do. Within a few bounds he had passed Leta and the two youths turned to run. The snow dog would soon catch them up and they ran off the road into the marshes. Ruff stopped on the edge and watched them go. Some of the marshes were quagmires. He turned and padded quietly back to where Leta stood watching. He sat down in front of her. The neat and intelligent head, in its white ruff, was higher than her waist. She held out a hand and Ruff sniffed it.

Griot came up. 'This is Ruff, from the Ice, north, beyond the Middle Sea,' he said.

Now Ruff was walking around Leta, sniffing at the long pale hair, and he let out a small bark, which could have been a greeting.

Those two glimmering white things, in the scene of dark water, greyish weeds and bushes, they belonged together, a pair, a match – and Griot, who had found it hard to accept Leta's strangeness, was now accepting her, because of the snow dog.

Leta was carrying bundles and baskets. Griot took them and felt her trembling.

'You can manage to get to the Centre?'

She stood, brave but irresolute. Ruff went to her side and positioned himself: she saw he meant her to put her weight on him. He began slowly moving and she kept pace, leaning on him.

'Dann is very ill; he is talking about you.'

'And I think about him.'

At the Centre she at once went in to Dann. Ruff waited until she had placed herself close to Dann, then he lay down, his head on Dann's shoulder.

The two soldiers guarding Dann could not take their eyes off Leta, and her hair. The Albs in the army were white, it could be said, compared with the many not-white skin shades of the others, but none was as white as Leta, whose skin glistened. That hair of hers, it flowed down her back – and they hadn't seen anything like it. She pushed up her hair into a great bundle and said, 'Dann, it's Leta.'

He opened his eyes and smiled. 'Leta,' he said, and he put out his hand to the knot of hair and stroked it. 'It's you.'

But he did not get up, lay there, in a curve, and it seemed that his eyes were going to close again.

'Have you eaten today, Dann?'

Dann did not answer, but one of the soldiers said, 'No, he refused food.'

'I am going to make myself clean, Dann, and have something to eat, and I'll come back at once and feed you.'

Dann closed his eyes.

Leta went with Griot to a nearby room, asked for water to wash off the mud of that long wet road, and then for something to eat – anything quick and easy.

When Leta returned to Dann she carried a jug of medicine she had mixed from herbs, and knelt by him, holding it to his lips. He took a gulp and grimaced, and then drank, because of her determination.

She made him take a few mouthfuls of food and began talking. She talked of the things they had done together, she, and Mara, and Daulis, and Shabis, and Dann. Amazing journeys and dangers. 'Do you remember?' she asked. 'Do you remember, Dann?' At last he seemed able to keep his eyes open and even to respond with a smile or a nod. 'Do you remember the inn, Dann? The inn where the water came through the roof? And we were all ill, except you, and you and the river woman nursed us; we would have died without you – do you remember?'

And then, as he showed signs of lapsing into sleep, she told some tale that did not seem wilder than what she had already told, but he opened his eyes and said, 'No, Leta, we did not do that.'

She went on with the true story, and as he seemed to lose grasp of it, allowed her tale to go off into improbability – at least, it was to Griot – and he smiled as he said, 'Naughty Leta, you know we didn't do that.'

He was more animated.

'I am going to use some of my medicines to wash you, Dann.' As he made a movement that refused her, she said, 'When we were sick at the river woman's inn, you washed me – do you remember?'

'Yes, I do. You told me what herbs to use.'

'And I shall wash you now.'

She ordered warm water, poured into it a strong-smelling liquid and then began taking off Dann's singlet and trousers. He sat up and took them off himself. His body, so bony and meagre, had to shock: it hurt Griot very much. This was General Dann, the powerful General Dann who had been the handsome and strong General Dann – and he was such a thin, poor thing. Leta got Dann to sit right inside a wide flat basin, full of the strong-smelling water, and she sponged and poured and sponged and all the time she talked: 'Do you remember how we saw that sky machine that crashed, so long ago, and there were lines of people worshipping it?'

'Yes. Of course. Long, long ago – and that's what we like. Isn't that disgusting, Leta? – the long ago?'

Leta poured and sponged; the snow dog crept forward and lapped at the water, for curiosity, and then sneezed. She laughed and stroked him and said, 'You have a wonderful new friend, Dann.'

'Yes. Yes, I do have a friend.'

Leta saw Griot react to this and turn away. Dann saw Leta's concerned face and understood. 'Griot, without you nothing would have happened. You have made it all happen.' Griot heard an undertone here and smiled a little, reproachful and ironical. Would Dann have preferred nothing to have been done while he was away? Yes, probably.

Leta said, 'I've understood that sometimes it is only when a friend leaves that you know what she was. When Mara died . . .' She did glance here at Dann, but went on, 'When she died, I knew what she had been, for all of us.'

Dann sat stiff and silent in the water, and Leta went on talking about Mara, how brave she had been, then said unexpectedly, 'Dann, what would Mara say if she could see you now? Have you thought of that?'

Dann let his eyes shut, sighed, and after a good long moment said, 'But as you see, Leta, she's not here and she doesn't say anything.'

And he began to weep.

Griot signalled to the soldiers to leave. What they

had heard until now could only strengthen their idea of General Dann the wonder worker – and to that had been added Dann the healer, Dann the tender nurse – and the exploits they had heard from Leta would be told and retold in the camp.

But weeping – no.

The snow dog groaned in sympathy and put his muzzle to Dann's face.

Dann stroked the snow dog and said to Leta, 'I don't want to live, Leta. Why should I?' As she hesitated, showing that it was not a thought unknown to her, 'No, I want you to tell me: what for, Leta?'

'For one thing, there's the child.'

'Oh, she'll never be my child. Kira wouldn't allow it.'

'No, you are right, but there's Mara's child.'

Dann got out of the basin, wrapped himself in a drying cloth and lay in his usual position, a curve like a bent arrow or flexed stick. 'Tamar has a father,' he said.

Leta hesitated, and then said, 'Shabis wants to return to Agre. They are waiting for him there. He can't take Tamar with him on that journey. Do you remember the journey, Dann? How dangerous it was?'

No movement from Dann, but his eyes were open.

'And Daulis wants to travel with Shabis as far as Bilma.' And now Leta lost her composure and broke into a wail. 'Yes, and he will go, he'll go, Dann.'

She sat sobbing.

Dann slowly sat up and pulled Leta to him past the great basin that was sending out its aromatic odours. 'Oh, Leta, I'm sorry. I'm so sorry, Leta.'

She wailed in his arms, and the snow dog whined in sympathy.

Griot thought, *A pity the soldiers have gone. It would go down well in the camps, kindly Dann, comforting the Alb.*

Then he saw the soldiers had not gone, they were spying and eavesdropping – four of them, the two ordered out and the two due to replace them. They were just outside the big doors to the drill ground. Griot pretended he hadn't seen them.

Dann was rocking Leta.

'It's been the only time in my life I wasn't alone – with Daulis,' she said.

'Yes, I know; poor Leta.'

'But I can't go back with him. I'd be caught and sent back to – Mother. Daulis knows that but he's still going, Dann.' And she wept, painfully, while Dann sat rocking her and the snow dog got as close as he could to both of them, his muzzle on Leta's shoulder.

'I want to come here, Dann. I'll bring the little girl and she'll be safe here. She's never safe anywhere near Kira.'

'I know.'

'And she hates you, Dann. Kira hates you.'

'What will Kira say about Shabis going off?'

'You're right. She wants him. She wants him for herself. So far she hasn't got him and now she is beginning to hate him too. She's starting something new. She's collecting people – refugees – and making an army.'

'What is she going to do with her army?'

'She doesn't talk to us, Dann. She hates us all.'

'But what would we do with a child here – in this dead place?'

Dann lay back again and covered himself with the damp drying cloth; Griot took that from him and replaced it with a rug.

'Thank you, Griot. Don't think I'm not grateful to you.'

Griot thought, *grateful*, that's a word that needs thinking about.

Leta watched and smiled, and let Griot know she felt for him. She said, 'I'm going to rest now. I'll come back later. There's so much I must tell you, Dann.'

Dann had closed his eyes. He seemed to be asleep.

Leta came back, and sat by Dann and talked. 'Do you remember, Dann?' and when after a long time he had not moved, she raised her voice, or lowered it sharply. What she remembered was always astonishing. The guards coming to watch Dann arrived earlier, and those due to leave stayed on. Sometimes as many as six squatted by the wall, listening.

It seemed as if Dann did not hear, but several times, when Leta invented, to check, Dann said, 'No, Leta, that didn't happen.'

Yet what had happened and what hadn't seemed equally improbable.

When she said, 'That night, when you and Mara killed Kulik, on the mountain, in the fog,' the listeners, and Griot too, expected him to say, 'No, Leta, that isn't true,' but he only said, 'Yes, but it was Mara's poisoned snake that did for him. If it did. You didn't know that when I was down in the Bottom Sea some men came to catch me and one had a scar.'

'No. I didn't. But I was so afraid that night. You and Mara were always so brave. But there's no need to be afraid now of Kulik or of anyone, because there's no price on your head now, Dann. Shabis said so.'

'But if Kulik is alive, would he know that?'

'How could he be alive? One little scratch from Mara's snake would be enough. I was afraid of Mara's snake. But I'm scared of everything. I'm afraid of Kira now. She hates me because of my white skin. That's all it is. Isn't that strange, Dann?'

The listeners along the wall were uncomfortable. The soldier Albs were discussed, were argued about. Some people didn't mind them, but they were always noticed.

'And it's my hair, too. One night I woke and Kira was standing over me with that knife of hers – she was going to cut off my hair. Then Shabis told me to carry a knife too and make sure she knew it. He gave me the knife in her presence. And he sat there telling me all kinds of tricks – how to use it. So here it is.' She pulled out the handle of a knife from her tunic. 'Kira just laughed: you know how she laughs.'

'Yes,' said Dann. 'I know.'

And Leta seemed to catch her breath when he said it: it was the bitterness in it. The soldiers and Griot were hearing a new thing from Dann, and Griot was not pleased. Bitterness was a weakness and General Dann could not be weak.

'But about your hair, Leta. You shouldn't be surprised at that. In all my wanderings I've never seen anything like it. It's a wonder and that's all there is to it. I sometimes think: before the Ice, did those old people up there in Yerrup all have hair like yours? Now I am doing it: why should we care about *then* – it's a sickness.' He sat up and said to her, 'And you are a wonder, Leta, with your plants and your healing tricks. It's not the first time I've been rescued by a healing woman. That was before you joined us, before Bilma. It was when I was so ill in the Towers at Chelops. No, I've never told you, because I hate to think about it. But I was ill with the poppy and with – a lot else, too. A plant woman called Orphne cured me. I was nearly dead.' He lay back and yawned, and stretched. He was better.

'The thing is, you see, Leta, I was too far gone to want to live then. And now I don't want to get better – I think. You must understand, Leta. It's such a hard grind, living. When I think of what Mara and I did together, the effort and the drudge of it, how did we do it? How do we do it, Leta, living and keeping on?' He lifted his head and addressed the soldiers. 'You know what I'm saying. You've had it so bad, you've lost everything, war and running, always running, and don't you ever ask yourself, what for?' He waited for them to answer him, but while they acknowledged what he said, with nods, or rueful grins, or their eyes told him they understood him, they did not say anything.

He let his head fall back and he was asleep.

Leta said, very low, 'He's nearly back with us, he's nearly here again. But he could still slip the other way. He must be woken and made to sit in the bath with the herb water, and he must eat, and take the medicines I'll leave.'

She went out and sat with Griot in the hall and then

laid her head on her arms. 'It's hard, bringing a person back when they want to die.'

Griot could not imagine himself wanting to die: in front of him stretched a life full of effort and accomplishment, fuelled by what he counted on, as he did his own breath – Dann.

He was thinking now that he could bring himself to like Leta, despite her unnatural white skin, and that hair which close to was like a thousand spiders' threads when the early sun is on them. He gingerly put out a finger and touched a strand of gold that had escaped from her pile of tresses and lay on the table.

'Don't mind me,' said Leta. 'I'm used to it.' She got up, piled the masses of gleaming hair on her head, pinned it, and said, 'Now get together all the soldiers who know anything about medicine and bring them here.'

Griot himself went through the camp of huts and sheds, with their reed roofs that gleamed, palely, like Leta's hair, and explained what was needed. He saw how the soldiers were filling their idleness with a hundred games and little tasks. Griot knew how dangerous idleness could be. And as he returned to the main building a couple of Kharabs came running to say they wanted to take a unit quietly at night through the marshes to the Tundra grazing grounds and drive away some meat birds, the big ones, taller than people.

'We're hungry,' one said.

'Everyone is hungry,' agreed Griot. He was pleased with what he was hearing. 'You can drive them through the marshes – if you have a guide.'

'We have a guide.'

'And when you have the birds here there'll be enough for one big feast for everyone, that's all.'

The two looked as if they could say more, and Griot said it for them: these were two capable, strong men. 'What we need to plan are regular raids, but not always in the same place; there are different animals in different parts.'

He saw the men's faces strengthening in confidence and resolution. These two would do well. 'You go away and come back with plans for regular raids. And not just of the meat birds. There are herds of goats, too. But you must have a good plan. We have spies in Tundra and they have spies here. They arrive with the refugees. So you can only trust a few people for the raids.'

He watched them leave: it was a wonderful thing, to see men going soft with idleness come back into strength and confidence.

Then he went to the great hall where Leta was waiting for the soldiers who knew medicine. They were coming in and sitting around her, on the floor.

She had her baskets of plants and was holding them out to be recognised, so she could be told what was known about them.

Griot was at his table watching. What a wealth of talent and skills were there, among the refugees; he was every day surprised by them. And as always he wondered secretly about all those people, so various and so clever, some able to read and write, some of them powerful in their own countries – yet here they were, taking orders from him, Griot. Why should they? They arrived at the Centre, more dead than alive; he fed them and gave them their red fleecy blankets, and they never questioned his authority. His, and Dann's.

He sat and watched Leta. She spoke of her skills and heard of theirs. There were about sixty people there, men and women from so many different places along the coast and beyond. You'd think they had known each other always. What a picture he was seeing, the crowd of soldiers, their red shoulder blankets uniting them, and light coming from some high source up there in the top of the building; it struck Leta's hair that glittered and shone. Her whiteness and that hair made a centre for the crowd. Some of them were doctors in their own countries. Leta was deferring to them.

'Oh, no, no, I'm not a doctor, I'm just a plant woman; I know only what I've picked up.'

It all went on until the light left the top of the building where the apertures were, and soldiers brought in the rush lights and the fish-oil lamps. The confabulation ended when it was time for the evening meal.

Griot returned to Dann's room and found him asleep. But Dann did not seem so limp, so gone in sleep that you could imagine him dead, or near death.

Leta said she could stay a few days. Most of the time she was with Dann; now he always sat up and was awake when she was there.

Soldiers came to Griot with a formal request which was not the usual kind of thing – permission to use the drill ground for a feast, permission to view this or that part of the Centre: the old rooms and their treasures had a fascination for some of the soldiers. The two men were embarrassed and, having spoken, said, 'No harm is meant. We hope that the plant woman will take it in the spirit of the request.'

They wanted permission to touch Leta's hair. How could Griot be surprised, whose hand had seemed to creep out towards those tresses of its own accord?

He went in to Dann, who was lying down, but now not so lost to the world, and said, 'Sir, some of the soldiers have asked formally – they weren't being impertinent – to have a feel of Leta's hair.' Leta was there; Griot would have been uncomfortable, asking her direct.

Not uncomfortable enough: Leta's always pale face froze into a stiff whiteness and her lips trembled. Dann sat up, all concern, and said, 'It's all right, Leta, they don't understand . . .' And he went off into Mahondi, which Leta spoke, as she did, adequately, many other languages. An impassioned exchange, which Griot's skimpy Mahondi did not allow him to follow. Why such a reaction? He caught a word, a phrase or two: 'brothel' and 'Mother's house'.

Griot remembered that at the Farm Kira had taunted Leta about the brothel, and her cleverness with languages. 'Tools of your trade, Leta,' Kira had jeered. And to Griot, 'Didn't you know that Leta was a whore in Bilma?'

Not only had Griot not known, he didn't know what a whore was, or a brothel. The child soldier had, when he ransacked his memory for it, run errands for a house where the girls gave sex in return for food. But that was his present understanding: then he had thought only that they were kind and the house welcoming and always ready to feed him.

It had not lasted: he had to run away again. He had seen rape and thought it not much more than the rough-housing that went with fighting and looting. Then babies had been born and he had understood from that what rape led to, what sex was for. He had never heard the word whore until Kira used it. Brothel? A certain level of social order must be reached before the word can make sense. When he was a boy soldier in Agre he had relations with a female soldier but thought it a mere relieving of physical needs, and believed that was how she saw it too. Now there was a female soldier from Kharab he sometimes had sex with if there was a corner somewhere they could find privacy – not easy in that overcrowded camp. The whole question of sexual need, seen as something to be supplied like food or clothing, had not presented itself to him, until Kira's scorn of Leta. But when he thought about it, a brothel made sense. A sensible idea, surely? Yet Kira had only to use the word brothel for Leta to shrink, and now she was in tears. Leta and Dann had switched to Charad and Griot followed easily.

'They must have heard, or they wouldn't treat me like this.'

'They don't see it like that, Leta. I am sure of it. You are a bit of a wonder – surely you must see that?'

She kept shaking her head, imploring him with her great greeny-bluish eyes, that changed with the light. No one he had ever known had eyes like Leta's.

Dann said, 'There's a rumour in the camp that you have magic power, and that you keep it in your hair.'

She thought this over and then said, 'I see. Very well. But it must be done in this room, and with you here – and you too, Griot, please.'

The two soldiers on guard went out, ordered by Dann, and came back with half a dozen soldiers. Leta sat on a pile of cushions and looked at them, as if it were hurting her to do this.

'Very well,' she said.

A youth stepped forward, grinning with eagerness, shyness, and there was a touch of fear there too. He touched the gleaming strands that lay on Leta's shoulders. He rubbed the gold between his fingers. He let out his breath, which he had been holding, in a sigh of wonderment. And stepped back. Another soldier took his place. A single gold hair had caught in the first soldier's red blanket, and now he picked it off and stood admiring it. The second soldier touched Leta's hair: his face was tense with the ordeal.

Leta sat with a bent head and did not look at them.

The third soldier was bold. He stroked Leta's hair with his flat palm and breathed, 'So pretty, so pretty.' And stepped back. The three were smiling, bashful and pleased, like boys. Griot was smiling, because he knew these three would go back and say they had touched the magic hair and were alive to tell the story. Dann was concerned, his eyes full of sorrow, for Leta. A fourth soldier, a fifth. Outside the doors lines of soldiers stretched across the drill ground, and then another began forming beside it. Leta could not see this from where she sat, with bent head.

The soldiers coming in were smiling because the four

that had left smiled. There was a gaiety to this occasion, a lightness; a gloom was being lifted.

They lived in a greyness that some had never known before, had found here as if it were the air of their exile. All along that coast and over the marshes mists and fogs moved or, if the view was clear, globules of wet were like the pearly droplets on the retina. When an arrow of sunlight did shoot through a cloud of vapour it painted colour where it struck and the soldiers stopped what they were doing to stand smiling, as if they saw an apparition that promised an end of this expulsion from their own lands. Inside their sheds and huts the air seemed as heavy as water, so that often lamps would be brought in when it was daylight, in an effort to lift the dark. Then the glow of light was precious, a reminder that they were not natives of this land of grey air and whining winds. And such was the effect of Leta to the soldiers; the bright shine of her hair was more than itself, was light in a dull place: just like a shaft of sunlight on a dark day. Her hair was like distilled light near that very white skin – no one saw an Alb for the first time without thinking *That must be some kind of skin disease*. Yet this woman had brought healing, and all the medicine men in the camps commended her, said they had learned from her. Conflicting emotions had to seethe, because of that shining pale hair; gaiety and the curiosity that is not far from cruelty was beginning to show on those faces. A soldier laughed. Leta shrank. More laughter. Leta was trembling.

Dann said, 'The ones that have finished, leave.'

Leta looked up and saw what seemed to her hundreds of soldiers and their excited faces. She exclaimed and stood up.

'That's enough,' said Dann.

This order reached the outside and there was a mutter, then a grumble, then a roar of disappointment, and Leta stood shrinking, a creature hunted by the laughter she was hearing.

'Leta, it was a good thing you did that,' said Dann, and Griot admitted the next two duty guards and shut the door.

Leta was crying. Griot did not understand, but Dann went to her and put his arms round her. 'Poor Leta,' said Dann, and then, 'Don't you see, you are so strange to them?'

'I suppose I must expect always to be chosen for my hair. But I'll go grey one day and then I'll be like everybody else.'

Outside, the disappointed soldiers were going back to their huts, and Leta said to the two new guards, standing at the wall, 'Well, do you two want to touch my hair?'

Bashful but eager smiles, and awkwardly, like boys, they came and touched her hair, but gently; they were pleased and grateful, and for the first time Leta smiled and said, 'You're good boys. It's all right.'

Leta stayed on a few days, nearly all the time with Dann.

Now he would say to her, 'Do you remember . . .' And the listeners had no idea if what they were hearing was true or the wildest invention.

'Do you remember how you used that cunning little

knife of yours to cut the gold coins out of my flesh?'

'Yes, they were so close to the surface, they were just under the skin.'

'And do you remember how we saw the snow on the mountain? It was the first time we had seen snow and we ran about in the moonlight – and all the time Kulik could have killed us.'

When Leta left she and Dann embraced, Dann standing up, a tall thin rail of a man, but not now trembling with weakness.

'Dear Dann.'

'Dear Leta.'

'And if it gets too bad, may I bring the child here, to be safe?'

'Mara's child?'

'Yes, Mara's, Tamar.'

'I suppose so.'

Griot sent an escort of soldiers with Leta, ordered to keep her in their sight until she was with Shabis and in his care.

Griot was at his table in the great hall and thought how alone he was; it was all too much for him, he couldn't do it all. Then Dann came from his room, sat down with Griot and said, 'And so, Griot, here I am.' It had been a long time since he had done this.

Griot talked, telling him everything, and when he got to the raids planned to take beasts and meat birds, Dann said, 'So now we are attacking Tundra?'

'How am I going to feed all these people? There were nine new ones yesterday. They say there's a new war started up. The reed forests of Nilus are on fire, and there are many new dead.'

Dann put his head in his hands, then lifted it to look at Griot in a way that made him exclaim, 'What is it, sir? I don't understand.'

'No, Griot, you don't. Those reed forests – they may burn for years. And the cities there . . . and so it goes on, and on, and again, and again.'

'I hope they don't all come here. Someone's going to have to feed and clothe them.'

'Suppose you don't? Suppose you simply – don't?'

'Sir? General? *Dann, sir*?'

'Oh, never mind. And it's just as well you can't see how I am thinking – because it's a kind of poison, I suppose.'

'That's what Ali says, sir.'

'Ali?'

A small brown man, working by himself down the hall, lifted his head, hearing his name, and stood up.

Dann looked at him casually, then with attention.

Ali came slowly towards Dann, his thin hands clasped together on his chest, smiling. 'Do you remember me, sir?'

Dann slowly smiled. 'Yes, it was on the road. We talked, and I told you to come here.'

Ali stood in front of Dann and bowed. He lifted Dann's right hand and laid his forehead on it, then kissed the back of it and said, 'General, we have been waiting for you to get better.'

His eyes were full of tears and so, Griot saw with surprise, were Dann's.

'My king is dead,' said Ali. 'My heart is free. And now I shall serve you, sir. Until my death, or yours.'

'Until my death or yours,' responded Dann, who seemed unsurprised by the formula, for it was that. As were the other phrases: Ali's oath of loyalty was a series of known phrases for this occasion. But beyond the formality of the occasion was something more. These two men seemed to be sharing some sort of recognition, as if they had known each other long ago, and yet they could not have done. This was no matter of a few words spoken on a road. The hair was lifting on the back of Griot's neck and he was thinking, *What is it? What is happening?*

'Sir,' Ali was saying, 'while you were away we found marvels here. Griot will tell you. And when you are ready, there are things for you to see.' He indicated how, down the length of the hall, near the pillars, were set tables and at each a soldier worked over the deciphering of the scripts. If Dann had noticed them before, taken in all this activity, he had not been curious enough to ask about it.

Ali saluted and went back to his table, and Dann sat down again.

'So, Griot, now tell me.'

Griot told about the hidden place and what had been found; how Ali and others were clever, and knew old languages; so he went on, while Dann rested his head on his hand and nodded and listened, then said, 'So, Griot, here we go again, with more of the long, long ago, the here-we-go-again, the around-and-around-and-around-we-go . . .'

'Sir, all I know is, if we start thinking like that, then we might as well put our heads under our blankets and never take them out again.'

'Well, yes, Griot.'

'And we have these people to feed, sir.'

Dann put back his head and laughed. A long time since Dann had laughed. Griot now had tears in his eyes and he said, 'Dann, sir, to see you better again – to see you better . . .'

Up got Dann, carefully, a hand on the table for balance, and said, 'Griot, when I was in bed, wishing I were dead, I kept thinking, *at least I've got Griot. I can rely on Griot*. So, thank you, Griot.' He went to where Ali was sitting and joined him.

Ali talked and Dann listened, then Griot followed the two as Ali took Dann into the hidden ways that led to the secret place and shining shape of the non-glass inner room. Ali talked and Dann listened, as they moved around the transparent shape where the pages were, to be seen and not touched, until Dann had had enough and the three men returned to the misty outside air. Dann sat with Ali and Griot was at his table, just in earshot, if there were no soldiers coming to petition him.

Griot could understand most of what they said, but now he was understanding how ignorant he was, how many words he did not know, for as they talked, their words kept going into gibberish to him.

When Griot had been a boy soldier in Agre he did go to classes but there were many he did not attend; he had been engaged, with all of himself, with watching and admiring the young Captain Dann.

But Dann never missed a class. Yet, like Griot, he was learning how little he knew, compared with a really learned person, who had been educated in a king's school for scribes and translators. Ali knew of countries Dann had never heard of and, often, their languages.

Ali told Dann that behind that enclosing non-glass were books in many languages, and at first he had despaired of finding one he knew well enough to read, so ancient and crabbed were the scripts. Sometimes there were patterns of words he knew must have descended to him through the twists and turns of time, emerging so far from their past selves they remained out of his reach. And sometimes out of the reach of the other learned people he brought in to decipher the books. Ali believed that whoever had set up that great square bubble of a room had meant to preserve for the future specimens of what was being thought, and written, then, but it was a time so far in the past that Ali knew nothing except that it had existed.

Once in that long ago, before the whole of northern Ifrik began to melt into water and marsh, long before, even when the Ice had covered Yerrup, there had been sand everywhere. When the Ice threatened and the pale-skinned inhabitants had fled south they brought with them books in many languages, some old to them, even then. At first these books were in the cities they built, replicas of the cities of Yerrup now under the Ice, and then there were wars and invasion and danger, and the books were buried in the sand. There, and quite by chance, since anyone who knew anything about the old sand libraries was dead and forgotten, some people excavating for new foundations – this was before the Ice began to melt again and the earth started to turn into marsh – came on enormous pits, crammed full of old books, preserved by the dry sand. Whoever had found them tried to save them.

Ali said he believed the need to preserve these records of the past – and remember that these were the only records of that past – built the Centre: probably that was the main reason for building the Centre. For not only books and papers were found in the sandpits but every kind of artefact and machine. All these were put into the Centre, which then spread much further than it did today, before all its northern and western peripheries had gone under the marshes. But the books, the records, were put into the hidden secret heart of the Centre and presumably – this had to be deduced – there were people who understood at least something of the old languages, because they were not placed at random but in their categories. So well had that work been done that in all that time – and there was no way of calculating how long, no way of marking it, save by saying, 'There was no Ice over Yerrup, then the Ice came down and now the Ice is going' – the transparent shell which was not-glass had stood there intact, while the Centre crumbled around it. But the records and books remained safe, in the not-glass case that must be airless, because otherwise they would have crumbled long ago.

And what was that transparent wall made of? In the recesses of the Centre there were objects made of it, vessels, containers, all sorts of things, and for generations people had been stealing them. Ali said that in his own city, which was far east beyond Kharab, were bowls and jugs of this almost indestructible stuff. And there had been a kingdom, Ali believed, where rulers had used the looted not-glass things to awe their people, saying the gods had made these marvels and they must be entrusted only to themselves, for they would bring a curse on the ignorant.

To all this Griot listened, in the intervals of soldiers coming up to his table with their demands. He sat half turned to that other table where Dann was with Ali, in consultation so intense that they did not seem to hear the colloquies at Griot's table or even to see Griot sitting there, half his attention on the entrance where a dark-red glow would move forward and become a soldier and his blanket.

So days went by, and Ali and Dann sat together, where they ended always at the same puzzling place: the old, very dead languages in scripts Ali did not know, and neither did any of the other scribes. What was in those records, now unreachable? They would sit with the sheets of flattened reed between them – with the unknowable and unreachable between them – and then they left these for later, more accessible, languages. All the scribes knew Mahondi, which had so recently been the lingua franca of all Ifrik. But before this Mahondi had been another language, its parent, recognisable by Ali, but not by Dann. That old Mahondi was related to another language which was the ancestor of what Ali spoke, and that was a variety of Kharab. Held flat against the glasslike walls of the bubble-room were pages of books in that very old Mahondi and the very old Kharab. Six or eight pages was all that was left of those faraway peoples whose voices could almost be heard, words related to what was spoken now.

And there the two sat, and Griot listened; often between the men lay a sheet on which had been copied lines from a page pressed against the not-glass. Once Ali showed Dann a line he translated as 'Here is the formula for making the panes'. He said, 'It took me long enough to work out that much, sir. But the bit we want, the formula, it is not a language, it is numbers, and they aren't the same as ours.'

Dann was spreading his fingers on the table. 'One, two, three, four, five,' he said. 'Those numbers must be the same for everyone.'

'Yes,' said Ali. 'Numbers. And here are six, and seven and eight and nine and ten. But that is only part of what is here. These – marks. No one knows them.'

'Like birds' marks on sand,' said Dann. 'Like marks made by a great lizard's claws in mud.'

Ali laid before Dann a sheet that had all the marks and signs on it. 'There's a woman just arrived in camp who says she recognises them from a rock wall near her village. That's way over on the east of Ifrik down the coast. They're all at war, sir. It seems as if everything, the whole world – the world we know – is at war.'

Dann said, angry, as he always was at such times, 'Of course. And what for, Ali? For what purpose?'

Ali said quietly, 'That is the voice of your grief speaking, sir.'

'Is it, Ali? And why not?'

'Because it is dangerous for you. I was a doctor for a

while; some thoughts are not good for us, sir. They are not good for you.'

Dann sat with his head on his hand and was silent. He looked at the sheet with the difficult marks on it and said, 'Is there no one in the camps who understands any of this?'

'So far, this kind of knowledge is beyond us, beyond anything we know.'

Dann brought out from his tunic an object from one of the museums about the length of his hand and as wide as four fingers. It was black, a dense hard substance, dull, without a scratch or a mark. On it were numbers. Ten of them. 'One, two, three, four, five, six, seven, eight, nine, zero,' said Dann, counting out the numbers on his fingers. 'So, these old people had ten fingers and ten toes, just like us. And how far back does that go, I wonder? I've seen a monkey spread out his hand and look at the fingers. Perhaps it was wondering, how many fingers have I got?'

'Perhaps one day the monkey will work it out,' said Ali gently.

'They knew it all, those old people,' said Dann. 'But we know nothing at all. I can't bear it, Ali,' he said, fretful, like a child. 'How can you stand it, Ali? We are as ignorant as – monkeys.'

'If we were,' said Ali, 'then I'd feel like you, sir.' Ali was speaking firmly, as if Dann were a child.

Griot was watching them with an emotion nearer to despair than anything. He could never have spoken to Dann like that. The two men were sitting in a patch of bright light from the high ceiling. They were so different.

Ali was brown, different from Griot's brown, more yellowish, with thin fine features and eyes deep under his brows. He was too thin, but that was because none of them ever ate their fill. There was a pride and self-possession about him – like Dann. Griot did not have that. He knew himself to be thick-fibred and heavy compared with the elegant little man with his gentle, thoughtful face.

'The woman who recognises the numbers – get her to write them down.'

'She has written them already.'

Now Dann got up, came to Griot's table, sat and said, 'Griot, every person who arrives here must be asked what they know.'

'It's being done already, sir.'

'Did you know about the woman and the numbers?'

'No, we hadn't thought of numbers, beyond what we need for tallying supplies and stores.'

'There you are, that's it. We don't even know what questions to put. We have to work out the questions and how to put them. Every person who comes here might be holding knowledge that could disappear with them. When Mara and I arrived on a boat in Agre there was a thing on the boat that trapped sun. The boat woman knew how they worked. Once sun traps were stuck all around the Centre but no one knew what they were for. The woman on the boat was killed and that knowledge went with her. It must be happening all the time. When we arrived here no one knew how the sun traps worked. There they are, now, stuck up there and people think they're bird traps.'

He sat, silent, remembering, and Griot and Ali watched.

'Sir,' prompted Ali.

'When my sister met Shabis she told him things she knew but he had never heard of, and he told her things she didn't know. Everywhere there are people who know things but they don't know their knowledge is precious. If we could put together all the things that different people know, it might add up to – it would be something enormous.'

Ali said, 'But I don't think anyone alive now knows how to unlock this – formula. That is what it is called. Formula.'

'How do we know that?'

'If it were known, then it would be made – the stuff like glass. Or this thing here . . .' he touched the smooth black of the thing that was like stone, but was not stone, that Dann had left lying on the table. 'Or some of the things in the Centre.'

'So, we have to be ignorant,' said Dann. 'Those people, those old people, they knew so much. They were so clever.'

'If they were so clever, then where are they?' said Ali.

This was a new thought for Dann. He sat silent, surprised, and then he laughed. Ali laughed with him. Griot did not laugh. If that was funny, then . . . he stood up and said, 'Dann, sir, I would like you to come with me to inspect the camp. It would be good for the soldiers, sir.'

'But, Griot,' said Dann, mocking him gently, 'you

don't need me for that, you do it all so well. You're a wonder, Griot. Isn't he, Decipherer Ali?'

'Yes, he is,' said Ali, meaning it. 'We all think so. But Griot's right. They need to see you, sir.' And then, 'You perhaps don't know, General, that another twenty came in this morning.'

'Very well, I'll come – tomorrow perhaps?'

'Sir, I'd like you to come now.' Griot persisted with this stubbornness, partly because he needed to take Dann away from Ali: their closeness hurt him. Partly he knew it was time Dann was seen around the camp. There he sat, his General, languid from his illness, too thin, but with such an air of . . . Griot wished he could somehow vanish into Dann and learn what it was Dann held there inside him that made people love him. As Ali did. As he did. Everyone had seen and heard Dann humble himself in front of them all, but they still loved him.

Now Ali surprised Griot by rising and saying to Dann, 'Why don't we all three go, sir?' He was allying himself with Griot.

'Very well,' said Dann. He put himself between Ali and Griot, and the three men made their way out, reaching the drill ground just as newly arrived refugees did. Short, thin people: at first it would be easy to think them not yet grown, or even children. Compared with the soldiers who commanded them they were poor wretches. Yet the soldiers had been in as bad a way when they came.

'Ask where they are from,' said Dann.

The soldiers tried phrases in various languages. Then

Ali went forward with his repertoire. At last a man answered, with what seemed like the last of his breath.

'They've come from a long way up the great river. There's a war there.'

'Where is there not war?' said Dann.

A pot of soup was being brought out from the huts, slung on a stick held on the shoulders of two female soldiers. They knelt by the new arrivals and dipped mugs into the soup, which they held to the mouths that reached out and seemed to strive after the soup.

'Untie their hands,' said Griot.

This was done, and now they could hold the mugs.

'Give them their blankets,' said Griot.

'Sir,' said one of the soldiers, 'our blankets are running short.'

'Then weave some more,' said Griot.

'We'll have to make another raid, sir. We simply don't have enough fleeces.'

Dann was walking into the huts, and Ali and Griot followed.

These were the first that had been put up, before such a compression of people had been thought of. They were well spaced, with good windows. Then, as the refugees kept on coming, the huts were put closer together. In the newest part, built between the cliff and the marshes on either side of the track that led east, they were not huts, but lines of building, with doors every few paces. Inside it was dark. The air was bad. Although it was midday there were low flickers of light from the fish-oil lamps. Soldiers were lying about on their beds, or sitting around between them, gambling. Ahead, beyond the lines, were huddles of newly arrived people sitting on the damp earth, and red blankets had been stretched over reed screens.

Dann looked, but did not speak. Griot was ashamed and did not say anything. He had thought that everyone had at least found a place in the lines. Ali walked over to the cliff's edge and was staring down. Dann joined him. Ruff too.

Griot knew what they would see. Down the slope of the cliff precarious shelves and platforms of rock and earth had been built, and on them reed shelters.

Griot knew about these ingenious attempts at housing, but had said nothing. Dann was angry and said to Griot, 'This is impossible, Captain.'

'Yes, I know,' said Griot.

Dann said, 'Griot, we will not take in any more refugees.'

'But, sir, where will they go?'

'They will walk onwards into Tundra and reach the border with Bilma, or they will go on to the Farm.'

'And if they do that Kira will make them part of her army.'

'Yes, Griot, that will probably happen. And she will feed them and look after them.'

'Sir, aren't you afraid that Kira will use her army against the Centre – against you?'

'Yes, Griot, I think that will probably happen.'

'Sir, all these people are saying the same thing – why are they stuck out here in the wind and the rain when there are empty places in the Centre?'

'Are they, Griot? And you are telling them the reason,

I hope? If some of them are in the Centre and some outside, then the ones inside will think they are better than the ones outside and they'll be fighting each other before we know it. Isn't that so, Ali?'

'Yes, I think so.'

'Human nature,' said Dann, grim, but as if the thought pleased him. 'We are up against human nature, Griot.'

'Yes, sir.'

'Aren't we, Ali?'

'Yes, sir.'

'Now, Griot, you will post soldiers just there where the lines end, and you will turn away any more refugees who arrive here. Send them away but tell them that if people walk for a few days along the road west they'll come to a lovely woman called Kira, and she'll make them Kira's soldiers.' He sounded amused, and he stood laughing, while the other two watched him, not laughing.

Then Dann left and said, without turning round, 'I've given you an order, Captain Griot. Have you understood that? Not one more person. No more.'

As he was about to go into the Centre, Ali joined him and the two men went in together.

Griot stood on the edge of the great cliff, looking down at the pitiful makeshift shacks and shelters, and listened to a baby crying. He thought that Dann had never given him an order before about how he organised his army. He had mixed feelings about this. Dann was acknowledging him, in a way Griot felt was overdue. But it was a criticism, a severe one, and Griot was sorry for himself. It's all very well, he thought, but he just leaves me to get on with it . . . He turned and saw the wretched newcomers under their skimpy red blanket shelters, already darkened by the wet, and he went forward, calling some soldiers to go with him.

He had to give orders. He set his mind to it and gave them, and they meant that these shelters would be removed and the people in them would be sent on their way.

He went back through the drill ground and there still squatted the refugees from that morning, chatting with the soldiers. They already looked better; they were like plants that had been watered.

Griot told the soldiers that they must set up a feeding station, just where the lines ended, serving soup and bread, and as the refugees arrived who must be sent on their way each would be given a mug of soup and a loaf.

Griot was thinking of the many times in his life he had walked, or run, or stumbled, for his life, wanting food, wanting water . . . at least no one in these parts need want water. He was sending people on their way, who might have been on their feet for . . . sometimes, he himself had not known how long he had been running, or staggering: the condition of being empty-stomached so long with him he had forgotten what it was not to be hungry. If Dann was right – and how could he be wrong? – then he, Griot, was sending people away who might die because of him. And yet Griot was hearing like an echo the baby crying in its shelter of reeds that could be tumbled down the cliff by any puff of wind or falling stone . . . a crying child . . . yes, back on the night of fire and fighting, babies had been crying, and had been in this war and that war ever since. There was a nagging at his attention, 'Remember me, remember me . . .'

Griot sat at his table in the hall, and a few paces away were Dann and Ali, in their usual close conversation, while the packs of reed pages piled up between them. The two of them pored over those – to Griot – indecipherable lines of writing, and often from one of the other tables a soldier came with another reed sheet, and laid it down, smiling, or bending to indicate something discovered there.

There were now twenty or more – always more – tables set out down the length of that very long hall, and at each sat one or two scholars, wise men, and women, who had been poor wretches like those Griot could imagine weeping and stumbling at that moment on their way through or past the dangerous marshes.

Each of these had been into the secret place, with Ali, had copied through the not-glass a page of some ancient text and returned with it. Outside the secret place stood guards. No one might go in who didn't have Ali with him, and that meant Griot too, he discovered, to his shame and surprise. When the order was given Griot had not been mentioned. Who had given the order? Dann had. And yet if Griot was standing near the table shared by Dann and Ali, when they planned a visit, Griot went along too, by right, Dann talking to him and Ali about camp matters, to Ali about the old books. Dann hadn't thought: that was all it was.

It was Sabir who supervised the dispensation of the tables, he who walked up and down, watching, stopping to talk, or joke. It was a pleasant, easy scene, that one, in the great hall, where the light changed according to how the sky sent sharp or mild winds, sent dark or light clouds, and even, sometimes, fragments of sunlight that lay patchily all down the hall, and over the busy tables.

Dann often left Ali at work on his transcripts, and wandered off down the hall. He stopped at every table, and if he didn't know the language of the scholar working there, Sabir called out for someone to come who did. Dann sat there, joking, laughing, and above all listening. Griot, making an excuse to go past, heard that the man was telling Dann his story, his wretch's story, for no matter how many languages he knew, present and ancient, he had had to flee from his equivalent of the night of flames and fighting, where he – or she – might have lost everything. Dann sat on, listening, his head on his hand, or with bent head, nodding, and once Griot, passing by, saw tears on his cheeks. He was so gentle, this Dann, so courteous in his sympathy, and Ali, too, when it was he who knew the language in question, and sat there with him, gentle and listening, always listening . . . Griot thought that Dann had never asked him about his own night of fire and shouting – and yes, babies crying – but now it was too late, there was the right time for that, and for these poor men, and one or two women, it was their time to sit, talking, talking, the words burning in their mouths and making their eyes burn too. Dann might sit listening at one of the tables all day, then next day it was another table. A woman scribe, the daughter of a wise man who had insisted on her being taught what her brothers knew, told how she had saved her children and run, but while she was strong, they were little and had died, of heat and hunger. That was far to the east; she was a sand-eater, she tried to joke, like Ali and Sabir.

Or Dann sat with Ali, and Griot hoped no soldier would come in for advice, because he was listening.

Ali: 'The pages they left pressed against that glass stuff, they were chosen because they were important. But each was chosen from a whole book, so that whole book is important.'

Dann: 'But we'll never know what was in the whole book, only that one page.'

Ali: 'And that page only partially, since the languages are so old – it's like seeing the worlds of ghosts – the ghosts of ghosts, and the meaning is like words heard in a wind, blowing them away. We are looking at words that were copied from others, written by people who lived long before them – long, long depths of time, sir. So long.'

'Yes.'

'So, if there are ghosts, then they must be pretty well past their best, sir.' Dann laughed. 'Yes. When we stand by those glass walls in there, and look, it's like looking into Time, and our eyes are not made for that.'

Griot thought, *If I could talk like him, talk like Ali, if I could read all those languages, if only I could . . .*

And now Dann indicated a shiny new sheet of pressed

reed and said, 'So, what's this? It's not broken up, like some.'

'It's a history, sir.'

'When? Where? What?'

'That information isn't on this sheet, sir. It must be in the hidden pages of that book.'

Dann actually groaned, and held his head between his impatient palms.

'I'll read what there is, but it's only an approximation.'

And Ali slowly read, hesitating sometimes for what seemed long moments, '*When it was clear the Ice was going to come down from the North* . . . a bit I can't read . . . *lamentation, because of what would be lost. The greatest civilisation in history* . . . a good lot missing here. *It was decided to replicate some cities so that at least some of our civilisation would be remembered. Fighting broke out over which cities should* . . .'

'Oh yes,' said Dann. 'Exactly. Fighting. Well, what else? At least that hasn't changed.'

'. . . *so many cities. Each city wanted to be rebuilt in North Afrique*. This spelling has changed. *Some were richer than others. The rich ones succeeded. The Ice advancing faster than* . . . *People fought to get away from the Ice* . . . *into the south* . . . *Millions* . . . we don't know how many a million was . . . *The new cities were built everywhere over northern Afrique* . . . *mostly on sand. The old cities of Urrup were large. Each* . . . *centre* . . . *usually older than the peripheries, but no attempt was made to replicate the suburbs because they were considered ugly and* . . . *not enough supplies of building materials. When a new generation was told, this city is a replica of Rome, or Paris . . . it was forgotten that this could only be a small part of the old city . . . forgotten how vast the old cities had been.*

'The inhabitants of Afrique fought the refugees coming in from Urrup and there were many wars. While the cities were still a great wonder, they began to empty. The technologies that made them function had gone. The cities that had been meant to carry the name and the idea and the fame of old Urrup stood empty for hundreds of years, and began to fall into ruins, and then – but a long time after – the permafrost began to melt and the cities sank down into the water. And we will never know what was in the rest of that book.'

'If we break the glass, then . . .'

'All that old mass of books will crumble.'

'How did they get the air out?'

Ali shrugged. 'We don't know.'

'They must have pumped it out. Sucked it out?'

Ali shrugged.

'Who did? Who were *they*?'

Ali shrugged.

'They wanted to be known. They wanted us to know them.'

'I think they didn't visualise us – so long after. A nearer succession of descendants, perhaps . . . and they were so long ago . . . we have a tale in our country, about the Centre.'

'About the Centre?'

Griot intervened: 'There are stories about the Centre

everywhere. As the refugees come in, we collect their stories.'

'Our fragment goes like this – it is part of a children's tale':

> The place where Princes do not guess
> The secrets that their servants know.
> Hidden windows clearly show
> Lost wisdom from the long ago.
>
> Do not try for it unless . . .

'Unless what?' Griot asked.

'Who can know, now?' said Ali.

'Servants,' said Dann. 'Those nasty old vultures who were here when Mara and I . . .' The name seemed to drain his attention away from them, the two with him. He stared, breathing hard.

Ali and Griot sat quietly, waiting. Dann came back to himself and went on, 'They knew it all. They knew about the hidden place.' And now he laughed aloud, not pleasantly, and said, 'And for what were those nasty old crows keeping their secrets?'

'Probably you,' Griot ventured. 'If you had agreed to go along with the old prince and princess.'

'And now we've found it anyway – *You* found it, Griot. Without Mara and me having to dance to their tune.' And he stopped again, staring, his breathing checked, his face cold.

Griot looked at Dann's hands lying on the table. Fists, then they began clenching and unclenching. Long, fine hands, and there was a small trembling in the fingers. Dann saw it and shut his hands tight.

Ali's hands, folded together, those thin, clever hands, seemed to be listening.

Griot's hands, palms down, were large, solid, strong with energy. One could not imagine in those fingers the slender reed pen that lay near Ali, with the little clay pot of ink.

'Sir,' said Ali loudly to Dann. 'Sir.'

Dann returned.

'Sir, in the Centre there are boats we do not have. I am having scribes write down their measurements and descriptions. If I ever get to my country I'll take them with me.'

'Well done,' said Dann. 'At least not guns. Guns copied from the Centre are all over Ifrik.'

'But in our country we already have a great many things that are in the Centre as exhibits.'

'That means you are far in advance of us.'

'We were in advance, sir, by more than you can imagine. There are records – our records are in our tales – we were once a great civilisation, before Yerrup, when Yerrup lived like savages in dirt and never washed themselves.'

'And, so, what happened?'

'Yerrup ceased to be savages. They acquired science – as you can see from the Centre . . . and then when the Ice came down they ran from Yerrup like rats from a disaster, overran us and destroyed what we had – except for the records in our tales, which we use to start again. We are starting all over again, sir.'

Dann sat, grinning, as if to himself, but they were meant to notice it. 'So you are beginning again. Tell me, Ali, don't you get tired of it?'

And Griot was listening as he never had. He knew he was near what it was that was deep inside Dann, that he could not reach, or imagine.

'I know what you are thinking, sir,' said Ali. 'Yes, I know that thought.'

'Over and over again,' said Dann. 'Never mind about the Ice, we don't even need that. We can destroy everything without that. Again and again.'

'Sir,' said Ali steadily, 'if you let that thought take over you might as well put one of these red blankets over your head and turn your face to the dark.'

'Exactly,' said Dann. 'Yes. Well done, Ali.'

Griot could not hold back. 'Sir . . . Dann . . . General . . . no. You can't. Don't you see . . .' He stopped, his voice shaking.

'Don't I see what, Griot?' He smiled, not his terrible smile, but the kind of smile he used listening to the tales he heard of famine and loss and fires and fighting. 'Poor Griot,' he said. He put out his elegant hand and laid it on Griot's arm. Griot could feel the trembling of it. Never had Dann spoken to Griot as he did now: kind, even tender, and Ali's smile at Griot was kind. 'Poor Griot. Well . . . what can we say?' He said to Ali, withdrawing that cold, trembling hand, 'Here is a man who has never had that thought. If it crept into his mind he wouldn't know what it was.'

'Then fortunate Captain Griot,' said Ali.

'Yes. Griot, when that thought does come knocking

at your mind, remember I foresaw it and was sorry for you.'

'Yes, sir,' said Griot.

Griot slept in a room between Dann's and the hall, and he woke to hear the snow dog's bark, not from Dann's room but from somewhere in the Centre. He looked into Dann's room, but he wasn't there. Griot ran out and through the hall, where a grey light filled the spaces under the roof. A moon was up and, rarely, was not cloud-hidden. He ran when Ruff barked and stopped to listen when he stopped. The animal was somewhere near the hidden passages to the secret room. Griot saw the white mass of the snow dog ahead, where the way to the secret place began. Ruff was too big to insert himself through the narrow places. He stood on guard and turned to face Griot, threatening, then saw who it was and came to him, and took him in his jaws by the arm. He was wanting Griot to lead him into the secret place. When Griot had to leave him, the unhappiness of the animal's bark made Griot's heart beat uncomfortably. 'Wait,' he said to the snow dog, 'wait, Ruff.' Griot slid and wormed his way through. At the entrance to the chamber he saw a light ahead. Dann sat on the floor, his arms stretched out round the not-glass bubble, as if he intended it as an embrace. Dann seemed to be singing or crooning to himself but Griot could not make out the words. A wordless dirge of a song, as sad as the soft whines of the snow dog left outside.

Dann did not turn his head, but stopped his song and said, 'Griot, what are you doing here?'

'I came to see if you are all right.'

'But I already have one dog on guard, Griot.' Dann got up and lifted his little flame high, so that the red glow fell on a shining page that was pressed to the transparency. Dann turned and Griot saw his face: eyes wild, and sick.

Dann walked past Griot to the exit and slid through, and now Griot was in the dark, and he was afraid. Tonight Griot could believe that ghosts guarded this place. He slid out quickly and saw Dann ahead, with his lantern, waiting for him.

'This place smells. It smells, Griot.'

'I suppose we get used to it.'

'I haven't got used to it.'

'Sir, it is time we left here.'

'Yes, I suppose it is. But we haven't finished with what we can learn from – that place in there.'

The moon went dark. Dann's lantern was like a little red eye in the darkness. The moon shone again. Wraiths of mist floated about through the roofs and courtyards.

'Do you believe in ghosts, Griot?'

'I have never seen one.'

'Oh, yes – now that's the safe approach to it. But suppose you feel them, you don't have to see them?'

'And I haven't felt them either. Sir . . .' Griot attempted to joke, 'I'd rather not talk about ghosts here, if you don't mind.'

'Always sensible, Griot. Come on.' And he went ahead, with Ruff, to his room, where he sat on his bed with Ruff by him.

Dann said over the dog's head, 'Griot, I'm not well.'

'No, sir, I can see that.'

For a while Dann sat, stirring his fingers about in the dog's mane.

'Sir?'

'Yes, Griot?'

'Could you say in what way you aren't well?'

'It's The Other One, Griot. He wants to take me over.'

'I see. *Sir*?'

'Well, do you see? You have seen The Other One. You saw him.'

'Yes, I have. But I'd say he's not here now.'

'He's here all right. I'm here, aren't I?'

Griot did not reply.

The dog whined softly. Griot was tired. It would soon be morning. He wanted to go to his room, lie down and sleep.

'The thing is, Griot, it is easier being *him* than being me. If I just let myself become *him* I'd never have to think again. That would be wonderful, Griot.'

Griot sat down, not knowing he was going to, on a low seat, close to Dann and Ruff. He yawned.

'Poor Griot,' said Dann. 'I know I am a disappointment to you.'

'Oh, no,' said Griot, shocked. 'How could you be?'

'It was in this very room that I first understood. It was when I knew there was The Other One. Before that I had not understood it. You see, I nearly betrayed Mara. Well, not for the first time. I gambled Mara – to slavers. Did you know that, Griot?'

'No, how could I know that?'

'They might have told you, at the Farm. I am sure Kira would never let a chance slip of making me sound – interesting.'

'But Mara was there. And Shabis. He'd never let Kira say bad things about you – he always stopped her.'

'Oh, yes, Shabis.' And Dann flung himself back, and then was asleep – just like that. Griot dared to go quietly to him, bend over, look at that face, so sorrowful it was, and even in sleep, tense. The snow dog lay beside Dann and licked Griot's hand.

Griot's eyes filled with tears. He thought, *There it is – love. But the beast loves him. He likes me well enough. And Dann called me his dog. Well, am I ashamed to be like Ruff?*

He went back to his room, lay down and was instantly asleep.

The next night he was again awakened by the snow dog, but this time it was from the front of the Centre. Out he went and there was Dann, the snow dog beside him.

'There you are, Griot.'

'Yes, sir.'

'I've been thinking, Griot, but no matter how hard I think I can't make sense of it. Mara and I came towards the Centre for the first time along this road here. That's how we came, the two of us. But we aren't walking there now. Do you see?'

'No, sir.'

Griot thought that Dann was worse than he had been last night.

'And then, along this road, the one going to the Farm, Mara and I walked together. She and I – together. But she's not there.'

'No, sir.'

'Have you ever lost someone, Griot, has someone died?'

This was such an absurd thing to say, Griot could not answer. Dann knew Griot's history.

After quite a silence, while he tried to find words that would fit, he said, 'No, no one died. Not the way you mean it. Not like Mara dying, for you.'

'You see,' said Dann in a quiet, reasonable sort of way, 'that's it, you see. That's the whole point. Someone is here. She was here. Then, they aren't here. *She isn't here*. That's the whole point, do you see, Griot?'

The two men stood together, close, on the wet road, in a wet dawn light. Over the marshes gleams of light were appearing. Mists were rising. Dann was peering into Griot's face, while his hand clutched at Ruff's mane. Too tightly: Ruff whined.

'Sorry, Ruff,' said Dann. And to Griot, 'I simply can't understand it, you see, Griot?'

Dann was appealing to Griot, leaning right forward, eyes on Griot's face.

Griot said, 'Dann – sir, but we know when someone is dead they are gone.'

'Exactly,' said Dann. 'There. You understand. Come along, Ruff,' and he walked back to his room, his hand on the snow dog's head.

* * *

A few nights later a soldier came to wake Griot, apologetic, worried. He kept saying, 'I'm sorry, Captain, but we don't know what to do.'

Again, Dann stood in the early light with his Ruff, and now there were soldiers, one on either side, who were holding his arms. Ruff was barking.

'Griot,' said Dann, 'they're arresting me. They think I'm on poppy.'

Griot advanced to Dann. He had not thought of poppy and he was right: Dann's eyes were strained and sad, but they didn't have the mad shine of poppy.

'The General was behaving oddly, sir. He didn't seem to be himself.'

'It's all right,' said Griot and the soldiers let Dann go. It was obvious he had struggled and perhaps hit out at them.

'You have orders to arrest me if you think I am on poppy,' said Dann.

'Yes, sir. You were shouting. The sentries heard and came to wake us up.'

'How do you know I wasn't shouting to – raise some ghosts?' He laughed.

'It's all right,' said Griot to the soldiers.

'The Captain says it's all right,' said Dann to the soldiers, who began to leave.

'Go back to sleep,' said Griot.

'The Captain is telling you to go back to bed,' said Dann, who was finding all this very funny.

'Yes, sir. Goodnight, sir.' The soldiers disappeared into the gloom of the parade ground.

'Come on, Griot. Come on, Ruff.' The three walked

back to Dann's door where he said to Griot, 'Goodnight. And thank you, Griot.'

'Goodnight, sir.'

As the door closed he saw Dann, sitting on the foot of his bed, his arms round the snow dog. 'What shall I do, Ruff, what shall I do?'

And in his room Griot sat with his head in his hands: 'What shall I do?'

That ghost of a man, wandering through the Centre, appearing at night on the roads outside, was Dann, the great General, on whom everything depended. It was not Captain Griot whose name was used among the soldiery as a talisman for the future; and in Tundra it was General Dann they talked about, waiting for the invasion that would not only rescue them but begin a wonderful new life. (Nothing in Griot mocked at these hopes; he envisaged the new life rather like the organisation of the army back in Agre: justice, order, fairness, kindness as a ruling idea.) It was Dann's name that had the magic, for whatever reason, and Griot often enough brooded about that reason, while he watched Dann, trying not to let Dann see that he did. Suppose in his camp out there, the soldiers and the refugees who would become soldiers, those who – in spite of everything Griot could do – sneaked in and found themselves corners to hide in, suppose they no longer said in voices hushed because of the great thoughts General Dann's name evoked, 'General Dann – there he is. Yes, there he is.'

Griot had to suppose they saw something different from what he did, a gaunt man shambling about, stopping to stare at – well, ghosts, really, or one ghost in particular. Painful to see, this unhappy man, but in the camps they said, 'There's the General' – and saw the future.

Which had to start soon, before all these precarious arrangements fell apart.

Before – and this was a new urgency – the waters did actually come up and flood the Centre. On a tall white wall in the very heart of the Centre Griot had seen a blanket of black mould creeping up from its foot, that was apparently set firm in a stone foundation. It must be standing in water. Griot took Dann to see the black furry film on the wall.

'Very well, Griot, I see. We have to hurry.'

'Yes, sir, we do.'

'I will – but first . . .'

Griot took the road west to the Farm. He was going to appeal to Shabis. He stopped for a night at the inn below the mountain and found there Shabis and the child, Tamar. Time had certainly passed: this was no small child. Six years old, she must be, but she was tall – a child, yes, but thoughtful and noticing.

Griot and Shabis and Tamar sat together in a room well out of the common traffic of the inn, and kept a watch on the door. Soldiers wearing a black blanket as a unifying mark showed that someone had copied Griot's idea. Kira had. The common-room was full of soldiers wearing the black identifier. Griot's entrance would have been noticed and already runners would have departed for the Farm.

'You must go back,' said Shabis. 'Go back at once.

No, we'll leave separately. We got here unobserved. I know a way through the marshes. I can take Tamar with me, but three would be too much.'

'You are . . .' He had been going to say, running away, and Shabis heard it and said, 'Yes, we are running away. If I am to keep my child alive she mustn't be anywhere near Kira. But there's no time to talk now. We'll come to the Centre. Tell Dann to expect us in a day or two. And now you, Griot – go.' He knocked on the table and in came the landlord.

Shabis said, 'Show Griot the secret way out. He will use it as soon as he has eaten.' He put coins down on the table.

The landlord said, 'Soldiers, so many soldiers. Good for custom, but not for peace of mind.'

Shabis and Tamar got up, put packets of food into their bundles, listened at the door, and then went out quietly. The landlord stood listening. Griot joined him. Two shadows moved across the road and disappeared into the marshes. The moon shone intermittently, there were half-gleams of water and wisps of mist, and among them a tall figure and a smaller one, shadows among shadows.

The landlord brought a bundle of food and said that Griot must not be out at night on the road in his red blanket. He gave Griot an ordinary brown tunic of the kind worn in Tundra. 'I'll swap it for your red blanket. Never know when it will come in useful.'

In an hour Griot, looking like a Tundra labourer, slipped out of the inn and began the walk back to the Centre. It was full daylight when he got there. The sentry challenged him and only with difficulty recognised Captain Griot.

Griot chose his time to tell Dann who was coming to the Centre, though he did not know any details.

'But I do know this. Kira's army is getting strong. I got that from talking to people on the road. She plans to attack Tundra and grab everything she can.'

'But from what I hear you already have so many of our people in strategic places she is not likely to do well – eh, Griot?'

'Yes, many. Spies and informers. But she has them too. She plans to be ruler of all Tundra and use the Centre as HQ.'

'And Tamar is taking refuge with me, for safety?'

'Yes, sir. Mara's daughter.'

Dann and his attendant Ruff placed themselves at a table in the great hall where they could see the Centre's entrance. Ali was with them. Griot, feverish and anxious, paced the hall up and down between the tables with their attentive scribes, until Dann told him to come and sit down. 'They either got through or they didn't,' he told Griot – told himself? – and then, cancelling the finality of his words, dropped his head into his hands and sat suffering. When the top of the hall was filling with a watery golden evening light there were knocks on the outer doors, and there appeared two figures who seemed to float towards them in garments that changed as you looked, like water running over a stream bed, from white and pale to black and dark with foldings and flickerings of gold and brown. Dann seemed not to be breathing. He lifted his hand in greeting to Shabis and let it fall, loose, on the snow dog's back. He was looking under his brows at the tall child, his head slightly averted, to avoid a hurtful direct stare, as if at an apparition that might take itself off again.

The child came to a stop just outside the reach of his arm, and stood there gravely, looking.

And Griot, who had known Mara, knew why Dann had to sit there, silent with shock. This Tamar was like Mara, and like Dann too. And Shabis who was now sprawling as he sat, from tiredness, his head on his hand, was one of their kind, looking like them and feeling with them. Ali knew only that this was a moment when the destinies of these people were meshing. He put out his hand to calm the snow dog, who was whining with the tension.

Griot was thinking that an outside observer might well marvel at the differences between the people at that table. He knew how he looked, having had to make comparisons so often with the many kinds and types who inhabited the soldiers' camp, and could see himself, a solid man, squarish grey-green eyes in a sturdy face, limbs that could make you think of wrestlers'. And there across the table was Ali, brown and slight and light, not tall, but like a marsh bird, quick and elusive. And here were the three Mahondis, tall, slender, fine, with their long hands, dark eyes, and their hair, black, long, shining and straight. And their skins, the colour of the inner bark of the rare marsh tree, that grew only where marsh edge climbed to solid land.

So beautiful, they were, these Mahondis . . . and Griot

was choosing to forget Kira, who might be a Mahondi but had nothing of their grace.

Now Tamar was putting out her hand to the snow dog, who sniffed at it, while all the time her eyes were on Dann's face.

'His name is Ruff,' said Dann. 'Ruff, this is Tamar.'

The snow dog lifted his muzzle and barked twice, softly.

'And I am Dann, and I am your uncle.'

Tamar took a step closer, so that she was at Dann's knee. Never had two people confronted each other with such a passionate shyness, such need. Both trembled. Tamar put her hand on Dann's knee, for support.

She might as well have hit Dann, from the look on his face. She let her hand fall and he snatched it up and held it.

'You knew my mother,' said Tamar. 'But I didn't know her.'

Dann shook his head, meaning *I can't talk*.

The others could see the child wanted him to tell her she was like her mother, for she had heard this so often, but he could not speak.

At last he said, 'That thing you've got on . . .' And he put out his other hand to touch the garment . . . 'Your mother and I wore them all the way up Ifrik. You can disappear in them, if the light is right.'

Shabis said, 'I told Tamar that we both must wear them and we wouldn't be seen.' On him it came to his hips and he wore it over the baggy Tundra trousers. On her it was a dress, halfway down her legs.

'You are so like Mara,' said Dann at last, through the pain of saying it, and she was in his arms and they were both crying. But as she stood in his embrace, the sleeve of her garment fell back and there on her upper arm was a crimson weal.

Dann caught his breath, but before he could ask, Shabis said, 'That was the latest of the so-called accidents and it is why we left.'

'A whip made that,' said Dann.

'It was apparently meant for Kira's house slave.'

'So there are slaves at the Farm now?'

'Yes, slaves. Bought and sold.'

'So, Kira got her way.'

'How could we have stopped her?'

Dann nodded. 'Yes.'

Tamar said to him, 'Why are there bad people, Dann? Why are there good people and bad people?'

Dann laughed with surprise. 'Well, little one, that is a real question. But I don't think anyone knows.'

'It seems so funny. I mean so strange, that there are good people at the Farm and bad people. Kira and Rhea are very bad and . . .'

'I think you are talking about my daughter,' said Dann. He still held the child, and now lifted her on to his knees. Tamar's face was near to Dann's: two such similar faces.

Tamar said, 'Kira says that Rhea is Shabis's daughter.'

Shabis was angry. 'That isn't possible. I keep telling you, Tamar. Your mother and Kira got pregnant at the same time: Mara with you and Kira with Rhea. When Dann was still living there.'

'Yes,' said Dann. 'Rhea is my daughter. At least, that's what she told me, and it is true.'

The child was crying again. This time in relief to hear the truth, and from the one person she could believe.

'Hush,' said Dann. 'And now tell me. Is my daughter Rhea really so very bad?'

'Yes, she is,' said Tamar and Shabis together. And Shabis added, 'the pair of them, mother and daughter.'

'In our country,' said Ali, 'we say that some people are the devil's spawn.'

'Ah, now, the devil,' said Dann, and he was stroking Tamar's hair. 'You'd be surprised how much there is about him in the sand libraries.'

'Who was the devil?' said Tamar.

'Another very good question,' said Dann.

'I think you'll find Tamar always asks good questions,' said her father. 'But that doesn't mean there are answers.'

'Do you know why Kira hates me so much?' Tamar asked Dann.

'Yes, because she hated your mother.'

'But why did she?'

'Now that is an easy question,' said Shabis. 'Because Mara was better than Kira. And much more beautiful.'

'I don't think that is an easy question,' said Tamar.

'But the fact is,' said Shabis, 'Kira does hate Tamar and we must not think Tamar is safe because she is here. People are coming in and out of the Centre all the time, and there's no way of preventing that.'

Dann nodded. 'And we know that Kira has a very long reach.'

Ali said, 'I will guard the child.'

'Thank you, Ali,' said Dann. 'But that's not enough.'

Dann put his long thin hand, that still trembled a little, on the animal's head, bent to Ruff and said, 'Ruff, we want you to guard Tamar.' And he gently directed Ruff's muzzle into the space between Tamar's body and her upper arm. He held his arms round the pair of them.

Ruff let out a deep groan.

'Yes, Ruff, I am asking you.'

The big tail flopped on the floor, and now the snow dog's face was out of sight, under Tamar's arm.

'Ruff?' said Dann gently.

Ruff's face reappeared. He lay down at Tamar's feet.

'There's a good dog,' said Dann, and patted Ruff, who groaned again.

'You'll be all right with Ali and with Ruff,' said Dann.

'I will tell them in the camp to keep a lookout, always,' said Griot, speaking for the first time.

'Yes, Griot,' said Dann. 'You must. Everyone must keep watch. This one must be . . . *this* one must stay alive.'

Tamar seemed to shiver. She slipped out of Dann's arms and sat on a stool near him. The snow dog moved to lie near her. She stroked and stroked the animal's head, but her eyes never left the adults' faces as they talked.

'And now, you must tell us everything,' said Dann to Shabis.

The talk went on, then, through the evening meal, and until the child slid off her stool and lay asleep with her head on Ruff's side.

This was the situation. Shabis had been sent another message from Agre. The army wanted him back. Only one person could unite Agre – Shabis. It was not possible to take the child on that dangerous journey south, though if Shabis did succeed in unifying Agre Tamar might come and join him. 'But don't forget: I have a wife,' said Shabis. 'She would not welcome Tamar. And it must not be forgotten that my wife intrigued with the Hennes to have Mara kidnapped. Tamar might find herself, with my wife, in the same situation she has been in with Kira.'

Of the people still at the Farm, Leta was virtually Kira's prisoner. Kira used her as a doctor for her army. But Leta intended to slip away when she saw her opportunity and come here. Daulis would return to Bilma. It was thought too dangerous for him to go with Shabis. He, too, would take his time, but Kira would not try to prevent his leaving, as she would Leta. Donna, Leta's friend, would come here, to the Centre.

At this point Griot intervened again with, 'Then they should be quick. The Centre won't be here for ever.'

Dann said to Shabis, 'Griot intends us to invade Tundra.'

Shabis said only, 'Then you had certainly better be quick, before Kira does, too.'

'We have one advantage that Kira doesn't have,' said Griot.

'Yes,' said Shabis. 'I know. Everyone knows. You have Dann. You have the wonderful General Dann. And Kira knows, too. So you had better be careful, Dann – or you'll find a scorpion in your bed or poison in your food.'

'I will taste everything the General eats,' said Ali.

Now it was late and Griot was thinking where people would sleep.

He said – it came hard to him to say it and his voice showed it – 'I will give up my room to Tamar and Shabis . . .'

But before he could go on Shabis said, 'Not me. I'll be off before morning.'

Dann said at once, 'Yes, much safer.'

'Kira has her assassins out for me. She's the kind of person who has to kill what she can't have. Well, she wanted me long enough – and I'll be happier when I'm well out of her reach. I've already delayed longer than she expected. So – that's it. Shall we put the child to bed?' And he lifted Tamar away from Ruff, and went with Griot and Dann to the room next to Dann's – Griot's – from where he kept an eye on Dann. All went behind him.

On the low bed Shabis deposited Tamar and said to Dann, 'I think this must be the room Mara was in when you were here together?'

'Yes,' said Dann. 'Here.'

Griot had never been told that this had been Mara's room, but now he understood all kinds of nuances in Dann's voice.

'I'll go before Tamar wakes,' said Shabis.

'No,' said Griot, as Ali said, 'No.' 'It would be better if you woke her and told her yourself.' Griot's voice was raw and emotional, surprising himself. 'Don't you see, she'll wake and find you gone . . . gone . . . and she'll never forget that.'

But he, Griot, had forgotten whatever it was that

made his voice wild now. Somewhere, at some time, Griot, a child, had woken and found – whoever it was – gone. And he would never know . . .

'Griot's right,' said Dann, and he laid his hand on Griot's shoulders. So rare was this kind of thing, a moment of recognition from Dann, that Griot's eyes filled with tears. Dann's hand fell and he said, 'Griot understands this kind of thing.'

Shabis nodded and lifted Tamar up into his arms. Tamar did struggle to wake, rubbing her eyes and yawning. Shabis said gently, 'Tamar, I am going away. I'm going now.'

Tamar slid from his arms to the bed and stood there on it, already forlorn, abandoned. 'How, going? Where? No, no, no,' she wailed.

'Tamar, I have to go and you can't come with me.'

'And when will you come back?'

Now tears were running down Shabis's face, too. 'I don't know, Tamar.'

'You're leaving me, you're going.'

'We'll both be alive, Tamar. If I don't go now I don't think I'll be alive for long. And if you come too . . . no, Tamar, no, I'm sorry.'

The child sobbed, standing there, still half asleep. Ruff stepped up on to the bed and put his great head on the child's shoulder. The weight collapsed her and she lay, her thumb in her mouth, staring. Ruff lay beside her, as he did with Dann.

Ali said passionately, 'This is hard on the animal. It is very hard on Ruff.' He looked pleadingly at Dann.

'But what can we do?' asked Dann.

'He loves you,' said Ali wildly. And everyone looked at Ali, always so quiet and wise and, well, always there.

Love, Griot was thinking. Well, when I saw my sand girl this afternoon it was very nice, it was really very nice. *And if I never saw her again?*

Dann turned away from Ali, suffering.

Ruff's eyes didn't leave Dann's face. Dann sat on the bed and put his hand on the animal's head.

Shabis said, 'I need food for the road.'

'I'll get it,' said Ali. He wanted to get out of that room and its painful emotions.

Shabis knelt on the bed beside his child. 'You mustn't think I am leaving you behind because I want to.'

'But you are going away from me,' came Tamar's little voice.

She put her arms round Ruff's neck and sobbed.

'Oh, Tamar,' said Shabis. 'The way I look at it is that I've had the great privilege of being with you – of being with you and, before you, your mother. But I suppose I was asking too much when I thought it would last.'

'Ask who?' said Tamar. 'Who were you asking?'

'It's a way of speaking,' said Dann. 'And I think like that, or I try to. I was lucky enough to be with Mara – yes, I did have that, so I should be grateful . . .' His voice cracked and the two men, Dann and Shabis, both weeping, were looking at each other, unable to speak.

'Grateful to who?' asked Tamar. 'I want to know. Why won't you tell me?'

Ruff was licking her cheek. Her eyes were heavy, and closed. She began to sob, in her sleep.

'This is awful,' said Dann. 'It's awful.'

'Yes,' said Shabis and got off the bed as Ali came in with a brown bag of provisions.

'Brown, good, not noticeable,' said Shabis. 'Which reminds me. Those garments Tamar and I came in. See that one gets back to Leta. They are very good for escaping in.'

And now he stood there, at the door, already a fugitive, looking back at them all. 'When I see you all again . . .' he began, could not go on, and with his last look for Tamar, who was lying between the paws of the snow dog, he went out.

'I'll sleep outside the door, here,' said Ali. And he showed them the slender curved knife of his people, where it hung under his tunic.

'I'll go to the room through there,' said Griot.

'When the child wakes – I'll be awake early,' said Dann.

Ali said, 'Sir, remember your – friend.'

'Yes,' said Dann. He called softly to Ruff and the two ran out down to the gates and out on to the road. There Dann stopped and embraced the snow dog, and then the animal began racing around Dann, leaping and woofing, in greeting.

Griot and Ali, watching, exchanged smiles.

'In my country I had two hunting dogs,' said Ali. 'They were my friends.'

Griot returned to the room that had been his. Tamar was in a heavy sleep. He sat down as carefully as he could on the foot of the bed. On the pillow by the girl's head was a smear of dirty white – Ruff's shed fur. He needed a good wash. And the child would need . . . Ali, who had had a family, would know what she needed. Griot was beginning to suspect that it was a lack in him, a place uncultivated, not knowing anything about children, a family. Tamar was younger than he had been on that night of fire and fighting. Would she perhaps forget she had had a father? Would that be good, saving her from pain? *Saving her from conscious pain.* Griot contemplated this steadily. But if you started thinking like this . . . in Griot's mind, walls, barriers, screens of all kinds were shaking, threatening to collapse: he sat hunched there, staring at the child, holding fast to a little sense of his wholeness . . . his woman down in the lines; she had never said she wanted a child. She had had a child, he believed, and it had disappeared in some raid, or battle. He himself had never once thought: I'd like a child. Well, now the subject was here, in his mind, did he want a child? He thought, no; suppose he and his woman in the lines did have a child, it would be a constant torment of worry. And a child could disappear, just like that. For the very first time he thought, *On that night, I've always taken it for granted my parents were killed. But suppose they are alive somewhere, wondering about me?* This was such an intolerable burden on him that he thrust it away. Too much, it was all too much. No, it was a good thing he was alone, had no child, no family; look what was happening now. One small girl and three people were concerned with her: Dann, himself, Ali. And, of course, the snow dog.

Barks and Dann's voice outside, and the two appeared in the doorway. Ruff was a ball of fuzzy wetness; his fur was covered with minute drops. There was mist out there, or fine rain. Just as Ruff was about to shake himself Dann enveloped him in a cloth and the two rolled over and over on the floor, Dann laughing, Ruff woofing in play, and Tamar woke and cried, 'Where's my father, where's my Shabis?' Dann at once sprang up; Ruff bounded to the child and lay down near her.

'Your father is well down towards the river and the boats,' said Dann. 'He will travel a good way by water. It'll be safer.'

'But won't it be dangerous, on the water?'

'There's marsh sickness and river sickness. But luckily if you bribe the boatmen well they protect you from – bandits.'

'Bandits?' said Tamar. 'Will there be bandits?'

'He'll be safer on the water,' said Dann again. 'Kira won't know where to look for him. It's good that it's drizzling. It will be harder to see him. Slippery, of course, but Shabis knows how to move through the marshes. Better, perhaps, if he lies up when the light comes – plenty of bushes and rushes and reeds to hide in.' Dann was out in the night with Shabis.

Ali said, 'They say that in Agre it is sandy and dry. That's what he's used to.' Meaning that was what he was used to.

Dann said, 'It seems we can be lizards in sand and then take to water like birds. All our early lives Mara and I were dying of drought and then we became water people.'

Tamar was quiet now. Dann went to the bed and laid his hand on Ruff's head. The snow dog let out his sad protesting groan, but watched Dann go without him to his room.

Griot extinguished all the candles but one and went out past Ali, who was already drowsing, leaning against a wall.

Griot tried to sleep, but could not, thinking of that child, so helpless there, asleep, guarded by Ruff. Well, yes, but was that enough? And Ali, that little thin man, but he was asleep . . . Griot went to the door of the child's room and saw Ruff's great head lift, then, when the animal saw who it was, the head dropped down again. But Ruff's eyes gleamed there: he was awake, on guard. Dann was in the opposite doorway, outlined by the rush light behind him. Ruff's tail beat once, twice, on the bed. Dann saw Griot and raised his hand silently in greeting. This was a precious moment for Griot: he and Dann, standing silently there, acknowledging each other. Then Dann turned and left: his light went out.

Griot stepped carefully past Ali and made his way through the hall, nodded to the sentries, and stood for a while on the road running east to west, empty now, this dangerous marsh road, that was usually so busy.

A sentry left his place and came to Griot. 'Sir.'

'Yes, soldier?'

'Some pretty suspicious types have gone past, but they didn't take the path General Shabis took.'

'If they come back, send them east.'

'Yes, sir.'

The sentry went back to his place.

Griot returned to his room, tossed and turned, and was pleased when the light came seeping in.

Outside Tamar's room – his room, that had been – Ali was waking. Dann was emerging. And the child was beginning to stir, then sat up, with a cry. She was wan, she was tear-stained, and on her upper arm where a sleeve had fallen back showed the thin red scar.

Ruff licked the scar, and Tamar began to cry and put her arms round the animal's neck. The little arms disappeared into the thick white fur. There was something so sad about this, and Ali turned away, hiding tears.

'Oh, Tamar,' said Dann humbly, 'don't be sad. You'll see, we'll look after you.'

'Perhaps I'll never see my father again,' said Tamar, but she tried to compose herself.

Ali took her to where she could wash. Soldiers brought food to the table out in the hall. Dann, and Tamar, Griot and Ali, sat at the table. Ruff was between Dann and the girl, who fed her breakfast to the animal.

Then Dann said, 'Now, Tamar, I'm going to send you with Ali through the Centre and he'll show you as much as possible in the time . . .' here he nodded at Griot, acknowledging what he had said, as a promise.

'And Ruff will come too?'

'Yes, Ruff will stay with you.'

'There won't be time to show you more than a little part of it . . .'

'Show me what?'

'Just a little, little part of the knowledge that they had once, the old people . . . long long ago . . . yes, I know that saying *long ago* doesn't tell you much, Tamar, but you'll understand, as much as any of us, and I'll explain, we'll explain . . .' And now Dann got up, pushing Ruff towards Tamar, to keep him from following him. 'You see, Tamar, in a certain place – and we'll show you – there is all that's left of a knowledge so wonderful, so extraordinary . . . even a tiny part of it . . . things so far beyond us that . . . and when we leave here, that will be the end of it all.'

'And why do we have to leave?'

'Griot will tell you. Griot knows. Yes, Griot, I do understand that we have to hurry. And I'm going to be as quick as I can.'

The scribes and savants were coming into the hall to take their places at the tables for the day's work.

Dann strode off, and the two men watching knew he was escaping from his emotions over the child, or trying to.

Now began a time when anywhere you looked, Dann was with Tamar, talking, explaining; at every meal it went on, and meanwhile Griot was watching, and waiting, then it all burst out of him, surprising Griot, but apparently not Dann.

'Dann, sir, you owe it to me.'

It seemed Griot did not have to explain, or to apologise, for when Dann heard these reproachful words he only glanced at Griot, smiled and nodded.

'Yes, I do owe to you. What do I not owe you, Griot?' His smile was medicine for Griot's poor heart, which was sick and swollen with worry, so he felt.

'Well, then, Griot, what exactly do you want?'

The very next day, the square was filled with ranks of soldiers. Griot had ordered 'everyone not on duty'. How many? Griot knew there were well over a thousand people in the camp. All dependent on him, which was why anxiety accompanied him like an enemy. All these soldiers, and each distinguished by a red shoulder blanket. Dann walked out from his room; Tamar was with him and, behind her, the snow dog. Dann had his red blanket folded in his arms, like the last time he stood there before them, and Tamar had a little red strip on her shoulder. She had tied a loop of red round Ruff's neck. A platform had been erected at the end of the square, for Tamar to stand on. Dann stood near the platform by Tamar, and the snow dog was on the platform with her. What a tall man Dann was, though he lounged there, making no attempt at a soldierly stance. Griot was watching from a doorway. Dann had said Griot should be there by him, but Griot knew better. His General, General Dann, should be there with the child.

Dann smiled and took his time, looking over the ranks of the soldiers, as if memorising their many faces. Every soldier was smiling, because of the child. How many of them were thinking of their lost or left behind or captured children? Most of them, Griot knew. And here was this child, fresh and lovely, unmarked by war – so they could all think; though every one of them would have been told about that red scar on her arm and know who caused it.

Dann said, not shouting, not even raising his voice much, more conversational, as if he were talking with each one of them alone, 'Welcome to you all. I want to introduce you to this girl, my relative, the daughter of my sister Mara and General Shabis, who is on his way back to Charad, to the Agre armies, which he will command. Hands up anyone who knows about Charad, or about Agre?'

A few hands went up.

'Beyond Bilma, beyond Shari, are the countries of the Hennes and the Agre. They have been at war for a long time. General Shabis will be commanding the armies of Agre. And this is his daughter.'

Everyone looked at Tamar. The child was stiff with the responsibility of her position. She smiled and was brave, but those close to her could see that she trembled. She put out a hand to rest it on Ruff's back. And then unexpected cheers rang out. Griot was pleased no one was near him. He was weeping: he had to; those three, Dann, so handsome, and the lovely child, so like him, and the snow dog, the shining animal with its thick white ruff into which Tamar's little hand had disappeared. A gleam of weak sunlight fell at this propitious moment from a wet cloud, and at first Dann, Tamar and the snow dog, and then the whole square, were touched with a gold light.

'And I promise you that soon you will hear the news I know you are all longing for,' said Dann. The cheers rang out again, alarming Griot because of their intensity. How badly every person there wanted to leave; how sick they all were of being cramped up on these edges of land, and the rumours that never seemed to come to anything: 'We'll be off next week.' 'We'll be off soon.'

As they cheered, the phalanx of snow dogs who stood

in their place in the middle of the soldiers began to bark, and Ruff barked back once, twice, as if they were saluting him and he was acknowledging their salutation.

Dann put out his hand to help Tamar jump down. The dog stepped down. Dann saluted the soldiers, and the man and the girl left the cheering soldiers and the barking snow dogs.

Ali was taking the child and the snow dog around the endless rooms and halls and museums of the Centre, showing her what he had decided, or Dann had told him, was important.

In the evenings, at the supper table, there was something new. It had begun with Dann's saying casually, 'And what did you see today?'

Tamar had chatted happily: 'Oh, so many things, didn't we, Ali, and some of them were so funny.'

'Now, choose one of them – in your mind. Tamar, have you done that?'

'Yes.' And Tamar sobered, because of Dann's seriousness.

'And now, look at it in your mind's eye. Now, what do you see?'

At first she said, 'It was big. It was black. It was full of sharp bits.' That was how the game had begun, which Dann said he and Mara had played.

Now Tamar was choosing this or that special item for the evening game.

'What did you see?'

'The best thing was a flying thing. It is a tube, with wings, but one is broken, and it had flakes of red on it.

Once it was all red. Inside there are twenty seats. But it is too small for even one or two people, so it is a model. I think most of the things in the museums are models. I didn't understand that to begin with. There are a lot of things that were meant for flying. They are mostly broken.'

'Once they flew all over the world. You know what that means, Tamar. You saw the maps at the Farm.'

'How do you know that they did?'

'It is known.' This had become the short way of saying, 'We know because the information is in the sand libraries.'

'You say *once*,' said Tamar. 'What does it mean, once?'

'A long time ago.'

'But there are different long times ago. You say *once*, and so does Ali but I never know which long time ago you mean.'

'Almost the longest time ago was before the Ice,' said Ali. 'In my country there are tales every child is taught, about times before the Ice when they had stories about *their* long time ago.'

Griot said warningly, 'Dann, Ali . . .' The child's eyes were filling with tears.

'Yes,' said Dann. 'You're right, Griot. But she should try and remember everything she sees because there will come a time when the Centre is gone, and no one will know about these things.'

Ali said, 'I think it is time this little one went to bed.'

Griot watched Ali take Tamar by the hand and, with her other hand on the snow dog's back, the girl went to her bed. 'When I'm asleep you can have Ruff back,' she said to Dann. 'But please let him be there when I wake up tomorrow.'

'You're asking a lot of her,' said Griot.

'I'm asking a lot of you too,' said Dann.

These acknowledgements from Dann were new and part frightened Griot. He did not like a sadness, a desperation, he saw in his General. More than once he thought, *The poppy? Is that it?* But no, he thought not.

Quietly, not hiding it, but not telling Dann, he was planning the move out of the Centre. He was sending small parties ahead, five or six at a time, to find places in Tundra's cities, which were so chaotic, turbulent, that a few more arrivals could not draw much attention. They were well prepared, these advance parties. All day he spent with his soldiers, explaining, instructing, training scouts – the women were good at that, the ones that went and came back to report – teaching the geography of Tundra. For while the area of Tundra that was south of the Centre, and a short way east, was lake and marsh and mud, this was only a small portion of Tundra, which stretched all the way to the great river in the east. Tundra was enormous. Many of the refugees knew about a part of it. In the Centre was a room filled with maps drawn with coloured inks on prepared skins. Some of the skins were snow dogs', which were being bartered and bought and sold in the markets of Tundra. Griot ordered that every platoon should have its maps. This meant a lot of work.

Sometimes he found Tamar in the map-making room, Ali with her, explaining, showing her . . . 'See here, all this is high dry land, and here is a line of mountains.' When Ali talked everyone stopped to listen. He had been an important man, educated, an adviser; now he was nurse to a little girl. That's what he wryly called himself.

'Nurse?' said Dann. 'You are educating her. What could be more important than training that child? One day she will rule Tundra.'

'If we ever get there,' joked Griot.

'We'll get there. I see that some of us are already there – eh, Griot? But Griot, you must see that I am not going to make old bones.'

Griot's ears could not accept this. He did not hear it.

Dann was taking Tamar to the secret place. There he held her up level with the pages pressed against the transparent wall and read to her from the languages he knew. He told her that what she saw there were ancient variations of those spoken now. Sometimes one had to puzzle out meaning from the old, crooked words. Did she see that while there were languages he did not know – that no one knew – the three he did know gave up their meaning to him? It was essential that she should learn Mahondi well, not just the baby Mahondi she spoke now, but grown-up language; and she must know Charad, and Agre, because it was her father's language. And the languages of Tundra. The child was possessed with the need to please him. She sat with Ali in the great hall in the fleeting or sometimes steady light from the damp skies and followed Ali's finger, repeating after him words in one language after another. Ali, whose several children had been blown away by tempests of war, bent tenderly over his charge, always patient, always ready to repeat, explain, and when he saw tears trickling he took her on his knee and held her tight.

'Little one, don't cry, you're doing so well.'

'Dann will be cross with me,' wept Tamar. 'He won't love me. I'm so slow and stupid.'

'No, you're not, you're quick and clever. And of course Dann won't be cross with you.'

'He's disappointed in me, I know that.'

Ali went to find Dann. 'General, you're trying the child too hard.'

'Oh, nonsense. She's all right.'

'General, not every little girl is like your sister, who had to learn hard lessons when she was not more than a baby. You mustn't match Tamar with what happened to you and Mara.'

'Is that what I'm doing, Ali?'

'Yes, I think you are.'

He told Dann the child had been weeping and Dann was angry – with himself. He found Tamar lying on her bed, her thumb in her mouth, with Ruff, and sat by her, humble with apologies. 'Tamar, am I being so hard on you?'

And Tamar flung herself into his arms and wept there.

Then Dann asked if he might borrow Ruff for a while and the two went out to play. When the play was over Tamar reclaimed Ruff, who went with her, looking back at Dann.

But her lessons were fewer and Dann said to Griot, 'All I wanted was to speed everything up.'

'But Dann, sir, surely our leaving doesn't depend on Tamar cramming her head with all that old stuff?'

'It's important, Griot.'

And Tamar's head was fuller every day with what she learned from the Centre. She came out with a hundred bits of information, about how a device she thought was a water pump worked, or she told them an old tale. 'A goddess . . . what's a goddess, Ali? She was bathing with her women and a man saw her naked and she was so angry she turned him into a deer – what's a deer, Griot? And then her dogs tore him to pieces. I think that was a cruel woman. Like Kira. I don't like her. And I am sure Ruff wouldn't tear anyone to pieces, would you, Ruff?

'Once it rained forty days and forty nights – that must have been here, on the marshes, and a man called No built a boat and filled it with friends and then when the flood went down they built houses on high ground. Like us going to Tundra where it is high and doesn't have marshes everywhere. Oh, I'm so sick of the marshes, Griot. You can't take a step without getting your feet wet or slipping in the mud. And think how pleased Ruff will be. He can run about as he likes. He can't get a good straight run here, there's always a puddle or a pond or something.'

Dann asked Griot if he thought people were coming from the Farm – from Kira. 'Spies, Griot, are they here?'

'Bound to be. All they have to do is to throw off their black blankets and put on a red one. Some people have escaped from Kira to join us – we don't turn them away. They don't like what goes on there.'

'When I was walking with Ruff there was a man on

the road, coming from the west. I am sure I knew him. I'm in danger, Griot.'

'But we always have soldiers on guard, keeping an eye.'

'There was something about him . . .'

'But, sir, have you ever thought how many people you and your sister met on your way up Ifrik? How could you remember them all?'

'How could I forget – some of them?'

Dann was all anxiety, looking over his shoulder, turning round suddenly to see if he was being followed. He told Tamar not to come with him when he went out to exercise the snow dog. 'I'm in danger, Tamar.'

The snow dog was taken out twice a day, once with Dann and once with Tamar.

Dann said to Griot, 'Do you know what this reminds me of? I used to tell Mara I'm in danger, but she didn't believe me.'

'But, sir, we know you are in danger. So is the child. That is what the soldiers are for.'

'Mara didn't believe me but all the time Kulik was on our trail.'

'Kulik is dead. When you were down in the Bottom Sea I went up to the top of the mountain because we all know that story, sir. There are the bones up there. The crows did their work well but the big bones are there, and the skull.'

'Why should the bones be Kulik's? That mountain is full of falls and steep places. Anyone could die up there – fugitives, refugees – they may think they are safe up the mountain but Mara and I weren't safe, were we?'

Dann was frowning, deep inside his thoughts and his memories. His words were a muttering, almost incomprehensible.

'Dann, sir, you must take hold of yourself. You are asking for – well, trouble, if you go on like this.'

Now Dann came to himself and laughed. 'So, it's trouble I am asking for?' And he slapped Griot across the shoulders and then hugged him. 'Griot,' he said, 'Griot, you are a prize. You're splendid. I don't deserve you, Griot, and don't think I don't know it.'

And off he shambled, to his favourite place by the not-glass walls.

Then they were at supper at their table in the great hall, Dann, Griot, Tamar, Ali and Ruff. He had his dish on the floor between Dann and Tamar. When he had finished his meal in a couple of gulps, he sat calmly, watching them all eat. The sentries sent in a message that a man had come from the Farm and wanted to see them.

Out from the shadows at the entrance door emerged a man with the black blanket on his shoulder, and at the sight Dann half rose and put his hand to his knife. He sat down again.

The man dropped the blanket on to the back of a chair and stood grinning, waiting to be invited to sit.

Tamar said in a little, brave voice, 'This is Joss. He's Kira's friend.'

Joss had not stopped grinning, an insolent cold baring of the teeth, and his bold black eyes took in every detail of the scene.

'Sit down,' said Dann. 'Join us.'

Joss sat, careless, at ease, always grinning. In the light from the lamps his red lips showed in a black beard, and white teeth that were biting off bread as if he were hungry. In the beard, on one cheekbone, was an old scar, showing white among the black hairs. Dann kept glancing at it and then away, as if it hurt him to see it.

Ruff began a low, rumbling growl.

Joss stared at the snow dog and said, 'Very useful, these snow dogs. We have a regiment of them. We know you have them too. But ours are trained to kill.' Then, to Tamar, 'You are well guarded, I see.' And he laughed, a theatrical soundless laugh, all his white teeth showing, and more than that, for his mouth was full of food.

Tamar sat primly, her voice trembling with her effort at bravery. 'It's rude to eat with your mouth open.'

'Quite right,' said Dann. Then he said to Joss, his hand seeking his knife hilt, 'Were you ever in Chelops?'

'No, I was never in Chelops. I came from the south up the coast, but you remember me because I asked for work at the Farm and you refused me, saying you didn't need labour. Well, you might not have needed it then, but Kira took me on.' And he gave his great, heaving, soundless laugh.

Dann shook his head. He didn't remember. But he could not stop staring. 'You are very like someone who was in the Towers at Chelops.'

'We all know the story,' said Joss, helping himself generously to the food. It was really unpleasant to see him eat. 'It is a story that gains in the telling.'

Dann asked, 'Where did you get that scar?'

'I was swimming in the sea and a wave threw me against a rock. No, it wasn't a fight. I am a peaceable man – when I get my way. I am getting my way.'

Griot said, 'I think you should deliver your message and then, if you have had enough to eat, you must leave.'

Ruff was still growling, but because of Tamar's restraining hand it was low, more like a vibration in the throat.

Joss reached inside his tunic, brought out a piece of food and threw it to Ruff who caught it – but before he could swallow it Ali was round the table and wrenching it out of the dog's jaws.

He wrapped the food in a piece of cloth and summoned a soldier to take it. 'Burn it,' he said. 'It's poisoned. Be careful.'

Though Ruff had not done more than hold the morsel in his teeth he was now shivering and sick.

'Go,' said Dann.

Joss stood up. 'Kira told me to say to General Dann that she will be seeing you before long.'

'And is that all?' asked Griot.

'It's enough,' said Dann.

'And Leta sends a message. She says to Dann, "Thanks for your invitation, but once a whore always a whore." She's running a House of Ease for us.'

There was enough of Leta in this to tell them the message was accurately conveyed.

Dann stood up. 'You are keeping her a prisoner,' he said.

'And a most efficient whore keeper she is,' said Joss.

'Her house is filled with Albs and with blacks from the river region. We captured some more Albs, just to keep her company.'

Tamar began to cry. 'Poor Leta,' she whispered, 'poor Leta.' And she knelt by Ruff and put her face into his fur. He was trembling and whimpering.

Dann had made a signal to the guards and now some soldiers came in.

Joss said, 'The men who came with me had orders to fetch some of the good poppy from the east. Kira likes her poppy – but only the best.'

Dann said, 'We don't allow poppy in our army.'

'Don't you? Some of the refugees from the east were taking poppy with their mothers' milk. Isn't that so?' – and he addressed Ali.

'Yes, it is true,' said Ali. 'But only a few fools go on with it.'

'And who is this brave slave, insulting me?' said Joss.

'No slave,' said Dann. 'This is Ali, our very good friend.'

Now Joss looked hard at Dann, straight down the table, with his insolent grin, that he seemed to imagine was affable, or at least attractive. He said, proving that he knew perfectly well who Ali was, 'And so I hope you have a good food taster, General.'

'A very good food taster, thank you.'

'Then look out, General – you might lose your food taster one of these days.'

Ali said, 'I think I can match anything you can come up with in a knowledge of poisons.'

Joss laughed at him. 'Goodbye, then. Goodbye,

Tamar. Goodbye, Dann. Goodbye, Captain Griot. Till we meet again.' And he went out laughing, the soldiers surrounding him, their knives drawn.

Ali had taken packets of herbs from his tunic and was sprinkling them on to Ruff's tongue. 'Don't worry, little one,' he said to Tamar. 'Your friend will be better very soon.'

Dann abruptly left them and went to his room. Griot followed him. Dann was sitting on his bed.

'Griot, I think that man was in the Towers. In Chelops.'

'But Dann, sir, he's the kind that would be boasting of the dirty work in the Towers, if he was there.'

'Griot, when I was ill you nursed me, you think I don't remember, but I do – and you saw my scars.'

'Yes, I did.'

'I had only to look at that man and my scars began to hurt.'

And Dann was prowling about the room, hitting out at the walls, and then at himself with his fists, on his stomach, his chest, his shoulders. 'Spies,' he was muttering, 'spies everywhere, and they think I don't know.'

'Yes, of course there are spies everywhere.'

Now Dann was fumbling with the door of a cupboard, and he stood with his back to Griot, in a ludicrous attempt at secrecy. He had brought out a small lump of black stuff and was sniffing at it. Griot was beside him and had the lump away from him. 'Sir, allow me.'

'But I don't allow you, Griot. What are you doing?'

'You don't want to start that again, Dann, sir.'

Dann sat on his bed and put his head in his hands. 'You're right, Griot. You're always right, Griot. Griot, I'm ill. I'm not myself.' And then, rearing as he sat, in a movement like a striking snake, he grabbed at Griot and stared into his face. Now Griot could smell the sickly breath, see dilated pupils.

'How do I know you aren't a spy, Griot?'

'Sir, you aren't well. Go to bed.'

From the door to the square, Griot called out to summon Dann's guards, and from the door to the hall he called for Ali, who looked at Dann and said there were still medicines left from what Leta had brought. Griot mustn't worry. Dann would be all right.

'Yes, he should worry,' said Dann, from his bed, where he lay stiff and stretched out.

Griot said, 'I'll make sure Tamar doesn't come in.'

'I want Ruff,' said Dann. 'I want my friend.'

'Sir,' said Ali, 'Ruff is with Tamar,' but Dann didn't reply. Ali went out and came back with Ruff; Dann grabbed him, sank his face into the thick fur and hugged him. Griot shut the door on the two. Just outside stood Tamar, with Ali.

'Don't cry, little one,' said Ali. 'Let Dann have his old friend for a while.'

'I'm not crying,' said Tamar. She was listening to Ruff's barks and Dann's voice, talking to the snow dog.

'Come, we'll learn some new things and surprise Dann when he's really better.' Griot watched Ali lead the child away to one of the old museum halls. This one, Tamar had not been in. Ali had found in it machines he could not make sense of. Sometimes Tamar had ingenious ideas.

Inside the enormous building machines stood about, many long ago collapsed or fallen over.

In front of a machine like a vast grasshopper, Ali stood with Tamar, who was trying not to cry. Ali put his hand on her shoulder and said, 'Tamar, what do you think that thing was for?'

Tamar said in a desolate little voice, but it was steady now, 'If that is a model it must have been as hard to make as it was when it was of iron.'

Great wooden balls dangled from chains carved of wood.

'They certainly wanted us to know what they had then,' said Ali. 'Well, then, imagine it in – what, iron? Yes, you're right. It must have been iron.'

'Because the whole point was, heavy iron balls. If they were of iron they'd have rusted long ago, with all the wetness, Ali.'

'But it wasn't always wet here.'

'Anything they dropped those great balls on would have smashed. Perhaps they used them to break up big boulders?'

'They could have done. Yes. Very useful.'

'Or an enemy could use them to smash down a house.'

'Yes. Even a big house.'

'Yes.' Her voice was quavering again.

'Tamar, would you like to learn some more words in Tundra? Or some really difficult Mahondi?'

'No, it's all right, Ali. Let's look at some more machines, and look and look until I remember them, and you can ask me questions.' Her voice broke: she sobbed and then stopped and insisted on sticking it out until they had looked over six more of the mysterious machines.

'Now they're in my head for ever and ever, and if they sink into the marsh they will still be in my head.'

'They're going to do that soon enough – look.'

At the end of the enormous building a couple of machines were standing in water.

'I'm tired,' said Tamar. 'Can I go and see Dann?'

'I think it would be better if you didn't, for a little while,' said Ali. Tamar accepted this, but her face made Ali put his arms round her again. They returned to the hall where the scribes were working at their tables. There they had a place near a pillar, of rugs and cushions.

'When it is evening, Ruff will need his walk,' said Tamar. 'May I take him?'

'I am sure you may.' When Griot came out he was asked, and he agreed.

'What's wrong with Dann?' Tamar asked.

Griot squatted by her and, on her level, spoke what he had clearly been preparing. 'Tamar, I don't want you to worry too much. I've seen Dann like this before. He'll get over it. Do you know about the marsh sickness, Tamar? It comes and goes. Well, what Dann has is a mind sickness, and that comes and goes too.'

'Is it poppy?' she asked. 'I know about poppy.'

'I don't think so – not really. He had some poppy, but he had it for only a short time. And I've got it away from him. You see, he's very sad. When someone is as sad as Dann is, he's better alone. I'll fetch out Ruff for you.'

Soon Ruff came padding out of Dann's room, saw Tamar, barked his welcome and bounded around her. The effects of the poison had gone.

Tamar and the snow dog ran about and played between the buildings of the Centre, then she had to take Ruff back to Dann's door.

She stood with her arms round him, her face buried in his fur, and wept. Ali and Griot, watching, looked at each other, helpless. Then Tamar stood back, and Griot opened Dann's door. Ruff padded in with a long look back at Tamar, and a little bark of farewell. He bounded forward to be welcomed by Dann. Barks and Dann's voice; whines and the man's voice.

Tamar, long past the age when she could allow herself this comfort, had her thumb in her mouth. She let herself be taken off to the cushions by Ali.

'Poor little one,' he said. And to Griot, over the child's head, 'We ask too much, too much is being asked.'

'Yes, it is. And there's worse. Tamar mustn't go out of the Centre. Some of the people on the road today were Joss's. The road is full of the black blankets.'

And so Tamar ran with her snow dog around and about between the buildings and played with him, the next day and the next, morning and evening. Ruff came out to her and there was a great reunion, then he had to go back – he wanted to go back, because he loved Dann. But he loved Tamar and wanted to be with her.

'Perhaps it is Ruff we are asking too much of,' said Ali. 'He's not looking well and he's not eating, either.'

'Dann will be better soon,' said Griot. 'I am sure he will.'

Ali sat with Tamar and they did lessons. The child was a pupil any teacher might dream of, she was so intent on learning. She was like a little flame, consuming everything she was told, her eyes on Ali's, listening with all her being.

'Dann'll be pleased when I tell him I know this,' she said often. And then it came out. 'Dann will love me again.'

'But Tamar, you mustn't think he doesn't love you.'

'But he doesn't want to see me.'

'He does. He doesn't want you to be unhappy too.'

'Ruff can be with him, but I can't.'

She wept. Ali, sitting by her, held her and rocked her. She wept herself to sleep and then Ali slept too, holding her, the little thin man with his sad face, and the child, her head by his. Griot went past and smiled, seeing them. It was touching, the trust she had in him, the love he had for her, this man who had lost his children. Then, as the evening shadows deepened, Ruff appeared, padding towards them and, observing them there asleep, sat down on his furry backside, waiting. And then Dann came too, and stood by Ruff, and bent, peering at the girl. The sound *Mara* seemed to emanate from the air, and he said it again with his lips, not sounding it, '*Mara*.'

Griot appeared behind Dann, and when Dann did not move, only bent there, staring, he dared to put his hand on Dann's arm. Dann turned, his fist raised to strike, saw Griot, hesitated, let his arm fall, and without a word went back to his room. Ruff stayed with the sleeping pair and lay down, his muzzle on Tamar's arm.

They woke, and Tamar exclaimed it was time for Ruff's evening walk. Off the pair went, racing about among the old buildings and through the puddles in the courts and then . . . round a corner sped Tamar and there in front of her was Joss, grinning, arms stretched to catch her . . . she almost ran into them but turned to run back and Ruff was with her. Black blanket soldiers rushed from the buildings to catch Tamar, catch Ruff, but the girl and the snow dog were too quick for them; they arrived back in safety at the great hall where Griot heard the news that Joss was in the Centre with equanimity.

'Then, Tamar, you must exercise the snow dog only out on the square.'

'But Joss is here, in the Centre.'

'More than Joss, I think. A good few of his followers are hiding in the nooks and corners of the Centre. No, don't you worry. It's a good thing. We are feeding them poppy, we give them all they ask for, and they'll be fit for nothing. But you, Tamar, you must have your eyes open every moment, all the time. And you too, Ruff,' Griot said to the dog, as a bit of a joke, but Ruff seemed to understand, and barked and wagged his tail.

'When are we going to leave, when?' begged Tamar.

'Believe me, it will be soon,' said Griot.

He ordered soldiers to make a double line of defence, shoulder to shoulder, looking in, looking out, defending that part of the Centre used by the red blankets. Next morning Tamar and her snow dog were playing and racing on the drill square. Soldiers watched the two, the girl and her playmate, and thought of their lost families. Dann watched from his windows. Griot told him that even if he was not well completely in fourteen days he must face up to leaving. They would go when the moon was dark, through the marshes. Meanwhile Dann must not go past the lines of soldiers.

'I'm not leaving until we've got everything we can from the secret room.'

The next thing was that a soldier came from sentry duty on the outside road to report that a man wearing the black blanket said he was Dann's friend; he was Daulis. As he entered, Daulis handed his black blanket to a guard and said, 'I am sure this will come in useful.'

He was outside Dann's quarters when Tamar rushed up, 'Daulis, Daulis,' but he went in, the snow dog with him.

'Daulis,' cried Tamar. 'Daulis is my friend, too.'

Growing up, the motherless girl had had four good friends – her father, Daulis, Leta and Donna, who stood between her and Kira's malice. Her father had left her, but here was Daulis. She flung herself down on the cushions, ready to dissolve into tears. But then she leaped up and ran out, and in a moment returned wearing her shadow dress, which Daulis would recognise. He would be pleased . . . She went floating up and down the long hall between the working scribes, singing, 'Daulis, my Daulis.'

Inside, Daulis had found Dann face down, asleep. Daulis bent to put his hand on Dann's shoulder but jumped back to avoid Dann's leap up, knife in hand.

'Oh, Daulis,' said Dann. 'I wondered when you'd come to join us.' And he sank down, the snow dog beside him.

'What's wrong with you, Dann?'

'I'm no good,' said Dann. 'Inside here are two people and one of them is out to destroy me.'

'Leta told me you were ill.'

'And how is Leta? Joss told us she had chosen to go back to her told trade.'

'She didn't choose. She was forced. No, I'm not saying she doesn't do it well.' And now he laughed, unpleasantly, and for the flicker of a moment another Daulis looked through his eyes. Then he was himself again; that is, the Daulis who would have hated the one who had so briefly appeared – if he had caught sight of him. 'We have to remember she was a child when she was taken to the whorehouse.' He handed Dann a packet. 'She sent you this. She told me to tell you that these are strong. Strong herbs. They will cure you if you want to be cured. That was her message, Dann.'

'A very clever woman,' said Dann.

'Ali will know how to use these herbs, Leta says. Yes, we know about Ali.'

'Your spies?' said Dann.

'And you know all about us.'

'So you know that Joss and some of his men are already in the further parts of the Centre. But did you know that they are drunk and mad with poppy every night?'

'No, we didn't know about the poppy.'

'And so now, you can come with us when we go into Tundra?'

'I'm going back to Bilma.'

'Well, Councillor Daulis, will Bilma be pleased to see you?'

'Some will be pleased. There is civil war.'

'And where isn't there civil war, where, Daulis?'

'Sometimes I think that there's a star up there that loves war and killing – that's what the soothsayers from the River Towns say.'

'So,' said Dann, 'then it's not our fault. It's the star. Well, we can't do anything about that, can we, a death-hungry star?'

'We can make sure we win the wars,' said Daulis. He got up. 'And now I'm going to beg some rations. I'm off.'

'Goodbye, then,' said Dann.

'Goodbye, Dann.'

'Daulis, have you ever thought how many people are in your life, for life and death, and then they're off and you never see them again?'

'I'll come and visit you in Tundra.'

'And perhaps I'll visit you in Bilma.'

'Goodbye. I'll never forget how you nursed me, at that inn where we were all so sick. I owe you my life, Dann.' He went out.

Daulis emerged into the great hall and in the spaces between the working scribes flitted or danced or whirled – what? A great moth? A bird? Something shadowy, and then as light fell on it from the roof openings a black and white thing, and then a creamy whirl of light –

Tamar, dancing her delight at his coming. She rushed up to him, he caught her and knelt to hold her.

'Tamar, it is so good to see you.'

She was bubbling with excitement. He could feel the drumming of her heart. He let her go and went with her to the piled cushions.

'Let me look at you. Tamar, you are so like your mother. And look how you have grown and it hasn't been all that long since you left us.'

'Daulis, are you going to stay with us now, are you, please do, did you know my father left here, Shabis left me here, Daulis?'

'Yes, I know. And haven't you heard? Your father sent a message saying he had got halfway, and he is safe.'

'Why did you get the message but we didn't?'

'Messengers get lost, or . . . that is why he sent two, one to us at the Farm and one to you.'

'But my father is safe?'

'So far, he is safe.'

He could not stop looking at the lovely child who knelt before him in her magical frock that changed its colours, shadow to light, black to gold, yellow to brown. 'How that thing you are wearing does take me back, Tamar. I can see her now, your mother, flitting along in it, now you'd see her, now she'd gone. But here you are. I do miss you so.'

'And so no one is left now at the Farm. Only Leta. And Donna?' Clearly Kira and Kira's daughter did not count in this reckoning.

'Yes, only Leta,' said Daulis gravely, meeting her

shamed, prim little gaze. 'Yes – but remember, it isn't what she chose to do.'

'Perhaps she'll come here to live with us.'

'I'm sure she wants to.'

'And you'll be with us.'

'Tamar, I have to go to my home. I'm needed there.'

'But I want you, Daulis. My father's gone . . . and Dann . . . Dann is . . .'

'Yes, I know. Dann is sick. But I've just been with him, and he is the old Dann still.'

She leaped up, scattering tears, singing, 'Daulis, Daulis, Daulis,' whirling and circling, because she was crying and didn't want him to see these little girl's tears. She danced on, while he stood, and turned to go, and left, as from Dann's room came Ruff's voice. He was barking. 'My Ruff and my Dann,' she sang. As if the ban on her going into Dann's room had never been, she rushed to his door and flung it open, just as Ali, who had been on watch, ran to stop her. But she was in, dancing, in Dann's room. Dann rose from his bed and stared, then advanced at her, fist up, and in it, a knife.

'Go away,' he shouted at her. 'Leave me alone. You never leave me alone, you . . .'

And now there was a howl from Ruff. This time he didn't leap to catch Dann's arm and bring it down, he stood on his hindlegs, put his great paws on Dann's chest and fell on Dann as Dann fell back. Tamar stood there, her mouth a tragic 'O' of horror.

Ali came forward, pulled Tamar away, and knelt by the two, Dann with Ruff still on top of him. 'Ruff, Ruff, good dog,' said Ali. 'It's all right.' Dann was trying to break free of the animal's weight, but Ruff did not move. He lay panting, then whimpered, and at last crept off Dann. Still crawling he went to a wall where he lay near a guard, who was only just recovering himself, so quickly had events gone. Ruff was in distress. He coughed and panted.

Griot came in and stood staring.

Dann was sitting on his bed, his head in his hands.

Tamar ran to the snow dog. 'Ali, Ali, Ruff's sick.'

Griot picked up the knife, lying on the floor, wiped it, and not knowing what to do with it, laid it on a shelf. Dann watched him from between his fingers.

Now, Ali was lying beside the snow dog, his ear on his chest. After a moment he got up and squatted there, stroking Ruff. 'Good dog, Ruff, good dog.'

Tamar, in her scrap of a shadow dress, sat weeping by the animal.

Ali said, 'This animal's heart is not good. He is very ill.'

Now he said, looking with severity at Tamar and at Dann, 'Ruff must belong to one of you, not both. He must be Tamar's dog or Dann's dog. You are asking too much, too much. Now let him rest. I'll fetch medicine.' He went out, running.

Dann said to Tamar, who sat there, her hand on Ruff, 'Tamar, don't be afraid, he's gone.'

'Who's gone? Who? Daulis? I know Daulis has gone.'

'No, not Daulis. The Other One.'

'Who is the other one?' And she sat trembling, trying to steady herself.

'The Other One is a very bad man. Griot knows him,' said Dann.

Ali returned, running. Now he made Ruff open his mouth and he poured in some medicine. He stood up and said severely to Dann and to Tamar, 'Please, if you love this animal, then be kind.'

Dann said, 'When I took Ruff out of the marsh – he was just a little pup then – he was nearly dead. I thought he was dead. Perhaps his heart was damaged then.'

'This animal's heart has been broken every day,' said Ali, 'with you two, pulling him different ways.'

Ruff was trembling and his claws rattled on the reed flooring. He seemed to want to be sick. He retched and coughed, and whined and shivered.

'Poor lovely Ruff,' whispered Tamar.

'I'll take him for a while,' said Ali. 'I'll have him in my room and look after him. He doesn't have to love me or care about me.'

Ali and Griot conferred, and Griot went out. Ali took one of Dann's rugs and covered the snow dog.

Now Tamar asked Dann, 'If you loved my mother, why do you want to kill her?'

Dann shut his eyes, shook his head, could not answer.

'I don't understand,' said Tamar.

Dann shook his head.

Griot came back with two soldiers and a board. Between them they lifted the heavy, inert animal on to the board and carried him out. Tamar was going to follow but Ali said, 'No, no, let the poor animal be alone for a while. He can lie in the dark and rest. Don't worry, I'll make him better. And he'll get well – if he doesn't have to choose between two people he loves.'

He went out. Griot stayed.

Dann sat trembling, like Ruff; his face seemed to have sunk into itself, and his eyes were dark and desolate. Tamar crept closer to him, close, and then, as she got within reach, his arms went out and he clutched her to him. The two of them, the man and the girl kneeling by him, were close and wept together.

Griot, standing there, watched and thought that if his own heart was cold stone then perhaps he had the best of it.

Dann lifted his head from Tamar and said, 'Griot, you have only one idea, to take me at the head of your armies into Tundra. Aren't you ever afraid that The Other One might take over and spoil your clever plans?'

Griot thought this out, and then said, 'No, he didn't get very far this time, did he?'

'Suppose I don't always have Ruff beside me to keep me in order?'

At this Tamar cried out, '*No*, no,' and tears threatened again.

But Dann said, 'Hush, Tamar.' And to Griot, 'But I'll always have you, is that it?'

'I hope you will,' said Griot.

'I hope so too,' said Dann. And there was no mockery in it, Griot thought.

Dann carefully stood up. 'Griot, before we leave this place there is just one thing we have to do. No, don't worry, it won't take long. We'll be in time for your new moon deadline.'

Griot still stood there, on guard, although the two soldiers were in their places, waiting and watching. He was not afraid for Tamar, now, but he was for Dann, who was so thin and ill.

Dann asked him to go and find out if the snow dog was recovering. Ali called out from his room that Ruff was asleep and would recover. Griot returned with this news and Tamar whispered to Dann, 'I think you must have Ruff. He's your snow dog. You rescued him from the marsh.'

'No, you must have him. I'll give him to you. Poor child, poor Tamar, your father's gone and your Uncle Dann has turned out such a disappointment.' And they hugged and reassured each other, and wept. And Griot watched.

When they emerged from Dann's room Daulis had left a message that he would tell them when he had reached Bilma, and Ali had sent a message that he was staying with Ruff, who had been given a strong soporific. Ali would stay with him, or make sure he was never left alone.

Now Dann ordered a parade of soldiers in the square. There were fewer than last time, so many had left already.

Dann stood there before them, this time alone, without Tamar, and said that they would have heard he had been ill again. Yes, it was poppy that had set it off, he thought, but he had taken very little. He hoped that they had the sense to leave poppy to the black blankets. They laughed.

Griot watched from a window and thought that he would never understand it. Those people out there loved Dann. The General might look like some wretch of a refugee who hadn't eaten for days, he was thin and feeble, but something shone from him. Griot saw there something fine and strong. Dredged from long-ago memories, perhaps not even his, or from old tales, a word came floating – noble. There was something noble in that poor sick creature out there. And what did it mean, saying that? Griot didn't know. He felt, in spite of everything, that he would die for Dann. And out there in the square they were cheering him. 'I don't understand it, but I am relying on it,' Griot thought. Messages were arriving from where his advance troops had reached. The people were waiting for General Dann. 'They talk about him. Everyone knows about him. They think he's bringing all kinds of great things from the secret place. And they love the girl too.'

All along the great hall the tables with their waiting scribes were ready. There was such excitement, such a fever. That bubble of not-glass was going to be broken into. Between the concealed entrance to the secret place and the hall, lines of soldiers stood waiting to hurry the released books and tablets and – whatever was there – to the tables where so many languages were known.

Dann, with Tamar, and Griot, and Ali, who had left watchers with Ruff, went into the hidden place. Griot had a great hammer, made of stone, and Ali a rock. They stood along the shining wall, looking at the leaves or pages held there, waiting, and at a well in the centre, where books were piled up, once in tidy heaps, but now slipping and sliding down.

Griot swung his hammer on to the shining wall and

it responded with a loud clanging that reverberated and sang. But it held.

'No one has ever dared to do that,' said Dann.

Ali hit the wall with his rock. Another singing note.

The bubble of not-glass stood intact. It had not even shaken, or vibrated.

'A pity we couldn't use that big machine with the weights,' said Tamar. 'I mean, when it was made of iron.'

'You're right,' said Ali. 'But it would never get in here, it's too big.'

'It would be easy to take those great balls off the chains and roll them at the wall,' said Tamar.

Ali was impressed: he often was, by Tamar.

'Together,' said Dann, and Griot and Ali swung their weapons together.

The sonorous clanging echoed around the room and seemed to want to burst it open.

They stood looking at their opponent, the glassy square. At its top it disappeared into a shadowy cleft. Ali stood back, ran at the wall, got a foot on it, and reached up: fingers scraped along the cleft, and he jumped down.

'It fits tight into something, but it's not rock,' he said.

'This thing has been here for so long, and it knows how to keep itself safe,' said Dann. 'What's under here?'

'You know what's under here,' said Griot. 'Water. The walls everywhere are mouldy with damp.'

Ali said, 'This is a sort of cell – like a square marsh bubble.'

'How did they make it?' exclaimed Dann in a fever of

despair. 'How did they? We don't know. We don't know anything.'

Tamar was resting her ear against the not-glass. 'It's still singing,' she said.

'Griot, you've got explosives. The ones you use to make roads along the cliffs.'

'It will destroy the books as well as the bubble.'

'Not all of them. We don't have a choice, Griot. If we just go, all this will disappear into the marshes. This way, we might perhaps save something.'

Griot went out and returned with sticks of explosive and fitted them in places around the walls at the bottom and at the top. He attached a long cord.

They went out, with the end of the cord, which Griot lit.

First, the thud of an explosion, then a bell-like ringing.

They ran in. The walls had split in two places, cleanly, and stood like shining leaves of solidified water. Air was hissing into the space. Water was trickling in from the sides of the room.

'Quick,' shouted Dann. He slid into the cell, or bubble, and grabbed at the books that were being held to the walls by hands of – what? Some kind of metal and strong glue. Now he, and Griot and Tamar and Ali, grabbed handfuls of the books from the walls and from the well-like middle, and handed them out to the waiting runners. They were dropping the books anyhow in front of the scribes and linguists at the tables and running back for more.

They were all working as fast as they could, but now water was rushing in to the centre of the shattered not-glass. Dann grabbed at the last of the books that were still dry, and leaped back as a jet of water shot up.

'That's it,' shouted Griot. 'General, we must run for it.'

Dann set down his final armful of books. The scribes were trying to sort the books into languages they knew, but the frail old things were falling apart. As each was opened, it began to crumble. Dann, desperate, grief-stricken, grabbed up book after book and saw it disintegrate in his hands. Fragments of paper bronzed and darkened as the air took it.

'And there goes the wisdom of a hundred civilisations,' said Dann. 'Look, there it goes. Going, going, gone.'

Dann was moving from table to table, hoping perhaps that at this one or that the books were still whole. He gently opened one after another, and watched it die, while odd words or lines of words sprang up clear and strong, like lines of writing being consumed by fire. Then he reached for another.

He was weeping. All the scholars working there in the hall were desperate, some crying, some trying to catch the fragments of paper as they blew about.

Dann stood watching, Tamar behind him, and then from the direction of the secret room there came a noise like a clang, that gurgled into silence. The not-glass cell had spoken its last. From its direction crept a trickle of water.

'It's time we all left,' said Griot.

All along the hall the scribes were scribbling down odd phrases, even words, as the books fell into dust in their hands.

. . . truths to be self evident . . .

Un vieux faun de terre cuite . . .

. . . be in England . . .

. . . Rose, thou art sick . . .

. . . all the oceans . . .

. . . rise from the dead to say the sun is shining . . .

. . . into a summer's day . . .

. . . Helen . . .

Western wind, when . . .

The Pleiades . . .

. . . and I lie here alone . . .

. . . and all roads lead to . . .

'Dann, sir, what has been made can be made again,' said Griot.

'And again, and again, and again,' said Dann.

He sat at his table and Ali's, and watched the people all down the hall scurrying and scrabbling over the bits of browning paper.

'It's the again and again, Griot. I can never understand why you don't see it.'

Griot sat down near Dann. 'Sir, you make things so hard for yourself.'

Tamar sat down too. In her hand was a bit of crumbling paper. She was crying. She said, 'When I get to Tundra I won't ever cry again. Never.'

A soldier appeared. 'General, sir, the snow dog's coming; he wouldn't stay, sir.'

The great white beast came crawling towards them, panting, but instead of putting his head on Tamar's knee, or Dann's, he went past them to the cushions, rolled on his side and lay still.

'Leave him,' said Ali. 'Let him rest.'

'Ruff, Ruff,' whispered Tamar. The snow dog flopped his tail once, twice, and lay with his eyes open, panting.

'He is afraid we are going to leave him behind,' said Dann. 'Aren't you, Ruff?'

The animal flapped his tail and lay still.

'Griot, how are we going to take him?'

'They are making a little carriage for him. We will carry him in it through the marshes, and then we'll fit on some wheels. If there's one thing there's plenty of in the centre, it's old wheels.'

'Ingenious, Griot,' said Dann. 'There you are. No need for the treasures of the Centre. Griot's going to do as well.'

'Yes,' said Griot, quite serious, 'that's what I think, too.'

There came a thunderous knock on the outer gate and a sentry walked in, immediately followed by Kira and a fat pouting child.

A high, imperious voice: 'Out of my way!'

'It's all right,' said Dann to the sentry. He was badly affected: that voice . . . that sweet, enticing, conniving voice. He was afraid of it.

There at the entrance stood a large woman with a mass of black hair, black dramatic eyes, and flashing jewellery that tinkled on her plump arms and ankles. The child Rhea was as highly coloured as her mother, with earrings, a gold band holding her black curls, and many rings on her fat fingers.

Kira was staring at Dann. 'Well,' she pronounced, 'you don't look up to much, Dann.' Behind her stepped a platoon of female soldiers with their black blankets draped and held with brooches made out of the claws of crabs. She signalled that they must close up around her, but Griot said, 'Wait a minute. You must send your soldiers round to the western entrance. You know where it is.'

He was speaking for Dann, because he could see Dann was not able to. He was breathing hard, fists clenched, a look of dread; but then his face cleared. Dann took a deep breath and shook himself free. That voice, with its singing sweetness – it had a hard edge to it, like an out-of-tune chord. There was in it the hint of a whine. Dann was free: she was no longer able to dominate him.

'How dare you?' began Kira. 'Griot, how dare . . .'

Dann said, 'Kira, do as you are ordered.'

His voice, calm and in control, stopped her.

'You and the child may come in, but your soldiers must go to join Joss and his troops.'

She pouted and dismissed her soldiers with what she intended to seem a commanding gesture. The hand was shaking.

'Sit down,' said Dann. 'Sit down, Rhea.'

The two sat, arranging their clothes, shaking out their voluminous curls; Kira at least was buying time.

Rhea now piped up, 'You needn't think you're my father, because you aren't.'

Kira gave her a look which was clearly a rebuke or reminder. Hard to read it: it was now evident that she was ill, or . . . her eyes were too bright, glassy, and the pupils were large. Her glances were moist and unsure.

'Poppy,' breathed Tamar, who was squeezed as close to Dann as she could.

And Rhea? She, too, was on poppy, and it had been no mean dose.

'Don't think I'm pleased to see you, Tamar,' said Rhea, in the same laboured, over-prepared way as her last pronouncement. She and her mother had rehearsed sentences, but now it seemed she had brought them out at the wrong time, and this was what Kira's glances meant: reproof.

Now Kira displayed her garment, which was long, and yellow, striped broadly with black. A Sahar robe.

'Do you see what I am wearing?' Kira said to Dann.

'Yes, I do – as I was meant to,' said Dann.

'I think this Sahar gown looks better on me than it did on Mara, don't you agree?' And she lifted her arm, to show off the pattern of the stripes. 'Mara was a lanky, lolling thing,' she said, and her sweet voice dripped dislike. 'I'm prettier than Mara, I always was,' she announced.

Dann said nothing: he was too angry to speak.

Griot said, 'Do you see those lines of soldiers, Kira? They are there for a reason.'

'I see them,' said Kira, focusing with difficulty. The sun had emerged from between labouring dark clouds and a strong yellow light, striking low, was hurting her eyes.

The snow dog, shifting his position, groaned. He was watching Kira and the child, prepared to attack if necessary – and if he could.

Ali got up and stood behind Tamar's chair, and he had his dagger in his hand.

'What a mess you are in,' said Kira, looking at the drifts of brittle browning paper over the floor.

'That', said Dann, 'is all that is left of the sand libraries of thousands of years. Preserved for us – and now, all gone.'

'No loss,' said Kira. 'We don't care about all that. What I wanted to say, Dann, was this. I, and Joss and Rhea, will stay here in the Centre, and get together everything usable before we move on to Tundra.'

'You're welcome to it,' said Dann.

Kira seemed to swell with anger. Rage sparked off her glistening locks, her jewels, her shining nails, her puffy pink lips.

'And I can tell you we'll make better use of the Centre than you do.'

The snow dog lifted his head, and growled, responding to her rage.

'Why do you have that dirty animal in here? Our snow dogs are trained as soldiers.'

'He's not dirty,' said Tamar. Ali put his hand on her shoulder.

'I have a snow puppy,' said Rhea, 'but my slave looks after it.'

'Ah, yes,' said Dann, 'I hear you have slaves now. I hope you are treating them as well as we were treated, when we were slaves.'

'How dare you!' said Kira. 'What lies!'

'What lies!' echoed Rhea. Her eyes were glazing.

Now they were looking at her, this stout, proud child,

the copy of her mother. Dann's daughter did not have much of him in her. The eyes, perhaps, a bit, the length of her hands – but they were too fat. It was Tamar who was Dann's child. Kira said spitefully to her, 'And I suppose you know your father is dead?'

Tamar cried out, 'No!' and Dann put his arm round her and said, 'Kira, you are lying. A messenger came this morning. Shabis was well down towards Charad when he sent the message.'

Now there began a great business of tossing locks, pouting puffy lips, flashing looks. But the whole show was off key, discordant, and the two of them, Kira and Rhea, were like dolls that had been wound up and were running down.

'Kira,' said Dann, 'my advice to you is you should go and lie down. Find Joss and lie down. You aren't well.'

'I've been travelling,' said Kira lugubriously.

'Then sleep it off,' said Dann. He stood up.

Kira tried to stand, sat down. Dann clapped his hands and a soldier appeared. 'Take the ladies out and to the western gate.'

Kira managed to get herself to her feet. 'I'm going this way,' she said, directing herself to go through the lines of soldiers.

'No, you aren't,' said Dann. 'They have orders to kill anyone from the black blankets who try their lines. You will go round.'

The two, mother and daughter, began an unsteady progress to the main gate. They moved with the over-caution of people who are drunk – but they weren't drunk.

The outer door banged shut.

'And now', said Griot, 'it's time we left.'

'Yes, I heard, Griot. Right. I'm ready.'

'Two days,' said Griot.

'But what are we to pack, Griot? Everything I own has always fitted into a bundle I can carry.'

'Do I have a bundle?' asked Tamar.

'I'll show you how to make one out of half a blanket,' said Dann.

'When we are in Tundra, will I have a room, like I do now?'

'Yes, I am sure you will.'

'And will I be near you?'

'Tamar, don't be afraid, we'll all be there.'

'And Ruff? will he be in your room or mine?'

Ali said, 'You should let him choose.'

That night, as the light left the sky, Griot set off into the western part of the Centre, with some soldiers, two on either side. They all wore red blankets. Two snow dogs went with them. They were likeable enough creatures, but when Griot looked for the loving intelligence he was used to in Ruff's eyes, it was not there.

Griot and his guards went through the double line of soldiers, telling them to be vigilant.

They were all used to seeing the Centre at night, dark, its towers and roofs and turrets and parapets standing out against skies that changed with the moon, but now as they moved through the courts and intervening spaces a flicker of fire showed in a corner, or even high up, in an angle of a roof, or at a ruinous window. Griot was not trying to avoid observation. He did not want to run into Kira, but thought it unlikely. She had found a great chair, like a throne, and she sat in one of the emptying museums. There, she and Joss were holding court, and feasted. Griot wanted to make the point that the Centre, until he chose to leave it, was Dann's, and that Kira was there on sufferance. More than that, he wanted to test something: how he stood with Kira's army.

At the western end he came on a company of troops, lying or squatting by their fires. He raised a commanding hand, as they seemed uncertain whether to attack or to run away, and asked them how they did. He stood there at ease, so they could have a good look at him. Most would know him. First, he was so unlike them, this solid, strong man, with his broad healthy face. Those eyes of his, greenish or grey; people noticed them. Nearly all these people that had come from the east, to beg asylum at the Centre, were refused. But they had been given food and drink to take with them. Griot had stood there, sometimes for hours, sad that he was turning them away, though he had understood Dann's rightness in giving orders that the army could accommodate no more. He had stood there monitoring what went on, to make sure that each was getting a fair share. They would remember him, associating him with food, with help; and he intended now that they should know him as the Captain Griot they would have heard Kira describe with contempt.

Many signalled their recognition of him, as he stood there. As he moved past this group and went to another he heard, 'When we are in Tundra, will you give me the red blanket?' *The red blanket, the red blanket* was what he heard as he moved about through the shadowy courts, among the cooking fires.

By the time he had finished his tour he knew that when Kira's army did reach Tundra, half of them would be deserting to him. Did he want them? He was taking a good look now, to see what effects drink and poppy had already had on these people. Kira had encouraged drinking and poppy: befuddled men were easier to control, she thought.

Griot did not want what Kira had spoiled, but there were plenty of unspoiled men and women there. But they were not in Tundra yet; Griot was pretty sure that Kira wouldn't be in a hurry to leave the Centre. There would be the fish coming up the roads he had built from the Bottom Sea. There were stores of food, and the farms growing grain and food beasts were flourishing. The refugees that came in streams from the east brought their supplies of poppy, and all kinds of goods unknown to the Farm or to the Centre. No, there would be plenty of time for Dann's army to take control of Tundra before Kira stirred her fat self to follow. That would not be the end of it, he knew. Kira and Joss were not a threat, one too self-indulgent and soft, one too rough and unskilled; not very clever, Griot judged. But there was Rhea, who when Dann was ruler of Tundra would remember she was his daughter after all. Some time in the future, probably a long time off, that imperious girl would arrive in Tundra, demanding her rights. Well, that was the future. And there was nothing to be done now. Rhea was too well guarded to slide a knife into her – not that Griot would have any reluctance to order that, if he thought it would succeed.

Griot reached the very end where the west wall stood, crumbling, but still strong. He turned; going round the south wall he saw a building with lights in it. He knocked. Leta appeared. At the sight of Griot she began to weep and flung herself into his arms.

She would not have done that before, when she was here; this woman had had a battering – from Kira, from Joss – and was all suppliant now.

Over Leta's head Griot saw her girls, some Albs, those pale creatures whose hair gleamed in the rushlights, and there were the girls from the River Towns, black and shining and smiling at him.

'Oh, Griot,' wept Leta. 'I hoped you'd never know we were here.'

'Don't cry,' ordered Griot and Leta tried to stop. 'Dann will be hurt you didn't tell him you were here.'

'I am so ashamed,' said Leta.

But before she could begin weeping again he said, 'Leta, stop. Please. I'm going to tell Dann you've come. He'd be angry with me if I didn't. He talks about you. He's so fond of you. Weren't you with him on that amazing journey?'

'Part of the journey. But things are different now. You can see for yourself.'

'Are you a prisoner?'

'Yes; we all are.'

'In a couple of days our army is moving to Tundra. All of us are leaving. They are expecting us. If you can be ready, I'll send some soldiers for you, and Kira can't stop them.'

'And the girls? My poor girls?'

Griot could not stop sending fascinated glances at those so different creatures, the white Albs, with the black River Towns girls, all sitting about half naked and bored.

'If you can't be ready when we leave, get to Tundra somehow and then you can decide what you want to do – you and the girls.'

And he left them with a salute; he thought they would like that.

What he was thinking – whether he should be thinking it or not – was that it wouldn't be a bad thing to have Leta, and the facilities she and the girls provided, in Tundra. He could see nothing wrong with that. He could not understand why she was behaving as if she had committed some crime or other. Obviously there was something here he didn't understand – he kept arriving at this conclusion again and again from various points of view. But there was that woman of his; what would he feel if she were one of Leta's girls? Yes, he could see he wouldn't like that. But she did have other men, he knew. He was always so busy and she got lonely; he didn't blame her. There he was again – there was something missing in him. When someone is confronted with the self accusation *there is something missing in me*, it is like arriving at the end of a journey to find you have left behind names of contacts, or special clothes, something important, which it is generally agreed you must have. 'Well, but I'm doing all right, surely? I can't be so bad.'

Anyway, he knew Dann wouldn't hear of it, if he

suggested putting Leta and her girls in some convenient house. Here was another problem he must postpone.

Griot found Dann sitting with Tamar just outside the door where Ruff could be glimpsed, asleep, with Ali on guard.

'Time you two were in bed,' said Griot in a low voice, so as not to disturb the snow dog. Ali smiled and raised his hand, meaning, *Thank you for removing Dann and Tamar, who shouldn't be here.*

Griot saw them into their beds, checked the sentries and went to his own.

Next evening, he walked through the interior courts – he was always coming on new places he hadn't seen, the Centre was so vast. Now he was stopping easily and without precautions, to talk to Kira's soldiers. Everywhere the black blankets lay about anyhow, in corners, or on the earth near the soldiers who were well warmed by the fires. But in Dann's army (or Griot's) the soldiers treated their blankets as precious, and looked after them, keeping them clean, mending them if they tore.

On this night Griot sent a rumour whispering through Kira's soldiers, 'There will be red blankets for honest soldiers who ask for them, in Tundra.'

And now, on the night of the new moon, it really was time to leave.

Four soldiers brought a box for Ruff, with long handles, and the animal was lifted into it. They all, Dann, Griot, Tamar and Ali, fetched their bundles and, with Ruff in his box, left the Centre for ever.

Dann stood on the east–west road to look back.

Through the great gates he could see the entrance to the secret place, from where water was oozing over that part of the courtyard.

The guides for the journey across the marshes were waiting at intervals along the track. Their own guide was a woman who had been one of Griot's best agents, often travelling back and forth across the marshes, and she knew the ponds and the meres, the slimes and quagmires and quicksands. She went in front, then Griot, then the snow dog in his litter, and behind him Dann, Tamar and Ali. They could see each other as dark shapes on heavier, wet dark. The moon was a fitful shred of white and, when it did appear, illuminating the edges of hurrying black cloud, it did not reach down to the night of the marshes.

Just before they had stepped from the track to the marsh path a shape with the black blanket across its face sidled up to Tamar and handed her a package. In it was a hideous wooden figurine filched from a museum, that had long sharp splinters of wood in its heart. They had been told not to talk, but when the group halted on the edge of a rushy place where the guide hesitated, Tamar whispered to Dann, 'Hate is a very funny thing. Why do Kira and Rhea hate me so much? When they look at me their eyes are like knives. I don't hate them but I'm so afraid of them.' In the dark her frightened little face could hardly be seen. Dann took the figurine she was showing him and threw it into a pool.

'I suppose you could say, not funnier than love,' whispered Dann.

Ali, just behind them, exclaimed his disapproval.

Tamar put her hand into Dann's, and her voice was high and afraid, 'Dann, Dann . . .'

'Yes, I know,' said Dann. 'But don't listen to me. I didn't mean it.'

'I think you did mean it,' whispered Tamar.

'We're moving,' said Ali.

It was a long night, so dark, and full of the noises of marsh birds and animals, frogs, fishes leaping away from them; lights moved, which could not be the army, forbidden to show lights. Everybody had to step exactly where the person in front had trodden, and on either side sometimes the water lapped close, and their feet squelched in mud. Once a cry told that a soldier had slipped in, and there were splashes and voices as he, or she, was hauled out. This little commotion in the great blackness sent fear through them, knowing how many people there were, all around them, and if so many, silently moving, why not enemies too?

The dawn came when they were in the middle of the marshes, hundreds of people, apparently walking or standing on water, greyish-brown figures on the greyish-green water; the red blankets had been stowed away in bundles. Getting a third of the way across had taken all night and, in the early light, which sent pink reflections rippling across the water, they looked back to where the Centre still loomed. There was a glow of fire and dirty smoke.

'I'm not surprised,' said Griot. 'They make these great fires every night. Well, there's so much water everywhere, fire won't get far.'

Dann said, 'Now we are gone, Kira and Joss will be

in our quarters, and they will be safe from the wet for a time.'

'Time, time,' said Tamar. 'Whenever you use the word time, it's different.'

'However you measure it, time will swallow the Centre, whether by water or by fire, or both.'

'It will seem funny without the Centre,' said Tamar. 'I've been hearing the Centre, the Centre, all my life.'

'We can make another one,' said Griot.

'But it took hundreds of years – thousands – to make the Centre,' said Dann.

'We can make a start, then,' said Griot.

'A Centre without the sand libraries, without records, without history.'

'But we're taking all the scribes and everything they wrote down. It's a mass of stuff,' said Griot.

'The tiniest little part of what there was.'

And on they went, through mists that curled up from the dank waters, stepping as carefully as they had when it was dark. Ali whispered to Tamar that she should let herself be carried, but she only said she was not tired. She was, but she remembered the tales about her mother, and how brave she had been.

They reached an island, a little higher than the marshes, about midday, and there successive batches of the travellers climbed to rest for a few minutes. There wasn't room for more than a few at a time. The snow dog had not made a sound all night. Tamar visited him. She did get a feeble recognition; his thumping tail acknowledged her, once, twice, but he lay on his side, eyes closed, and was not well.

So it went on that day, the armies of people moving through the marshes. Tamar watched the drowned cities going past, deep in the water. She had heard about them, but not seen them and Ali hadn't seen them either.

She tugged at Dann's arm. 'The people in the cities down there, were they drowned?'

'No, they would have had plenty of time to leave, as the buildings sank down.'

'Where did they go?'

'They couldn't have gone north, because of the Ice, so it must have been south.'

'Some went east to my country. There are old tales,' said Ali.

'Old tales . . . that was so long ago.'

'Long ago,' said Dann. 'The cities must have sunk down slowly. They didn't disappear into the water overnight.'

'Like the Centre now? The edges going into the water and wet creeping up?' said Tamar.

'Just like that. Long, long ago.'

Her face told them the immensities were frightening her, and Dann said, 'Ali, perhaps it is better for the horrors of the past to be in old tales. Not so bad when it's a tale and begins, "Our chroniclers tell us . . ."'

'I think so,' said Ali. 'Children should hear the past as "The storytellers say that . . ."'

Dann said, 'Our storytellers relate that once, long, long ago all of Yerrup was prosperous and full of cities and parks and forests and gardens, and everyone was happy; then the Ice appeared and soon the cities were under the Ice.'

And Ali said, 'And all the people went south and east and found new homes.'

Tamar's face was bleak, and prim, and small with exhaustion. Ali put his hand on her shoulder and said, 'Little Tamar, forget the long ago. We are here and we are now, and that is all. We are making a new start.'

When the dark came in again, the land at last lifted, and by the time the light of the sky was draining into the reflections on the water, the armies were standing all along the shores of the marshes, immensities of gleaming water and reeds, where the pathways they had used were now not visible, though they reached right to the mists which they knew were where the Middle Sea and its great cliffs were, and the east–west track running along its edges.

Still no lights were to be shown. The armies brought out their red blankets and wrapped themselves, and lay on dry earth among warm aromatic grasses and bushes where insects clicked and sang. Overhead was a deep, starry night and the white splinter of the moon.

The box where Ruff lay was carefully set down, and opened, so that he could crawl out and sniff around a little. Tamar knelt not far from him, so he could come to her if he wanted, and he did creep close and sniff her hand, but seeing Dann standing there, gave a low bark, and seemed glad to go back into his box.

All the army was exhausted, having not slept for a night and a day, and soon the red blankets were absorbed into the dark.

Tamar lay between Dann and Ali and slept at once. In the night she woke and saw that Dann was kneeling by Ruff's box. When he came back, she could just see his face, and what she saw on it made her put her hand into his.

'Ruff is afraid of me,' he said.

Tamar said, 'I'm not afraid of you.'

'You should be afraid of – Him. I am.'

'Who is he, do you know, Dann?'

'No. Tamar, sometimes when I wake in the morning I don't know who I am, Dann or – The Other.'

Tamar said fearfully, 'But Griot knows how to look after you.'

'Yes, I hope he does.' Then, after a long silence, 'Perhaps He won't come back. I think the Centre made him worse.' And then, very low, 'I believe the Centre is a bad place. Well – bad for me, then.'

It was morning, and everywhere hundreds of people were waking, getting up and eating bread, and standing about, letting the sun warm them.

Now the marshes were a dull shine where the earth dipped down from the grasses and bushes. Some grasses stood in rising water, though it could not rise far, because the ground lifted up fast, into high land and rocky hills.

When they all stopped for the midday meal the marshes were out of sight, and people came towards them from everywhere. The people of this part of Tundra, some of them sent ahead by Griot, were welcoming them. And they all wanted to see Dann.

Dann stood still, to be looked at, a tall, too thin, stooping man, his long black hair over his shoulders, his red blanket in his arms.

Griot thought, *It's all right. I knew it would be all right. I don't know why they love him, but they do. How strange it is* . . . He saw how they came to touch him, some stroking him, or the blanket. 'We've been waiting for you for a long time, General Dann.' One or two said, 'Prince, we've been waiting for you.'

Dann said, 'No, that was a long time ago, no princes now, and here is Griot, my captain, who looks after everything.'

But while they had heard of Griot – and how could they not? – it was Dann they wanted, Dann they needed to touch and smile at, through tears, 'Dann, Dann, you're here . . .'

Griot was content: this was how things should be, how he had known they would be. Here was his General, in his right place at the centre of everything.

The first town was a short march away. The army arranged itself into its parts, on the wide hillside, with plenty of room to spread out. Blocks of soldiers, with their officers, and in front went Dann with Tamar, and Griot and Ali, and just behind was Ruff, not in his closed box, but on a litter made of branches, carried by soldiers. There were trees here: parts of Tundra were all forest, and woods. No more reeds now, no more of the mosses and rushes and slimes of the wet.

So they went forward, between lines of townspeople who at first were silent, and then – when they could get a good look at Dann, with the beautiful child, and Griot and Ali, and the great white beast stretched out on his litter, gazing around at them – the cheering began, and it went on.

It went on for weeks, as they travelled over Tundra.

The four sat at their supper in an inn decorated for their arrival in a town in east Tundra, and Dann said to Griot, 'Well, Captain, are you satisfied now?'

'This is a wonderful place, Dann – sir. They told me today that the mountain over there is full of iron. The locals didn't know, but some of our soldiers did. The skills and knowledge we have in our army – it's a wonderful thing. We can make a wonderful thing of Tundra, sir.'

'The place is wonderful, Griot. But are we? Have you thought of that?'

'Just wait and see. A little while and – you'll see.'

'Ah, well, that's all right, then. If you're satisfied, Griot, then I have to be.'

Time had passed, measured by that tall girl walking down there in the garden, her hand on the head of a white animal who was not Ruff. She had wept so long over the loss of Ruff that a snow pup had been found, and he became her companion.

It was Griot who looked down from his window, where he was calculating the stocks of food in his warehouses. Tundra was prosperous and food was plentiful. In a square not far from here soldiers were drilling, but while they looked like the army that had marched into Tundra, few of the soldiers were the same. The wars in the east, or some of them, had ceased and many soldiers had gone home. But people fleeing from the droughts of the south came to the Northlands, more and more of them, and they took refuge in Tundra, happy to be fed and comfortable in return for becoming soldiers. Tundra did not go in for war. Dann joked that he was called General, and there was an army, but no war. 'Now, what do you make of that, Captain Griot?'

Griot could have replied, 'What's in a name?' for that is what he felt.

One thing he did secretly fear: that Ali might decide to go home. His country was at peace and a new ruler had sent messages to Ali to return.

Ali was Tamar's tutor, Dann's physician and Griot's adviser in everything: Griot could not imagine doing without him. He had never asked Ali for counsel and failed to get it.

Dann knew of this worry: Dann seemed to sense what everyone was thinking. He told Griot that if Ali left, there were good doctors, Tamar was clever enough to be a tutor herself and she didn't really need Ali. And why did Griot need advice? He underestimated himself.

'And there is no need to be anxious, Griot. Ali will never leave me. He says he was my brother in another life.'

'Easy enough to say that.'

'He says he knows, he remembers.'

'We can't argue with that, then.'

'Always sensible Griot. But do you know, I like playing with the idea.'

'I'm surprised, Dann, when you hate the idea of over and over and over again.'

'But there would be variations, wouldn't there? Suppose I were reborn as Kulik, whose one idea was to persecute Mara and Dann?'

'You're joking, Dann!'

'Now, would I do that, Griot?'

Leta had come to Tundra, all apologies for herself, and she had been given a building now called the School of Medicine, where she and her girls taught healing. The River Towns, it turned out, had a fine tradition of medicine and, as the drought sank them one by one in sand, their doctors were happy to come to Tundra, now famous in the Northlands, and beyond, for its skills.

The scribes and savants who had studied at the tables along the Great Hall in the Centre the material from the secret place had a building where what they had preserved was taught, and kept. Dann spent much of his time there; it was his favourite place. Tamar, too, who was going to be the Director of this College of Learning when she was grown up, which she nearly was.

Everyone entering this place was confronted with a tall, wide white wall, almost blank, and at its top was written,

> This great white expanse represents the area of knowledge of the Ancient World. The small black square in the lower right-hand corner represents the amount of knowledge we have. All visitors are asked to reflect for a few moments, asking themselves if they perhaps have information or learning which is not general, and which could be added to our common store. There was once, long ago, a shared culture covering the whole world: remember, we have only fragments of it.

This town had been chosen as capital of all Tundra because it was on a long, wide hill, with plenty of trees and pleasant buildings of mellow yellow brick, which was the colour of the soil of the region.

People came to this town, where there were all kinds of reception places for them, because they wanted to catch a sight of Dann and the girl who would be his successor.

Sometimes Dann would say, using a by now old joke, 'Yes, Griot, I owe it to you' – and a party of people went off to visit another town: Dann, Griot, the girl, and Ali.

On these occasions Dann was always ready to be seen and do what Griot wanted. He would walk around in public places and stop to talk and listen. He was not ill now, was healthy again, and did not seem much different from the Dann of before going off on his adventure to the Bottom Sea. If you looked closely, though, there was a sheen of grey on the black hair, and his eyes peered out from deeper in his head.

He was always courteous, patient, smiling, and he might sit for hours listening to whoever needed an auditor. He listened, nodded, and smiled and consoled and . . . well, he mostly listened. He was known everywhere for this, that he never turned anyone away who needed someone to hear them.

A tall, but stooping, smiling man . . . his smile was something that Griot had to watch and wonder over. Ironic, yes, always; tender, kind . . . but was there something else, too, a touch of . . . was that cruelty? No, it was a carefully hidden and held-down impatience. But this always patient Dann did sometimes flare into anger and it was usually with Griot, who pestered him – Griot knew Dann felt that. When this happened Griot was fearful and Dann was apologetic, with a bit of reproach – 'Don't worry, Griot, there's no need to be afraid. I've got *Him* well in hand, yes, I promise you.' And then he added, 'But sometimes I hear him howling on his chain – there, can you hear? – no, no, I'm only joking, Griot.'

When Dann had finished with the College of Learning for the day he went down into the garden where there was an unusual monument or memorial. In the middle of a platform made of slabs of yellowish stone was a tall irregular piece of white rock that looked like ice, but was a shard of crystal that had been brought from far away in Tundra. Dann wanted rock that looked like ice.

Here Ruff was buried. Dann sat on the edge of the platform, sometimes until it was dark. Griot went down to join him.

'You see, Griot, he loved me. He really did, Griot, you know . . . He was my friend.'

'Yes, Dann, sir, I know. He was your friend.'

Once, Griot would have gone off to find his sand girl – a woman now – but she had chosen to live with a reed worker from the great river. Griot had forced himself to think something like *plenty of fish in the sea* . . . but there had been no one he liked as much, and he never found the word to describe his feeling that she was irreplaceable and like nobody else. Lonely, he had taken to visiting Leta and her girls. There, a lively black girl, Nubis, from the River Towns, sang and told stories, and one day she said, 'Griot, come and sing with me; why don't you sing?

This surprised Griot, who had not thought of melody and song as a possibility for himself. 'I can't,' said he.

'Now, come on, Griot, you have a nice voice.'

So he learned the songs of her river and then she said, 'Griot, you must find your own tales to sing.'

Griot could not think of anything in his life that deserved a song, so he made up songs about Dann's and Mara's adventures. One evening he sat with Dann at Ruff's grave, and said, 'Now, listen, Dann,' and sang his version of Dann and Mara and the river dragons.

At first Dann seemed disturbed, but soon he smiled and said, 'You'll always surprise me, Griot. But why me? You forget Mara and I were among so many – so many, Griot. Who praises them? Who sings about them? The funny thing is, when I was one of them, running like them from the drought, I never thought of them like that. But now I do. I think of them a lot.'

'But Dann, a song about you must include them. People listening will imagine those others – won't they?'

'Will they? I hope they do. People just disappear, Griot; they vanish like – bits of straw in a whirlwind.'

Sunset, the hour Dann liked to sit there, with his Ruff, his dead snow dog; and the time Griot was free from his many labours. Sunset, the birds noisy, the dark soon to come, and supper; then, instead of sleep, as it had been once – people falling asleep as soon as the meal was done – all the old friends sat together, and Leta's girls too, and they sang their stories and exchanged news from all over Tundra. Griot was always asked to sing, and when he did he praised Dann most of all.

'But I notice you never sing of The Other One,' Dann said. 'Never about the Bad Dann.'

'I wouldn't like to do that, Dann.'

'A pity. He has interesting things to say, but only I hear them.'

Griot could not help suspecting that his voice, so commended by Nubis, was not as good as she made out. This charming girl, a drought orphan like so many, hoped to be Griot's favourite. Now, that really would be a triumph for her. Griot thought, *At least my sand girl never flattered me.* And then came the doleful knowledge: *Probably I will never again be able to trust in the truth from anybody, when they flatter.*

Griot began visiting the high moorland hills, making sure he was alone, with only the foxes and hawks to hear him. There, he sang to find out for himself what his voice was worth, but soon knew that no one could ever hear their own voice as others did. He sang for his own pleasure – and fancied that the foxes and birds came close to listen. This shocked him: surely not a thought for a practical man! When he sang about Dann, or Mara, and sometimes Tamar, no difficult thoughts appeared, but sometimes he let his voice go free, and sang without words or thoughts; then, more than once, his tentative voice, which seemed that it wanted to learn something, began a kind of howl, a tuneless sound; and this really did shock him. Why, Ruff could have howled like that. There was a bird he loved to hear, a small, grey, creeping bird that hopped about near him in the heather; its song sounded like 'To-do-again, to-do-again, to-do-again', and Griot heard Dann's voice instead of the bird's. This frightened him away from the moors, and he did not go back for a long time. Then he did; he seemed to be drawn there. When he stuck to his songs of Dann, nothing arrived to trouble him, yet the moment he was tempted into his wordless song his voice roughened into a yell, and then a howl. Griot blamed the place, the skies, those sunny, smiling, deceiving skies; after all, not so far away to the north-west they became the low, grey, sullen skies over the marshes.

He was tempted to tell Leta of this experience, but when he was at home away from the heather and the heath and the playfully treacherous skies, what he felt up there seemed fanciful, not worthy of him.

He did allow himself to think calmly, like a serious and practical man, that Dann told him he kept locked up a part of himself that wanted to destroy him. Was he, Griot, the same? *Was everyone?* He never shared these thoughts, not even with Dann. He felt that would be dangerous, like confessing a weakness.

A conversation between Dann and Tamar. They were watching Griot walking towards them, a solid, healthy, serious man.

'He is still young, and I am old,' said Dann – 'and yet, I am not much older than he is. The joke is, when he came to be a boy soldier under me in Agre, I was his Captain – and three years older than him.'

Tamar held his hand and did not say anything.

'Did you know the ancients lived to be eighty, ninety years?'

This upset Tamar. 'Oh, how could they? How awful.'

'Even a hundred sun-cycles, sometimes.'

'I'd hate that,' said Tamar.

'And we do well to live to be forty, or fifty.'

'Why, Dann?'

'It is not known why.'

Ali said to Griot, in his passionate and reproachful way, 'Poor Tamar, she works so hard. She's a young thing. She shouldn't always be so serious.'

Griot said to Dann that Ali thought Tamar needed some fun. 'She works so hard always.'

Dann said to Tamar that everyone was reproaching him for working her too hard. She needed some fun. 'Something of that kind, Tamar.'

'Fun?' said Tamar.

They were walking in the garden beyond Ruff's grave, where she would never go: it made her too sad.

'I suppose they mean dancing? Is that what they mean? I know the young girls dance and have festivals – that kind of thing, Mara?'

'I'm not Mara, I'm Tamar,' she said, and put her hand into his. 'Dear Dann, some day you'll have to let me be Tamar. And let my mother go.'

'Yes, I know,' said Dann. Then, 'Mara never danced in all her life. She was too busy – surviving. Poor Mara. She didn't have much fun, did she?'

'I did go and dance with the other girls,' said Tamar. 'But I'm not good at it. I'm too – stiff.'

'You're going to have to think of something to keep Ali and Griot pleased with me.'

'The girls made up a song about me. It's a game. Shall I tell you how it ends?'

And so she stands and bows her head.
Who cannot dance must bleed, we said.

'And she did, didn't she,' said Dann. 'Mara – did.'

'Dann,' said Tamar. 'Please.'

Dann stopped, put his hands on Tamar's shoulders and peered deep into her eyes. He often did this, and not only with Tamar. He seemed to feel that if he peered long enough the truth of that other person would be seen.

'Poor Dann,' said Tamar. 'And I'm still Tamar.'

'Yes, yes, you're right.'

'Ali isn't always right. It was he who said I must go and keep company with the other girls. But it would have been better if I hadn't. There's another verse of the song they made up':

And so she stands and bows her head.
Who cannot sing is dumb, we said.

'Don't they love you, the young women?'

'They love *you*, Dann. All of them, everybody. But they don't love me.'

This hurt Dann, and she said quickly, 'No, it's all right, they could never love me. They want to admire me, they want me to be perfect. I should sing wonderfully, dance better than they do, and I should play at least a dozen musical instruments – better than they do.

Don't you see, Dann?' She was coaxing him to laugh, and now he did.

'So, they wouldn't love you because you aren't perfect?'

'Oh, they wouldn't ever love me. They love you, because you are Dann.'

'Because I am such a . . . such a . . .'

'What are you?'

'A misfit. I don't – fit. I always expect them to throw me out. "What do you want with that – that poor thing," they'll say.'

'They love you because they think you are like them, and that forgives them for everything.'

'Little do they know. Oh, Tamar, if you knew how I long just to set off – somewhere, anywhere, walking somewhere, just to walk, you see?'

'Where would you go?'

'Perhaps I'd go with Ali, when he goes home. That's a whole sun-cycle – to get to his home.'

'And when you got there?'

'I'd walk on, and on – anywhere.'

'But you have to be here, Dann, and so do I.'

'We have to play our parts, yes.'

'Yes, until the story is finished.'

'When would that be? When I die? When you do?'

'Why are you talking of dying, Dann?'

'Did you know that long ago, long, long ago, they often said, "They lived happily ever after"?'

'Oh, I like that, Dann.'

'But what kind of people could say that? Or, perhaps they were just . . . whistling in the dark, the way we do.'

'No, no, Dann.' And Tamar was really upset now. 'Why do you laugh? The way I see my life . . .'

'Your long life . . .'

'Long enough, for me . . . it's moving from one bad dark place to a better – from the Farm to the Centre, and then to a good place. This is a good place, Dann, isn't it? The way I see it, this is living happily ever after.'

'Yes, of course it's a good place, of course it is.'

'Well, then, don't laugh when I say it. Why do you?'

'I'm sorry. You're right.'

Over in the Centre Kira was ill, old long before her time, and she sat on her throne-like chair sodden with poppy, and gave orders to everyone. Joss was dead: a knife fight. Kira replaced him with favourites who did not last long, because they didn't get much good from her. Most of her soldiers had joined Griot. Kira had a ragbag of soldiery, usually drunk or on poppy, who were nothing to fear.

Rhea had remembered she was the daughter of General Dann, the ruler of Tundra, and boasted that one day she would be ruler. Dann sent her a message inviting her to live in Tundra, with her own establishment. But she would have to obey its laws. She replied that when she did come it would be at the head of an army. She was very drunk, the messenger said.

Griot could not see her as a threat; he did not see danger coming from anywhere.

There were rumours that one of the kingdoms by the great river, south, towards the lakes, had plans for invading Tundra. They were suffering from the drought.

Griot said to Dann, 'You see, sir, I can't believe they would be so stupid. Tundra is very prosperous, we provide stability for all the Northlands and to the south and east too. We grow so much food there are always surpluses for sale. We are an example to everyone. So there would be no advantage in attacking us. I mean, it would be too stupid. I am pretty sure there is no need to lose sleep over it.'

'Well, yes, Griot, it would certainly be stupid. I agree with you there.'